Shadows Over Tanzlora

.

Secrets of Sage Manor Series

Book One: Through the Crystal Gate
Book Two: Shadows Over Tanzlora

Shadows Over Tanzlora

L G Rice

Disclaimer:

This book is a work of fiction. Any names, characters, events, and incidents are purely the product of the author's imagination or are used fictitiously. While this story may reference real locations and landmarks, these are included solely as a backdrop to the fictional narrative. Any resemblance to actual persons, living or dead, or real events is entirely coincidental.

For every family bound by love and unity, may you find strength in togetherness and courage in the face of challenge. This story is a testament to the power of standing united.

Beneath the twin suns of Tanzlora, the air shimmered with an ethereal glow, casting kaleidoscopic reflections across the endless canopy of the Lucidus Forest. The trees, towering like emerald spires, hummed with a subtle resonance, their translucent leaves catching light in a thousand colors. Rivers of liquid silver coursed through the land, weaving between crystalline cliffs that glistened like prisms. Every element of the planet pulsed with life, its vibrant energy unmistakable to those attuned to its rhythms.

At the heart of the forest, within a sacred grove untouched by time, Elder Sylvaris knelt. His tall form, draped in flowing robes spun from iridescent fibers, blended seamlessly with his surroundings. His blue-violet skin shimmered like polished opal, reflecting the radiant hues of the forest. Silver streaks in his hair framed his angular face, and his eyes, glowing like twin moons, were fixed on the ancient ceremonial pool before him.

The pool's surface, still as glass, held the secrets of Tanzlora's lifeblood. Sylvaris's long, graceful fingers hovered above it, and with a whispered incantation, the water began to ripple. Swirling images of the planet's energy web appeared, vibrant and whole. But as he continued the ritual, a dark tendril slithered across the vision, disrupting the harmony.

A deep, guttural hum reverberated through the grove, and Sylvaris's eyes widened. The tendril grew, morphing into a writhing mass of shadows that consumed the vibrant energy in its path. Trees blackened, rivers turned to ash, and the once-resonant hum of Tanzlora's life force fell silent.

"No," Sylvaris murmured, his voice trembling. The vision shifted violently, showing a massive, amorphous entity at the planet's core, its shadowy appendages reaching outward, spreading decay. It was not of Tanzlora—this was something ancient, malevolent, and unrelenting. The Umbralox.

With a sharp gasp, Sylvaris released his supernatural powers to counteract the evil vision. The pool's surface stilled, but the elder remained frozen, his breath uneven. The Lucidus Forest around him seemed to dim, as though it too had witnessed the devastation.

He rose to his full height, his robes billowing as if stirred by an unseen wind. The urgency in his movements betrayed the calm demeanor he usually carried. "The council must hear of this at once."

In the Tanzloran council chambers, a majestic amphitheater carved into a massive crystal formation, the other elders awaited Sylvaris's arrival. The room pulsed with faint light, the crystalline walls resonating softly as though amplifying the thoughts of those within.

Sylvaris glided into the chamber, his robes shimmering with each step. The other elders turned, their luminous eyes widening as they sensed his distress. Elder Brakar, her silver hair cascading like starlight, stepped forward.

"Sylvaris, what troubles you? The forest whispers of your unease."

He raised his hand, and the air around them shimmered, projecting the vision from the sacred pool. The council watched in horror as the darkness consumed their world.

"The Umbralox," Elder Draven breathed, visibly quivering. "We thought it vanquished eons ago."

"It slumbered," Sylvaris replied, his voice heavy. "And now it awakens, hungry for the life force of Tanzlora."

Each elder, tall and graceful, shared Sylvaris's shimmering blue-violet complexion, their features marked with the wisdom of countless cycles.

Elder Thaloria, her eyes a swirling nebula of purple and gold, stepped forward. "We must act swiftly. The Umbralox's awakening threatens not just Tanzlora, but the also the sister planets."

The council chamber hummed with tension as the elders conferred in hushed tones. Sylvaris's gaze swept over his peers, noting the fear etched on their ageless faces.

"There is but one hope," he said, his voice cutting through the murmurs. "The Beaumonts."

A collective gasp rippled through the chamber. Elder Draven, his robes shimmering like the wind given form, shook his head. "They won't come, Lincoln and Bethany Beaumont left to make their life on Earth with their family. The family has sacrificed enough, we must find another way so they can live in peace."

"Perhaps," Sylvaris conceded, "but the Beaumont family is intertwined with the Umbralox more than you realize and we must not forget the Triadorne. They are the only way to the weapon that will eradicate the Umbralox for eternity.

"Sylvaris is right", Elder Brakar said, "Tanzlora is in grave danger. The Beaumonts are the only hope."

The air in the chamber grew heavy as each of the Elders pondered the dire situation, their expressions grave.

Elder Brakar, the most revered among them, stood. Her voice, soft yet commanding, resonated like the chime of distant bells. "The Umbralox... if it has returned, then the danger is greater than we feared."

"What do we do?" Elder Draven asked, his tone laced with urgency.

Brakar turned her luminous gaze to Sylvaris. "We must summon Keelee. He is our most capable envoy and the only one who can bridge the gap between Tanzlora and the Beaumonts. If there is any hope of survival, it lies with them."

Sylvaris nodded. "I will bring Keelee at once."

Keelee stood on the edge of a shimmering plateau, the Lucidis Forest stretching out below him like a sea of light. His form, tall and graceful, radiated strength. His blue-violet skin glistened under the twin suns, and his long hair, a cascade of shimmering silver, flowed in the breeze.

Keelee's amber eyes, flecked with gold, scanned the horizon as he sensed Sylvaris's approach. He turned, bowing his head in respect as the Elder materialized beside him.

"Keelee," Sylvaris began, his voice grave, "the council requires your assistance. The fate of Tanzlora hangs in the balance."

Keelee's expression tightened, his jaw clenching as he absorbed the weight of Sylvaris's words. "What has happened, Elder?"

As Sylvaris recounted the vision and the council's decision, Keelee's eyes widened. The Umbralox, a name whispered in ancient legends, now threatened their very existence. And the Beaumonts—a family he knew all too well.

"You wish me to bring them back," Keelee stated, his voice a mixture of awe and trepidation.

Sylvaris nodded solemnly. "You are the only one who can, Keelee. Your connection to Earth and your history with the Beaumonts make you uniquely suited for this task."

Keelee turned his gaze back to the shimmering forest below, memories flooding his mind. He remembered the day he escorted Bethany Beaumont and her twins to Earth to join their family, their faces etched with both sorrow and hope. They had a simpler life on Earth, away from the cosmic battles. And now, he would have to shatter that peace.

Sylvaris placed a comforting hand on Keelee's shoulder. "I know the burden we place upon you."

Keelee took a deep breath, his chest rising and falling as he steeled himself for the task ahead. "I understand, Elder. I will bring them back."

Sylvaris nodded, relief flickering across his ethereal features. "Time is of the essence. The Umbralox grows stronger with each passing moment."

"I'll leave at once," Keelee said, his voice resolute.

Keelee closed his eyes, the weight of his mission settling heavily upon him. When he opened them again, determination burned in their amber depths. "I will not fail you, Elder. I will not fail Tanzlora."

Keelee left Sylvaris and quickly headed to the Reficiat Haven where the healer Sanodia could help him with the herbal mixture he would need to acclimate to Earth's environment.

Normally Keelee would appear holographically on Earth to communicate with the Beaumont family but this dire of a situation required a physical presence meeting. Preparations for this will take more effort.

Arriving at the Haven, Keelee immediately sought out the location of Sanodia. He strode through the crystalline halls of the Reficiat Haven, his footsteps echoing softly against the iridescent walls. The air was thick with the scent of exotic herbs and healing elixirs, a testament to the countless remedies prepared within these sacred chambers.

As he rounded a corner, he caught sight of Sanodia. The healer stood before a wall of shimmering vials, her slender fingers dancing over their surfaces as she murmured ancient incantations. Her skin, a deeper shade of violet than most Tanzlorans, seemed to pulse with an inner light.

"Sanodia," Keelee called, his voice cutting through the ambient hum of the Haven.

The healer turned, her eyes widening as she took in Keelee's tense posture. "Keelee, what brings you here with such urgency?"

Quickly, Keelee explained the situation—the awakening of the Umbralox, the council's decision for him to go to Earth and ask the Beaumont family for assistance.

Sanodia's expression grew grave as she listened. "I see. You'll need a potent mixture to withstand Earth's atmosphere and gravity. It's been some time since a Tanzloran physically traveled there."

She turned to her workstation, her robes flowing like liquid starlight. With practiced efficiency, she began selecting various herbs and crystals, grinding them into a fine powder.

"This will be stronger than what you're used to," Sanodia explained as she worked. "It will allow you to maintain your physical form on Earth for up to three of their days. Any longer, and you'll need to return or risk severe illness."

Keelee nodded, watching intently as Sanodia combined the ingredients in a small, ornate vial. The mixture glowed with an inner light, shifting through various hues of blue and violet.

"Drink this just before you depart through the portal," Sanodia instructed as she held the vial out for Keelee to take.

Keelee accepted the vial, carefully tucking it into a hidden pocket in his robes. "Thank you, Sanodia. Your skills may have saved not just me, but all of Tanzlora."

The healer's eyes softened. "May the light of the twin suns guide you, Keelee. And may the Beaumonts heed your call."

With a respectful nod, Keelee turned and strode out of the Reficiat Haven, his steps purposeful. The weight of his mission pressed upon him, urging him forward. He made his way to the Portal Chamber, an ancient structure hewn from living crystal at the heart of the Lucidus Forest.

As he approached, the massive doors of the chamber sensed his presence and slowly swung open. Inside, the air crackled with energy, and at the center stood the shimmering Crystal Gate.

Out of the entire universe, only three of these existed. Keelee stood in front of one, while another was located on the sister planet of Arcmyrin. The third one could be found on Earth, specifically at Sage Manor. Keelee would soon emerge from this third structure to initiate communication with the Beaumont family.

Keelee stood before the Crystal Gate, its surface rippling like liquid starlight. He took a deep breath, steadying himself for the journey ahead. With practiced movements, he retrieved the vial Sanodia had prepared and drank its contents in one swift motion. The mixture tingled as it coursed through his body, preparing him for Earth's foreign environment.

He placed his hand on the gate's surface, feeling the familiar hum of energy beneath his fingers. Closing his eyes, Keelee focused his thoughts on Earth, on Sage Manor, and on the Beaumont family. The gate responded to his intent, its surface swirling faster, forming a vortex of light and color.

With a final glance back at the lush, shimmering world of Tanzlora, Keelee stepped through the portal. The sensation of interdimensional travel was instantaneous – a rush of energy, a moment of weightlessness, and then the familiar pull. In a flash of blinding light, he was gone.

Moments later, Keelee materialized in the hidden chamber beneath Sage Manor's gazebo on Earth. The air felt heavy and thick compared to Tanzlora's, and he stumbled slightly as he adjusted for Earth's atmosphere.

After taking a moment to orient himself, he surveyed the stone walls, adorned with mystical symbols that faintly glowed in the dim light. He began his gradual climb up the stone stairs, the joyous sounds of singing and laughter growing louder as he approached the top. Finally, he reached the stone door and stepped onto the creaky wooden planks of the gazebo.

2

The gardens of Sage Manor were in full bloom, the late afternoon sun casting a golden glow over rows of vibrant roses, lilies, and wildflowers. A long table, adorned with pastel linens and bouquets, stretched beneath the shade of a grand oak tree. Balloons swayed gently in the breeze, and the sound of children's laughter mingled with the chirping of birds.

Maya and Maddox Beaumont, the youngest members of the family, were the center of attention, their wide smiles and sparkling eyes lighting up the gathering. Maya's curly auburn hair was adorned with flower clips, and Maddox, his blond locks slightly tousled, wore a crown of daisies he'd insisted on making himself.

"Happy birthday to you!" The family's voices harmonized as they gathered around a beautifully decorated cake, two sets of candles flickering atop it. The twins leaned forward, their small faces alight with excitement, and blew out the candles together.

Cheers erupted, and the twins laughed as bits of confetti rained down on them. Gran Celia clapped enthusiastically, her silver hair shining in the sunlight. "Perfect! Another year wiser for my little starlights."

Waverly handed out slices of cake, her movements graceful and precise. She smiled at the twins. "Six years old already. When did that happen?"

"Time moves differently when you're this close to the cosmos," Ridge said, smirking as he leaned against a nearby pillar. "These two are growing up faster than we can blink."

Bethany, the twins' mother, placed a gentle hand on their shoulders, her emerald eyes glowing with pride. "They've done so well since we came back to Earth. Better than I expected, really."

"It helps that they've got such a strong support system," Lincoln added, wrapping an arm around his wife. His deep voice carried warmth and admiration. "And a family that's a little too experienced with inter-planetary adaptation."

Lynx, lounging on a blanket nearby, raised an eyebrow. "Still, you have to admit, they're not like other Earth kids. Not entirely."

"No," Bethany admitted, her gaze lingering on Maddox, who was giggling with Maya as they chased butterflies. "But they're finding their way. Tanzlora will always be part of them, but Earth is their home now."

As the celebration continued, Maddox suddenly broke away from the group, his playful demeanor replaced by an expression of confusion. He made his way to his father, tugging on Lincoln's sleeve. "Dad?"

Lincoln crouched down to Maddox's level. "What's up, buddy?"

Maddox hesitated, looking down at his shoes before meeting his father's eyes. "I feel... funny."

"Funny how?" Lincoln asked, concern creeping into his voice.

"My head," Maddox said, tapping his temple. "It's humming. And kind of... vibrating. Like there's music I can't hear, but I know it's there."

Lincoln frowned, his brows knitting together. "Does it hurt?"

Maddox shook his head. "No, it's just... weird."

Lincoln patted his son's shoulder reassuringly. "Okay, let's talk to Mom about this."

He guided Maddox back to Bethany, who was arranging a platter of fruit. "Beth, Maddox says his head's humming. Vibrating, even."

Bethany froze mid-motion, her face turning serious. "Humming? Vibrating?" She crouched down and took Maddox's hands in hers. "Sweetheart, when did this start?"

"A little while ago. It got stronger when we were singing," Maddox said. "I didn't want to tell everyone, but it's like there's something... trying to talk to me."

Bethany exchanged a sharp look with Lincoln, her voice lowering. "He's picking up on something. A higher consciousness entity. The vibrations aren't random."

Lincoln's face darkened. "You think it's connected to Tanzlora?"

"It could be," Bethany said. "Or it could be something else. Either way, we can't ignore it."

"Ridge!" Lincoln called, his tone urgent. Ridge, who had been laughing at one of Waverly's quips, immediately straightened and came over.

"What's going on?" Ridge asked, his relaxed demeanor replaced with alertness.

Bethany quickly explained Maddox's symptoms. "It's possible the portal has been activated, or something is trying to come through. You and Lincoln need to check the chamber."

Ridge nodded, his jaw tightening. "Let's go."

While the others tried to maintain the festive atmosphere for the twin's sake, Lincoln and Ridge slipped away, heading for the chamber underneath the gazebo. The chamber, an ancient, hidden part of the estate, housed the portal that connected Earth to its sister planets, Tanzlora and Arcmyrin—an interplanetary gateway to the cosmos.

As they rounded the corner of the house, they could see a form standing in the middle of the gazebo. Immediately alarmed, Lincoln and Ridge slowed their approach, exchanging a wary glance.

The figure turned, revealing a tall, elegant form with blue-violet skin shimmering in the golden light of the setting sun. His silver hair, cascading like a waterfall, his vibrant eyes scanning the grounds before settling on Lincoln and Ridge.

"Keelee," Lincoln breathed, recognition dawning on his face.

Ridge tensed beside him. "What are you doing here? The portal wasn't supposed to be activated."

Keelee smiled, a gentle, sad expression. "I'm sorry for the intrusion, but I come with urgent news from the Elder Council of Tanzlora." His voice was melodic, carrying the whisper of cosmic winds.

Lincoln stepped forward, his heart racing. "What's happened?

"Elder Sylvaris has seen a vision," Keelee began, his tone steady but urgent. "A shadowy entity—an ancient force—is corrupting Tanzlora's core. The Umbralox is feeding on our life essence, and our world cannot withstand its assault for long."

Lincoln frowned. "The Umbralox? That's... ancient history. It hasn't been mentioned in—"

"In millennia," Keelee interrupted. "We believed it was destroyed. But now it has returned, stronger than ever."

"And you think we can help?" Ridge asked, crossing his arms.

Keelee's gaze fixed on him. "The Elders believe you are the only ones who can. Tanzlora's history and Earth's are more intertwined than you realize. The Beaumonts have faced threats of this magnitude before."

Lincoln exchanged a glance with Ridge. "Keelee, our family has already sacrificed so much. We've only just resettled here—our children are finally acclimating to life on Earth."

Keelee's face softened with understanding but remained resolute. "I wouldn't ask if it weren't absolutely necessary. The Umbralox will not stop with Tanzlora. Its corruption will spread across the cosmos, and Earth will not be spared."

Keelee stepped closer. "I understand your fears, Lincoln, but this time, your entire family must come. Ridge, Waverly and Lynx's unique abilities are crucial, and Bethany..." Keelee hesitated, his gaze locking in on the party in the distance. "The elders believe she holds a key to understanding this threat. Your family's connection to Tanzlora is deeper than you know."

Ridge shook his head. "No. They can't leave their children again."

Keelee's jaw tightened. "No, Ridge. The Elders were clear—all of you must come. Tanzlora's survival depends on it."

Lincoln stood quietly, his arms crossed. "If the Elders are right, then this isn't just about Tanzlora. If we don't heed this call for help, then the Umbralox's reach could spread here. Do we really have a choice?"

Ridge's voice faltered. "But Maddox and Maya... they've only just found their footing here. How can they endure more upheaval?"

Lincoln looked at his brother and then back to Keelee. "If we agree to this, you'll need to give us time to prepare. We won't leave without ensuring the children are settled."

Keelee inclined his head. "Of course. But please, do not delay for too long. Tanzlora's time is running out."

As the brothers exchanged determined glances, Keelee turned and started walking back towards the gazebo.

"Where are you going?" asked Ridge.

"To sit in the gazebo while you speak with your family," replied Keelee.

"Nonsense," exclaimed Lincoln, "you are coming with us to join the family at the party. Bethany and the twins will be happy to see you."

"Sure they will," drawled Ridge sarcastically, "until you tell them why you are here."

Keelee hesitated, his luminous eyes flickering between the brothers. "I... I'm not sure that's appropriate. My presence may cause alarm."

"Nonsense," Lincoln repeated, more firmly this time. "You're practically family. Besides, it's better we explain this situation together."

As they made their way back to the celebration, the sounds of laughter and chatter grew louder. Maya spotted them first, her eyes widening with delight.

"Keelee!" she squealed, breaking away from the group to run towards them. Maddox was close behind, his earlier discomfort forgotten in the excitement of seeing their Tanzlorian friend.

Bethany's head snapped up at Maya's exclamation, her smile faltering as she took in the serious expressions on Lincoln and Ridge's faces.

Keelee's stoic demeanor softened as he knelt to embrace the children. "My, how you've grown," he said, his melodic voice filled with warmth. "You're becoming quite the young Tanzlorians."

"We're Earth kids now," Maddox said proudly, puffing out his chest. "But we still remember how to do the star dance you taught us!"

Maya nodded eagerly. "Watch!" She began to twirl, her arms outstretched, fingers splayed like starbursts. Maddox joined in, their movements surprisingly graceful and synchronized for children their age.

Keelee's eyes shimmered with emotion as he watched them. "You haven't forgotten. That's wonderful. You are children of both worlds, and that makes you very special indeed."

By now, the rest of the family had gathered around, their expressions a mix of joy at seeing Keelee and concern at his unexpected appearance.

Gran Celia clapped her hands together. "Well, isn't this lovely! Another guest for the party. Waverly, dear, fetch another plate for Keelee, won't you?"

As Waverly moved to comply, Lynx caught Lincoln's eye and raised an eyebrow in silent question. Lincoln shrugged his shoulders and silently answered back 'later' to which Lynx gave a quick nod of understanding.

Bethany approached, her emerald eyes searching Keelee's face. "It's good to see you, old friend. But I sense this isn't just a social call."

Keelee straightened, his gaze meeting Bethany's. "You're right, of course. I'm afraid I bring news that may dampen the celebration so let's speak about it after the festivities are finished."

Waverly arrived with a plate of food and Keelee graciously accepted it. He was uncertain if the potion he had taken earlier had completely activated enough to allow him the enjoyment of Earth's food. He held the plate and pushed the food around with the utensils to make it appear he was eating.

Bethany noticed and leaned in to whisper, "Go easy, we don't have Tanzloran healers here to help if you get ill."

Before Keelee could answer her, Gran Celia was calling for everyone to gather around the gift table. It was time for the twins to open their presents.

3

The garden was still alive with the sounds of laughter and celebration. Maya and Maddox were now busy unwrapping presents under the watchful eyes of their grandmother, Gran Celia. Waverly, Lynx and Ridge stood nearby, chatting softly as the warm glow of early evening settled over Sage Manor.

Lincoln and Bethany invited Keelee to sit down at one of the cheerily decorated tables to further discuss the reason for his visit.

Keelee settled into a wrought iron chair, its cushion still warm from the afternoon sun. He cleared his throat, his eyes darting between Lincoln and Bethany.

"I hate to bring business to such a joyous occasion," he began, his voice low yet still melodic. "But I'm afraid time is of the essence."

Bethany leaned forward, her brow furrowing. "What is it, Keelee? You've got me worried now."

Bethany reached for her husband's hand, her fingers intertwining with his as she braced herself for whatever Keelee was about to reveal.

"Elder Sylvaris's had a vision unlike anything we have seen before," Keelee said, his voice soft but filled with gravity. "The Umbralox has returned to Tanzlora, spreading darkness across the land. The Elders believe it will only grow stronger unless it is confronted—and soon."

Lincoln frowned, leaning forward slightly as he processed Keelee's words. "How did it come back?" he questioned quietly. "I thought the Umbralox had been eradicated during the Galactic War."

Keelee inclined his head slightly. "So did we. But shadows, as we have learned, do not always stay buried. The Elders fear the Umbralox's return may be tied to a greater disturbance within the Triad—one that affects Earth as well."

Bethany's face tightened, her arms folding protectively across her chest. "And now the Elders want us to come to Tanzlora?" Her voice was steady, but there was no mistaking the edge of emotion beneath it.

Keelee met her gaze evenly, his expression sympathetic. "Yes. The elders have asked for your help, Bethany. Not just yours, but Lincoln's, Ridge's, Waverly's, and Lynx's as well. Together, with the elemental spirits, the Elders believe you are uniquely suited to stop the Umbralox."

Bethany's hands gripped the edge of the table, her knuckles pale against the bright tablecloth. "And what about Maya and Maddox?" she asked sharply, her voice rising. "They're only six, Keelee. We've barely begun to help them adjust to life on Earth. After five years on Tanzlora, this is finally starting to feel like home for them. I won't uproot them again. I can't leave them—not when they've come so far."

Lincoln reached out, resting a steady hand on Bethany's arm. "Beth, I know it's hard—"

She pulled back, turning to look at him. "It's not hard, Lincoln—it's impossible. We promised them stability. We promised them this life." Her voice broke slightly as she continued. "And now, after everything they've been through, we're supposed to leave them behind? Like we did Waverly and Lynx?"

Lincoln winced at her words.

Keelee's glow softened, his tone soothing. "Bethany, I understand your concerns. Truly, I do. The well-being of your children is always paramount. But this mission is about their future too. If the Umbralox is not stopped, its darkness will spread—beyond Tanzlora, beyond Arcmyrin. Earth will not remain untouched."

Bethany's expression wavered, tears welling in her eyes as she looked away. "They're just kids, Keelee. They don't deserve this."

Lincoln exhaled slowly, his voice calm but firm. "Bethany, we've always known that protecting the Triad was part of our legacy. We can't let the darkness spread—not if we can stop it."

"Legacy?" Bethany snapped, turning back to him. "This isn't about legacy—it's about our children. They need us here."

Keelee spoke gently, his words deliberate. "The council is aware of the sacrifices they are asking of you. That is why Elder Draven has suggested sending Tanzloran warriors to Earth. They will protect Sage Manor and your family while you are gone."

Bethany's brow furrowed as she considered his words. "Tanzloran warriors? Here?"

"Yes," Keelee said with a nod. "Callum, the son of Marellis, will lead the warriors. You know him well, Bethany. He will ensure your children—and Sage Manor—are protected."

At the mention of Callum, a flicker of recognition passed over Bethany's face. She fell silent for a moment, her shoulders slumping as she ran a hand through her hair. "Callum," she murmured. "I remember him. He was always kind... steady."

Lincoln squeezed her arm gently. "Beth, if there's anyone we can trust to keep the twins safe, it's Callum and the warriors."

Bethany closed her eyes briefly, taking a deep breath as the tension in her shoulders eased slightly. "It still feels like we're abandoning them."

Keelee's voice was soft but resolute. "You are not abandoning them, Bethany. You are fighting to ensure their future—a future free from the shadows. And when you return, it will be to a world you helped protect."

The trio fell silent for a moment, the weight of Keelee's words settling over them like a heavy blanket. Bethany sat back in her chair, her expression pained but determined. "We'll need to prepare them," she said quietly. "Maya and Maddox deserve to know why we're leaving, even if we can't explain everything."

Lincoln nodded, his expression steady. "We'll do this together, Beth. We'll make sure they're safe. And then we'll do what we have to do."

Keelee inclined his head in gratitude, his glow brightening slightly. "Thank you, Lincoln. Thank you, Bethany. The Elders and all of Tanzlora will not forget your sacrifice."

Bethany gave a small nod, her attention drawn to the children who were still eagerly unwrapping presents and proudly displaying them to Gran Celia, Lynx, Waverly, and Ridge. A bittersweet smile graced her lips as she thought about leaving the children behind, even if it was just for a short time.

Later that evening after the children had been tucked into their beds for the night, the family invited Keelee to sit with them in the parlor. It was steeped in a warm glow, the flickering light of a crackling fire casting dancing shadows across the intricately carved wooden walls. The family usually gathered for the evening taking their usual seats, the gravity of what they had heard from Keelee settling heavily on their shoulders.

Waverly and Lynx sat on the velvet sofa still not completely certain of the journey that lay before them. Lynx, being briefed by Ridge, was idly flipping through one of the old journals they'd retrieved from the manor's archives.

Lincoln leaned against the mantel, arms crossed, while Bethany relaxed on a chaise lounge, her brow furrowed as she took notes on a pad of paper. Gran Celia perched near the hearth, her calm presence anchoring the room, while Ridge sprawled comfortably in a wingback chair, sharpening a knife with practiced ease. Keelee was seated in the matching wingback chair next to Ridge.

Bethany exhaled deeply. "If we're really doing this, we need to be strategic. Tanzlora isn't Earth. The environment is different, the dangers are different, and we can't afford to be unprepared."

Lincoln nodded. "Agreed. But I am not so worried about reacclimating to the environment since we lived there. Beth, you and I will be fine, it's Ridge, Waverly and Lynx who will need more preparation." He sighed and continued, "What we really need is more information about the Umbralox. Maybe Sage Manor's library might have it."

"Keelee,what else can you tell us about this evil?" asked Bethany.

Before Keelee could answer, Lynx glanced up from his reading. "I found a mention of the Umbralox in this journal. It's vague, but there's a passage about a shadow entity that 'consumes life at its core.' It sounds like what Keelee described."

"Let me see that," Waverly said, leaning over to read the passage Lynx pointed out. Her eyes scanned the text, her expression growing darker with every line. "This isn't just some random threat. The Umbralox is older than Tanzlora's recorded history"

Ridge set his knife aside. "What about protection for the portal? If the Umbralox is as dangerous as it sounds, what's stopping it from using the Crystal Gate to come here?"

Lincoln's jaw tightened. "Good point. Keelee?"

"I realize," Keelee began, his tone calm but grave, "that many of you do not yet fully understand the nature of the Umbralox."

He paused, as if he were gathering his thoughts. "The Umbralox are not like any enemy you have faced before. They are not creatures in the traditional sense. They are manifestations of corruption—shadows born of an ancient darkness that predates the Galactic War. Where there is chaos, where there is fear, the Umbralox take hold. They do not merely destroy; they consume. They erode the life force of everything they touch."

Lynx, arms crossed, frowned deeply. "So, they're parasites? Feeding off fear and destruction?"

"In a way, yes," Keelee replied. "But the danger lies in their adaptability. They can infiltrate any environment—creeping through cracks in the physical world and anchoring themselves in places of power. Their goal is to spread, like a sickness, until everything is swallowed by shadow."

Bethany shivered slightly, wrapping her arms around herself. "How would they get through to Earth? What would they want here?"

Keelee sighed deeply, as if weighed down by the question. "The Umbralox have always sought out nexuses of power—places where energy flows strongest, where the boundaries between realms are thin. Sage Manor, as you know, is one such place. The portal beneath this chamber is a point of great energy, a link between worlds."

Waverly's sharp gaze fixed on Keelee. "You think they're trying to use the Crystal Gate to come through."

Keelee inclined his head. "Yes. If the Umbralox can anchor themselves to the gate and pass through fully, they could spread to Earth unchecked. If they gain a foothold here, it will be catastrophic."

Ridge shifted uneasily, "Then how do we stop them? How do we keep them from getting through the Crystal Gate?"

Keelee turned to Ridge, his voice steady but urgent. "The gate itself must remain pure. It is attuned to balance and harmony. The Umbralox cannot corrupt it outright, but they can exploit weaknesses in its energy—particularly if fear or doubt seeps into those connected to it."

Lincoln's brow furrowed as he processed Keelee's words. "So, it's not just about the gate—it's about us. If we're not strong enough, they'll use our own fears against us."

"Yes," Keelee said solemnly. "The bond you share with the elemental spirits and with one another is your greatest defense. The gate cannot be corrupted as long as its guardians—you—remain resolute."

Bethany's voice was tight with concern. "But if the Umbralox are already trying to come through, how do we strengthen the gate and stop them?"

Keelee brightened as he spoke. "The gate responds to purity of intent. The elemental spirits, when combined with your gifts, can reinforce the energy of the gate."

Lynx let out a slow breath, "It's like playing defense while preparing for offense. Keep the shadows out of here while we deal with the real fight on Tanzlora."

Keelee's expression softened slightly, admiration in his glowing gaze. "Precisely, Lynx. You understand what is at stake. The Umbralox cannot be allowed to cross into your world."

Lincoln stepped forward, his tone resolute. "Then we'll do what needs to be done. We'll protect the gate. We'll keep Sage Manor safe, and we'll stop the Umbralox on Tanzlora."

Bethany nodded, though worry lingered in her eyes. "We'll fight them, Keelee. But we can't lose sight of what's at home—our family, the twins."

Keelee gazed at Bethany reassuringly. "The Tanzloran warriors who arrive soon will guard Sage Manor while you are away. Callum understands the importance of what is happening here. Your family will be safe under his watch."

The room fell silent for a moment as the gravity of the situation sank in. Waverly broke the silence, her voice clear and determined. "Then we stop them. We guard the gate, we protect Earth, and we fight for Tanzlora."

Ridge smirked faintly, his confidence returning. "They're not going to know what hit them."

Lincoln placed a steady hand on Ridge's shoulder. "We fight as a family. And we don't let the darkness win."

Keelee bowed his head slightly, grateful for their willingness to join in the battle. "Be ready, Beaumonts. The shadows are watching, and the real fight is about to begin."

Just as Bethany opened her mouth to respond, a loud, insistent knocking echoed through the house. The sound was jarring, breaking the quiet tension of the parlor and startling everyone to their feet.

"Who could that be at this hour?" Gran Celia murmured, already moving toward the door. Lincoln and Ridge followed close behind, their expressions wary.

The knocking came again, faster and more frantic. Gran Celia opened the door to reveal their neighbor, Lorinda Rooney, standing on the porch with her young daughter, Monica. Both were in their night clothes and robes, their faces pale and eyes wide with fear.

4

"Lorinda," Gran Celia said, quickly ushering them inside. "What's happened? You both look terrified."

Lorinda stumbled into the parlor, clutching Monica's hand tightly. "Celia, I'm so sorry to come unannounced, but—" She hesitated, glancing nervously at the others in the room. Keelee had stepped into the library to avoid more fright for the newly arrived Earthlings. "Something strange happened at our house tonight. I didn't know where else to go."

"It's all right," Gran Celia said soothingly, leading them to the sofa. "Sit down, get warm. Take your time."

Monica, shivering slightly, clung to her mother's side as Lorinda sat down, her hands trembling. "It started a little after we went to bed. Monica woke me up, saying she heard voices—whispers coming from the walls."

"They weren't just whispers, Mama," Monica whispered, her voice trembling. "It sounded like... like someone trying to get in."

Waverly and Lynx exchanged uneasy glances. Lincoln knelt beside Monica, his tone calm and reassuring. "Did you see anything, sweetheart?"

The young girl nodded hesitantly. "Shadows. They were moving, even though there was no light."

Lorinda's eyes welled with tears. "When I checked the house, I felt... something. A pressure, like the air was thick. And then the lights started flickering. I grabbed Monica and ran. I came here because I did not know where else to go. The Sheriff would think we are looney tunes if we went there and told him we were fearful of shadows."

Bethany's face hardened. "You did the right thing coming here."

Gran Celia placed a comforting hand on Lorinda's shoulder. "You're safe now and we don't think you are looney at all. What you two experienced sounds frightening and whatever it was, it can't follow you here."

Waverly stood, her expression grim. "Shadows. We need to check their house. If this is connected to Keelee's urgent message, it means the threat is already here on Earth."

Lincoln rose as well. "Ridge and I will go. The rest of you stay here and make sure Lorinda and Monica are settled."

"No," Waverly said firmly. "I'm coming too. If this is connected to the Umbralox, I need to see it for myself."

Lorinda looked at Waverly very confused, "Who is Keelee? What is the Umbralox? What kind of threat are you talking about?"

Gran Celia nodded in agreement with Waverly while starting to pat Lorinda's shoulder in a reassuring manner. "Go to Lorinda's house, but be careful. And don't linger if you sense anything dangerous. Bethany and I can explain this to her."

As Lincoln, Ridge, and Waverly prepared to leave, Bethany sat beside Lorinda, speaking softly to calm her nerves. When the front door closed behind the trio, Gran Celia's gaze lingered on it, her unease growing.

Keelee was standing at the bottom of the front porch steps waiting on them. "I am coming with you, I heard the story of her fright," he said.

"Jump in," Ridge replied, as the group headed towards the garage where his vehicle was parked.

The Jeep rumbled down the winding country road, its headlights cutting through the dark. Ridge gripped the steering wheel tightly, his usual laid-back demeanor replaced by a steely focus. Lincoln sat in the passenger seat, his jaw set and eyes scanning the roadside for any signs of movement. Waverly and Keelee sat in the back, leaning forward slightly, their senses on high alert.

Lorinda and Monica's house was a couple of miles away from Sage Manor, nestled in a clearing surrounded by thick woods. It was quiet—too quiet, Waverly thought. Even the crickets seemed to hold their breath as the Jeep approached.

"Does anyone else feel like the air's heavier here?" Ridge said, breaking the silence.

"Not just heavy," Waverly murmured, her voice low. "It's charged. Like something's waiting."

Lincoln turned his head slightly, his expression dark. "We've felt this kind of energy before. It's never a good sign."

As Ridge pulled into the gravel driveway, the house loomed before them, its silhouette stark against the blackness of the forest. The lights inside were off, and the curtains drawn tight, giving the place an eerie, lifeless feel.

There was an unsettling shimmer around the edges of the windows, as if the glass itself was vibrating. The porch light flickered erratically, casting eerie shadows that seemed to move of their own accord.

"This is not good," Keelee whispered. "The Umbralox have definitely been here."

Ridge killed the engine, and the four of them stepped out of the Jeep. The air hit them immediately—dense, almost suffocating, with a faint metallic tang.

Waverly froze, her hand instinctively going to the small cloud shaped charm necklace she wore. She closed her eyes, letting her senses extend outward. The air hummed faintly, almost imperceptibly, but to her, it felt like a whisper brushing against her mind.

"There's something here," she said, her voice barely above a whisper. "It's not just inside the house. It's... everywhere."

Ridge's hand went to the knife holstered at his side. "Yeah, I feel it too. It's like the woods are watching us."

Lincoln led the way toward the house, his flashlight cutting a narrow path through the darkness. The gravel crunched under their boots, loud against the oppressive silence.

They approached the house cautiously, Waverly and Keelee bringing up the rear. As they neared the front porch, Waverly stopped abruptly.

"Wait," she said, holding up a hand.

Lincoln, Ridge and Keelee froze, their eyes darting around the clearing.

"What is it?" Lincoln asked.

Waverly pointed toward the edge of the woods, where the faint outline of something unnatural shimmered in the shadows. It was faint, almost imperceptible, but it pulsed faintly, like a heartbeat.

"Do you see that?" she whispered.

Lincoln followed her gaze, his flashlight beam slicing through the trees. It landed on the shimmering shape for a split second before it vanished, dissolving into the darkness.

"What the hell was that?" Ridge hissed, his voice tense.

"Something that doesn't belong here," Keelee said.

Waverly stepped closer to the edge of the porch, her hand outstretched as if feeling for the unseen.

Suddenly, the ground beneath their feet seemed to tremble, just slightly, but enough to make Ridge and Lincoln glance at each other.

"We're definitely not alone," Lincoln said grimly, his hand moving to the weapon holstered at his hip.

Waverly turned to face them, her expression resolute. "Whatever this is, it's testing us. It's trying to decide if we're a threat."

"Then let's show it we are," Ridge said, his tone sharp as he took a step forward.

Waverly shook her head. "Not yet. We don't know enough about it. Let's focus on the house first and figure out what spooked Lorinda and Monica."

The four of them moved cautiously up the porch steps, the old wood creaking under their weight.

Lincoln tested the door—it was locked. He glanced at Waverly, who nodded.

"Let's go around back," she suggested.

As they moved toward the rear of the house, the oppressive air seemed to thicken, and the faint hum grew louder. Ridge stopped abruptly, his eyes narrowing.

"Did you hear that?" he asked, his voice low.

Lincoln, Waverly and Keelee paused, listening intently. For a moment, there was nothing but the sound of their own breathing. Then, faint and distant, came a low whisper—a sound like wind moving through dead leaves, but with words hidden beneath.

"It's trying to communicate," Keelee said softly.

"Or lure us," Lincoln countered.

Ridge gripped his knife tighter. "Either way, I'm not a fan."

They rounded the corner of the house and found the back door ajar, swaying slightly in the faint breeze.

"I would venture to say that Lorinda would not have left that open," Lincoln said.

"Probably not," Waverly agreed, stepping closer. She motioned for the others to stay back as she peered inside.

The kitchen beyond was dark, the faint moonlight through the windows casting long shadows across the room. Nothing seemed out of place, but the humming sensation was stronger now, pressing against her mind like an insistent whisper.

"Stay close," she said, stepping inside.

Lincoln, Ridge and Keelee followed, their footsteps careful and deliberate. The house was silent, but the energy in the air was anything but calm.

"There is a strong presence here," Keelee whispered, his usually melodic voice tight with tension. "Be on your guard."

As they moved deeper into the house, the hum grew louder, and the shadows seemed to shift, stretching and twisting unnaturally. Waverly stopped in the center of the living room, her heart pounding.

"It's here," she said, her voice steady but strained. "Whatever it is, it's still here."

Lincoln and Ridge exchanged a tense glance, both gripping their weapons tightly.

"Then let's find it," Lincoln said, his tone firm.

Ridge nodded. "Before it finds us."

Waverly stood motionless in the center of Lorinda's living room, her eyes scanning the shifting shadows as the oppressive hum pressed against her senses.

The faint scent of something acrid—burnt wood or metal—hung in the air, mingling with the lingering traces of the Rooneys' everyday life. The dichotomy was unsettling.

"It's close," she murmured. "I can feel it moving."

Lincoln stood at her side, his flashlight sweeping the corners of the room. "Then why can't we see it?" he muttered, his voice taut.

"Because it doesn't want to be seen," Ridge said from the doorway, his knife glinting faintly in the dim light. "Whatever this thing is, it's toying with us."

A sudden creak sounded from the ceiling above them. All four froze, their heads snapping upward in unison. The noise came again—soft, deliberate, like someone pacing. Waverly exchanged a glance with Lincoln, whose jaw tightened.

"Second floor," he said.

Waverly nodded, already moving toward the staircase. "Stay close."

The stairs groaned under their weight as they ascended, the hum growing louder with each step. Ridge brought up the rear, his eyes scanning their surroundings, his knife ready. As they reached the landing, the air seemed to shift, colder and sharper.

"Something doesn't feel right," Ridge whispered.

Waverly pointed to a door at the end of the hall, where a faint light flickered under the frame. "There."

Lincoln moved forward, gripping the door handle tightly before glancing back at his daughter. She gave him a short nod. With one swift motion, he pushed the door open, flashlight beam cutting through the darkness.

The room was empty—or so it seemed at first glance. The bed was neatly made, and the curtains hung undisturbed. But the hum was almost deafening now, vibrating in their bones.

"Check the corners," Waverly said, stepping inside. Her gaze swept the room, landing on a large, ornate mirror hanging on the far wall. It seemed out of place—too ornate for the modest home.

"That doesn't fit in with the rest of the decor in this guest room," Ridge said, narrowing his eyes.

The surface of the mirror was strangely dull, as if it absorbed the light rather than reflecting it. Waverly approached cautiously, the hum growing louder with every step.

"This isn't just a mirror," she said, her voice barely audible over the sound. She reached out, her fingers just inches from the surface.

"Waverly, don't!" Keelee warned, but it was too late.

Her fingertips grazed the cold surface, and the room exploded with sound and light. The hum became a roar, and the mirror's surface rippled violently, as though it were liquid. Shadows poured out, spilling into the room like living smoke.

"Get back!" Ridge shouted, pulling Waverly away just as one of the shadows lashed out like a whip, striking the floor where she had stood.

Lincoln fired his weapon, the blast illuminating the room for a split second. The shadow recoiled, hissing like a wounded animal. Waverly scrambled to her feet, her heart pounding as the shadows coiled and writhed, filling the room with their oppressive presence.

"This must be the Umbralox," she gasped. "This is how it spreads—through objects. Through places."

"How do we stop it?" Ridge demanded, slashing at another tendril of shadow as it lunged toward him.

Keelee yelled. "The mirror! It's a conduit! You need to destroy it—"

Lincoln didn't wait for him to finish. He aimed his weapon at the mirror and fired. The shot hit its mark, shattering the glass into a thousand shards. The shadows shrieked, the sound almost unbearable, before collapsing inward and dissipating into the air.

Silence fell over the room, broken only by the sound of their ragged breathing. The oppressive hum was gone, and the air felt lighter—though not entirely safe.

"Is it over?" Ridge asked, his voice hoarse.

"For now," Waverly said, staring at the shattered remains of the mirror. "But I believe this was just a fragment of the Umbralox's power. A warning, maybe."

"Yes," Keelee confirmed.

Lincoln stepped closer, his expression grim. "Then we'd better be ready for whatever comes next."

The drive back to Sage Manor was tense and silent, each of them lost in thought. When they arrived, the house was still and quiet, the others asleep or waiting anxiously. Gran Celia was the first to greet them in the parlor, her sharp gaze immediately picking up on their shaken expressions.

"What happened?" she asked, her tone brisk.

Waverly explained everything—the mirror, the shadows, the suffocating presence that had seemed to permeate Lorinda's home. By the time she finished, Gran Celia's face was pale but resolute.

"This confirms it," she said. "Keelee, what you have communicated is true. The Umbralox is probably here on Earth too. If this evil entity is strong enough to influence Earth from Tanzlora, then the Elders are right, time is not on our side."

Bethany entered the room, her arms crossed tightly over her chest. "The twins are back asleep now. They felt something earlier—Maddox, especially. He said his dreams were full of shadows."

Gran Celia frowned. "The Umbralox is targeting him. His sensitivity to higher consciousness entities makes him vulnerable."

"Then I need to reach out to the Elders immediately to tell them what happened here tonight. We will need to leave for Tanzlora tomorrow," Keelee said firmly. "The longer we wait, the greater the risk to everyone—here and on Tanzlora."

The room fell silent as the weight of his words settled over them. Waverly met his gaze and nodded. "Tomorrow, then. Let's get some rest and start preparations early in the morning.We should be able to leave for Tanzlora in the afternoon."

As they dispersed, Waverly lingered in the parlor, staring out the window into the dark woods beyond. The shadows seemed deeper now, more alive. She could feel the Umbralox's presence pressing against her mind, a silent challenge.

"We're coming for you," she whispered. "And we'll be ready to destroy you."

5

The he dining room at Sage Manor was filled with the warm scents of freshly brewed coffee, buttery biscuits, maple syrup and sizzling bacon. Sunlight streamed through the tall windows, casting golden light across the long, polished table where the family and their guests were gathered. The twins, Maya and Maddox, were perched on high-backed chairs, giggling as they tried to stack pancakes into the tallest tower possible.

Gran Celia, seated at the head of the table, poured herself a cup of coffee with steady hands. Lorinda and Monica sat near her, looking far more relaxed than they had the previous night, though traces of unease still lingered in their expressions. The rest of the family filled the seats, each with varying degrees of focus on their breakfast.

"Lorinda," Gran Celia began in her soothing, maternal tone, "I want you and Monica to feel welcome here. You've been through a lot, and Sage Manor has always been a place of sanctuary."

Lorinda offered a grateful smile. "Thank you, Celia. I can't tell you how much it means to us. Monica barely slept last night."

The young girl, sitting quietly beside her mother, nodded, her hands wrapped around a glass of orange juice.

Gran Celia's gaze softened. "You're safe here. And I think it would be best if you stayed at the manor for a little while, just until things settle down."

Maya tilted her head, her curiosity piqued. "Why do things need to settle down, Gran? What's happening?"

Gran Celia smiled warmly but evasively. "Oh, just a little trip your parents and siblings need to take. It won't be long."

"Where are they going?" Maddox chimed in, his face alight with curiosity.

Bethany leaned forward, her tone light. "It's a grown-up thing, sweetheart. Nothing you need to worry about."

Maya frowned. "We're six now and not little kids anymore, you know."

"Sure you're not," Ridge said with a teasing grin, reaching over to ruffle her hair. "But trust me, this is boring adult stuff. You'd hate it."

Waverly cleared her throat, cutting through the tension. "Lorinda, I wanted to ask you about something we saw at your house last night. The mirror in the guest bedroom—the ornate one with the gilded frame and gemstones. Where did you get it?"

Lorinda froze mid-bite, her brow furrowing. "Mirror in the guest bedroom? What mirror?"

"The one hanging on the wall in the upstairs guest bedroom," Waverly said, her voice calm but insistent. "It's large, with intricate carvings and inlaid gemstones. It's hard to miss."

Lorinda glanced at Monica, who shook her head vehemently.

"We don't have any mirror like that," Lorinda said slowly, her tone laced with confusion. "Our house is minimalist—plain furniture, neutral colors. I wouldn't even know where to find a mirror like the one you're describing."

Monica chimed in, her voice small. "Mom's right. There's no mirror like that in our house. We definitely didn't buy one."

The room fell silent as everyone processed this information. Ridge set his coffee cup down, his brow furrowing. "Are you sure? Because we all saw it. It was hanging right there in plain sight."

Lorinda shook her head, her voice resolute. "I'm absolutely sure. I've lived in that house for five years. I have never even purchased a mirror for the house, all our mirrors came with the dressers when we bought the furniture. The bathroom mirrors are original from when the house was built."

"Yes," Monica added, her face pale, "We never needed to buy a mirror."

Waverly leaned back in her chair, her mind racing. "If it wasn't yours, then how did it get there? And why? Are you positive it was not there when you bought the house?"

"One hundred percent positive," Lorinda responded, "That house was completely empty when I purchased it. I stripped wallpaper off of all the upstairs walls and painted them so I know that a mirror like you are describing has never been on the wall of that guest room."

Lincoln exchanged a glance with Bethany, his expression dark. "The mirror wasn't just a decoration—it was a conduit for something. It shouldn't have been there."

The silence that followed was heavy, the weight of this revelation settling over the group.

Gran Celia, ever the matriarch, broke the tension. "Lorinda, why don't you and Monica take the twins for a stroll in the garden? They can show you the estate's playground. It's a beautiful morning, and I'm sure some fresh air will do everyone good."

Lorinda hesitated but then nodded. "That sounds nice. Monica?"

Monica gave a small smile and nodded, though her unease was still visible.

Maya and Maddox lit up at the mention of the playground. "Yes! Let's go!" Maddox exclaimed, already hopping down from his chair.

"Can we play with babydolls too?" asked Maya.

"Yes sweetie," Bethany said, "you can show Monica the playroom after you are finished playing outside."

"Fun!" declared Maya as she followed her brother.

As the four of them left the dining room, their chatter fading down the hallway, Lincoln turned to the remaining family members. "Let's go get Keelee and head to the gazebo," he said firmly.

"What's on your mind?" Ridge asked as they rose from the table.

"Answers," Lincoln replied, his tone grave. "If that mirror wasn't part of Lorinda's home, then something—or someone—put it there for a reason. We need to figure out what it was and how it's connected to the Umbralox."

"Maybe we should also check the library too," Waverly suggested.

Gran Celia placed a reassuring hand on Waverly's arm. "You'll find what you need in the archives. The manor holds more knowledge than most realize."

Bethany nodded, already moving toward the door. "Let's get started. Time isn't on our side."

The group filed out of the dining room, their earlier lightheartedness replaced with determination. Behind them, the sunlight continued to stream through the windows, but the shadows seemed to stretch just a little farther than they had before.

Lincoln and Ridge arrived at the chamber within the gazebo to find Keelee already there. He sat in silence, occupying the anteroom on the right side of the Crystal Gate. The room was home to a remarkable table with enough seats for four people, each chair resembling those used by astronauts on Earth. The table included hand-sized indentations in front of each seat, which activated the four screens adorning the walls when touched by whoever occupied that seat.

"Keelee, we need to talk," Lincoln said as he entered the chamber, his voice echoing slightly in the confined space.

Keelee looked up, his eyes tired but alert. "I assumed as much. What's happened?"

Ridge took a seat across from Keelee, his fingers hovering over the hand-sized indentation. "The mirror at Lorinda's house. It wasn't hers."

Keelee's brow furrowed. "What do you mean?"

"Exactly that," Ridge said, entering the room and taking his seat next to Keelee. "Lorinda and Monica both confirmed they've never seen it before. It just... appeared."

Keelee leaned back, his expression grave. "That's... concerning. Very concerning."

Lincoln placed his hand on the indentation in front of him, activating the screen on the wall.

"Show us the origin of the mirror that was used as a conduit for the Umbralox," he demanded.

The screen flickered to life, a swirl of colors and patterns coalescing into a clear image. It showed a dimly lit workshop, cluttered with arcane tools and mystical ingredients. In the center stood a figure shrouded in shadow, their hands moving with practiced precision over an ornate frame.

"That's it," Ridge breathed, leaning forward. "That's the mirror from Lorinda's house."

The shadowy figure continued to work, inlaying gemstones and etching intricate symbols into the frame. As they worked, a faint purple glow began to emanate from the mirror's surface.

"Can we get a clearer view of who that is?" Lincoln asked, his voice tense.

The image zoomed in, but the figure's face remained obscured, as if hidden by some magical means. However, a pendant around their neck became visible – a silver crescent moon with its edges intricately engraved with symbols that seemed to shift and shimmer in the dim light of the image.

"What is that?" Ridge asked, his brow furrowed as he leaned closer to the screen. "That pendant—it's not just decorative. It's doing something."

"The pendant," Keelee said slowly, "is not something I recognize immediately, but it appears to be tied to something supernatural. Those symbols... looks like they predate even the recorded history of Tanzlora. They may have roots in the early alliance between Earth and the sister planets."

Lincoln stood and stepped closer to the screen, his eyes narrowing as he studied the pendant. "Could it be connected to the mirror? If this figure had something to do with Lorinda's house, maybe the pendant and the mirror are part of the same design—some kind of anchor for the shadows."

Keelee nodded thoughtfully. "It's possible. Mirrors, especially ornate ones like the one in Lorinda's home, are often used as conduits or gateways for the supernatural. If the mirror was placed there intentionally, it could be an artifact meant to channel or amplify the Umbralox's influence."

Ridge frowned, now pacing the room as he processed the information. "But why Lorinda's house? Why not go directly after Sage Manor? It's the stronger nexus point."

Keelee stood and approached the screen, standing beside Lincoln as they both studied the image. "That's a critical question. If the mirror is indeed connected to the pendant and to this figure, it suggests that someone—or something—is testing the boundaries. They may be probing for weaknesses or looking for a way to destabilize your family's connection to the portal."

Lincoln crossed his arms, his voice tense. "Then we need to figure out where this pendant comes from and who this figure is. Keelee, can you track the source of the mirror?"

"The mirror's craftsmanship is distinctive. Its ornate frame, the gemstone inlays, and the supernatural residue it carries suggest it was not created on Earth," Keelee stated as he was walking back to his chair and placing his hands in the table's indentations. "Let me cross-reference its design with the archives on Tanzlora and Arcmyrin."

Closing his eyes and mumbling so quietly that Lincoln and Ridge could barely hear him, it only took less than a minute for the second screen to flicker to life. It was faint at first, but then started to display various artifacts cataloged from the two sister planets.

The images cycled quickly, Keelee's system searching for a match. After a few tense moments, the screen stopped on a similar-looking mirror. Its frame was gilded and adorned with gemstones, though it lacked the eerie glow of the one in Lorinda's house. Keelee opened his eyes.

"This," Keelee said, pointing to the image, "is a ceremonial mirror from the Age of Harmony on Arcmyrin. It was crafted to reflect energy and amplify it. While not inherently malevolent, if corrupted, it could be used for more sinister purposes."

Ridge rubbed the back of his neck, his expression dark. "So it's an Arcmyrin artifact. That means someone with knowledge of the sister planets brought it to Earth. But who? And why?"

Keelee sat gazing at the mirror on the screen as he considered the question. "The pendant may hold the answer. It is older than the mirror, tied to something supernatural that even I do not fully understand. We need to find someone who can interpret those symbols and trace their origin."

Lincoln sighed, his shoulders heavy with the weight of the situation. "We need Francis Roller. She's been studying our family history and ancient texts for years. If anyone can make sense of those symbols, it's her."

Keelee nodded. "That is a wise course of action. In the meantime, I will continue to investigate the pendant and the mirror's connection to the Umbralox. If this figure is indeed orchestrating these events, we need to uncover their motives before they gain more ground."

Ridge glanced back at the screen, his jaw tight. "And if we can't figure it out in time?"

Lincoln's gaze hardened as he placed a hand on Ridge's shoulder. "Then we stop them the old-fashioned way—with force, if necessary. We're not letting them tear apart what we've fought so hard to protect."

Keelee looked from one brother to the other. "I will alert the Elders of this development. For now, stay vigilant. The mirror was only the beginning."

As Keelee remained in the chamber to continue the investigation into the mystery surrounding the pendant and the mirror, Lincoln and Ridge left to return to the house. They needed to update the family and reach out to Francis.

6

The library of Sage Manor was a labyrinth of towering shelves, filled with books that spanned centuries and worlds. Dust motes danced in the beams of light streaming through the stained-glass windows, casting colorful patterns on the dark wooden floors.

Lincoln and Ridge entered to find Lynx standing near a ladder on the second level, craning his neck to look at the uppermost shelves. His sharp eyes caught sight of a set of oddly shaped volumes tucked behind a row of more conventional books.

"Hey," he called down to the others. "There's something up here. They're not... normal books."

"Define 'not normal,'" Ridge said, leaning casually against a table but clearly intrigued with what he walked into.

"They're shaped differently, like wooden boxes or something." Lynx climbed up the ladder and reached for one of the items. As he pulled it free, he realized it was indeed a carved wooden box, its surface engraved with intricate symbols that glowed faintly under his touch.

Lynx descended the ladder carefully, holding the box as though it might shatter. "Look at this."

Bethany took it from him, running her fingers over the carvings. "These aren't just decorations. These are symbols—Tanzloran symbols, but ancient. I've never seen some of these before."

Lincoln opened the box, revealing a stack of parchment bound together to form a journal. The writing inside was unlike anything they'd encountered—flowing and ornate, the characters resembling spirals and geometric patterns.

"Can you read it?" Ridge asked.

Bethany shook her head. "No. This is older than anything I studied on Tanzlora. Whoever wrote this had knowledge that predates even the Elders' archives."

"There's more of them," Lynx said, gesturing to the upper shelves. "I only grabbed one."

Ridge grabbed another ladder and climbed up to retrieve the remaining boxes. Soon, a small collection of wooden journals sat on the table, each one unique in design but filled with the same indecipherable text.

"We need help," Waverly said, pacing. "There's only one person I know who might be able to decipher these—Francis Roller. She's an expert in interplanetary ancient languages and symbology. If anyone can make sense of this, it's her."

Lincoln nodded. "Good, go call her. We also need her to look at some symbols we just saw on a pendant while in the chamber with Keelee."

Bethany and Waverly looked at him questioningly.

"Go get Francis on her way here and I will tell you more when you return," Lincoln said to Waverly, "the more we know about this threat, the better prepared we'll be."

Waverly didn't waste a second. She grabbed her phone and left the room, already dialing Francis's number.

Waverly returned to the library a few minutes later. "Francis is on her way," she informed the others. She laid her phone down on the table and turned to her father. "Well?" she prompted, her voice calm but edged with worry. "What did Keelee show you?"

Lincoln looked up from the journals he was inspecting, his eyes meeting hers. "It wasn't good, Waverly. Keelee showed us a figure—someone connected to the shadows. Their face was hidden, but they were wearing a pendant—a silver crescent moon, engraved with strange symbols."

"A pendant?" Waverly asked, leaning forward. "What does that have to do with anything?"

Lincoln motioned for her to sit, his expression serious. "The pendant was glowing, Waverly. It wasn't just decorative—it's supernatural, tied to the mirror that was in Lorinda's house."

Bethany's brows furrowed as she folded her arms. "The mirror? You're saying this figure has something to do with that mirror and what happened to Lorinda and Monica?"

"Yes," Lincoln said. "The mirror wasn't just some creepy artifact; it was placed there intentionally. Keelee thinks it was meant to channel or amplify the shadows' influence."

Ridge gestured toward Lincoln. "And the pendant this figure was wearing might be the key. It's older than the mirror—maybe even older than anything we've encountered before. The symbols on it don't match anything Keelee recognized as being from Tanzlora."

Lynx straightened, his eyes narrowing. "If Keelee didn't recognize it, then we're dealing with something really ancient. Maybe even something from before the Galactic War."

"Exactly," Ridge replied. "And that's where we need help. Keelee suggested cross-referencing it with the archives on Tanzlora, but we don't have that kind of time. We need someone here, someone who understands our family's history and the connections between Earth and the sister planets."

"Francis," Bethany said, realization dawning. "She's the only one who might know what those symbols mean."

Lincoln nodded. "She's been studying these things for years. If anyone can decipher those symbols or tell us where that pendant came from, it's her."

Waverly tapped her fingers against the table, her mind racing. "So, we're looking at someone who's deliberately using these artifacts to open a pathway for the shadows. And that pendant—it's part of the puzzle."

"It has to be," Ridge said. "Keelee thinks the pendant might be tied to a nexus of energy, like the Crystal Gate. Whoever this figure is, they're playing a long game. And if we don't figure out their plan, it could mean the shadows gaining more control—not just over Tanzlora, but here on Earth too."

Bethany's hands tightened on her arms, her voice firm. "Then we don't wait. Once Francis gets here, we show her everything, and see if she can help us piece this together. Whatever this pendant is, whatever connection it has to the shadows—we need to understand it before it's too late."

The crystalline walls of the Tanzloran council chambers glowed faintly, reflecting the gravity of the discussion taking place within. The five elders sat around a large circular table made of the same shimmering crystal as the walls, their expressions heavy with concern.

In the center of the table floated a holographic map of Tanzlora, its vibrant forests, rivers, and mountains marred by creeping black marks that indicated the spread of the Umbralox's corruption.

Lumorith, the oldest of the council and the keeper of Tanzlora's history, leaned forward, his silvery eyes scanning the others. "The Beaumonts will arrive soon. Their connection to the Origin Gift and the elemental spirits makes them our greatest chance of stopping the Umbralox. But we must tell them everything, including what lies in the ruins of Erevelle."

Brakar, the leader of the council, nodded solemnly. Her strong, commanding presence filled the room. "Agreed. The Beaumonts need to know the truth about the Triadorne and its purpose. It is time to reveal the role their ancestors played in its creation."

Sylvaris, the visionary member of the council, waved a hand over the holographic map, zooming in on a darkened region labeled The Shadowed Expanse. The once-vibrant area was now shrouded in corruption, its edges fading into ominous darkness. At the heart of the region lay the ruins of Erevelle, a faintly glowing marker indicating its location.

"The Shadowed Expanse has been a place of fear for generations," Sylvaris said, his violet eyes reflecting the glowing map. "Most Tanzlorans avoid it, believing it to be cursed. There are rumors—tales of those who ventured too close and vanished without a trace. The people call it a punishment place, a realm where the spirits abandon those who enter."

Draven, the overseer of the Tanzloran warriors, scoffed softly, his silver eyes sharp. "Superstition. The Shadowed Expanse is not cursed. It is infested. Wild entities have taken root there—predators that prey on anything that dares cross their path. The darkness of the Umbralox has made them more feral, more dangerous."

Thaloria, the youngest and most clairvoyant of the council, spoke next. Her soft voice carried an otherworldly weight. "Perhaps. But the fear of the Shadowed Expanse is not without reason. It is a place that thrives on despair, feeding on the fears of those who enter. This is why only those with pure intent can hope to navigate it."

Brakar turned her attention back to the map, gesturing to the marker over Erevelle. "The ruins of Erevelle are at the heart of this region, hidden by both the corruption of the Umbralox and the passage of time. It is there that Triadorne lies, waiting to be awakened."

Sylvaris nodded. "And the daggers. They were hidden on Earth, protected by Galen and the elemental spirits. Only those who are pure of heart and united in purpose can retrieve them."

Thaloria's eyes closed briefly, her hands glowing faintly as she tapped into her clairvoyant connection. "The spirits have been waiting for the Beaumonts. They sense their arrival and know that the time has come. The Triadorne will respond to them. We need the daggers transported safely here to Tanzlora."

"Keelee has a clear directive about the daggers," Brakar responded to Thaloria, "Celia has knowledge and will assist Keelee in that mission."

Lumorith spoke again, his deep voice filled with the weight of centuries. "Triadorne was not created lightly. During the Galactic War, when the Abasimtrox and Umbralox threatened the Triad for the first time, Galen Beaumont and his allies realized that conventional means would not suffice. The evil entities are not merely creatures of darkness; they are a force, entities that cannot be fought by physical means alone."

Draven's expression grew grimmer. "Which is why Triadorne was forged—not as a weapon of destruction, but as a weapon of disintegration and purification. It does not simply kill the Abasimtrox and Umbralox; it erases its very essence, ensuring that it cannot reform or return."

Sylvaris waved his hand again, and the holographic map shifted, displaying a detailed image of Triadorne. The weapon was massive, its core a glowing honeycomb structure surrounded by intricate carvings and conduits. At its base were four slots, evenly spaced and perfectly shaped to hold the daggers.

"The daggers are the keys," Sylvaris said. "Each one contains the essence of its corresponding elemental spirit—Mistara, Terraveta, Ignissa, and Ambreela. Together, they form the energy source needed to activate Triadorne."

Thaloria's voice grew softer, almost reverent. "The crystals in the daggers are unlike any others in the universe. They are formed from the heart of Tanzlora's ley lines, infused with the purest energy of the spirits. When the daggers are inserted into Triadorne, their combined power awakens the weapon."

Lumorith's voice grew more somber. "This is a weapon like no other ever formed. Galen and his son George were instrumental in the weapon's creation. Their connection to the Origin Gift and the spirits allowed them to forge the bond between the daggers and the weapon. But they also knew the dangers of such power."

Brakar's tone was resolute. "Which is why they chose to hide it. The Galactic War left the Triad fractured, and there were those who sought to exploit Triadorne for their own gain. To protect the weapon, Galen and George worked with Tanzloran and Arcmyrin allies to seal it within the ruins of Erevelle. The daggers were taken to Earth and hidden, both locations guarded by the spirits."

Thaloria opened her eyes, her clairvoyant glow fading. "The Beaumonts must retrieve the weapon. The spirits will guide them, but the journey will test their resolve and their unity. The Shadowed Expanse is not merely a place of physical danger; it is a place where fear and doubt can consume even the strongest."

7

The chamber beneath the gazebo glowed faintly with the steady hum of the portal. Keelee stood before the orb in the center of the room, his luminous form reflecting the tension in the air. With a deft motion, he extended his hand over the orb, the light intensifying as he activated its long-range projection capabilities.

The air shimmered as the connection formed, and moments later, the holographic images of the Tanzloran elder council appeared. Each elder was seated in their respective crystalline thrones within the grand council chamber of Tanzlora, their auras radiating the unique energy that defined their roles. Brakar, the leader of the council, sat at the forefront, her sharp gaze immediately locking onto Keelee.

"Keelee," she began, her voice resonant and commanding. "You have requested this session. What news do you bring us from Earth?"

Keelee inclined his head respectfully. "Elders, I bring troubling developments. Shadows—fragments of the Umbralox—have manifested on Earth, targeting a home near Sage Manor. These shadows whispered and caused disturbances, and they were accompanied by an artifact: a mirror that I believe is of Arcmyrin origin, corrupted and used as a conduit for their influence."

Sylvaris, the visionary elder, leaned forward, his luminous eyes narrowing. "The Umbralox on Earth? This is worse than we anticipated. The mirror—what do you know of its origin?"

"I have traced its design to ceremonial artifacts from Arcmyrin's Age of Harmony," Keelee explained. "While these mirrors were originally intended to reflect and amplify positive energies, this one has been corrupted, likely to channel the shadows' influence. Its presence in this neighbor's home was no coincidence."

Draven, the overseer of Tanzloran warriors, spoke next, his voice deep and steady. "Do you believe the Umbralox is attempting to anchor itself on Earth?"

"Yes," Keelee confirmed. "The mirror is only part of the story. The Beaumont family and I discovered a vision tied to the artifact—a shadowed figure, their face obscured, but they wore a pendant of a silver crescent moon engraved with ancient symbols. This pendant appears to predate recorded history on Tanzlora and Arcmyrin. I suspect it holds the key to their intentions."

Thaloria, the youngest and most clairvoyant elder, tilted her head as her eyes glimmered with insight. "The crescent moon. That symbol has appeared in fragments of our oldest texts, tied to the earliest days of the Triad's formation. If this pendant is tied to the Umbralox, then it may be more dangerous than we realize."

Lumorith, the oldest and keeper of Tanzlora's archives, stroked his shimmering beard thoughtfully. "If the pendant and the mirror are connected, then we are facing an ancient and deliberate force. The Umbralox is no longer merely spreading chaos—it is strategizing. It seeks to destabilize the Triad by eroding the foundations of its balance and harmony."

Brakar's expression hardened as she addressed Keelee. "You have done well to uncover this, Keelee. The connection between the artifacts and the shadows must be investigated further, but we cannot afford to lose focus on the larger goal. The Triadorne must be found and activated."

Keelee straightened, his glow steady. "Elders, I am ready to assist in whatever way is required."

Brakar nodded firmly. "You will accompany the Beaumont family to Erevelle once all of you return to Tanzlora. The ruins of Erevelle hold the key to locating the Triadorne, the weapon crafted by Galen Beaumont and our ancestors to entrap and eradicate the Umbralox. Without it, the Triad cannot survive this onslaught."

Draven added, "The journey to Erevelle will be perilous. The Umbralox's presence grows stronger near the ruins, and the terrain itself is treacherous. You must guide the Beaumonts and ensure they reach the weapon."

Keelee's light flickered slightly as he absorbed their words. "I understand, Elders. The Beaumont family has proven themselves capable, and with the elemental spirits at their side, I believe they will succeed."

Thaloria's voice softened, her gaze distant. "The Triadorne was created for this very moment in history. It has been waiting for them, for their unity, their connection to the spirits. Keelee, your role will be to ensure that they reach it—and that they understand its true power."

Brakar's tone was final as she concluded the session. "Prepare for their return, Keelee. The survival of the Triad depends on your combined efforts."

Keelee inclined his head respectfully. "Elder Brakar, I must raise another concern. As was previously discussed, while the Beaumont family journeys to Tanzlora to aid in this fight, Sage Manor and the family members left behind on Earth will remain vulnerable. The manor is more than just their home; it is a sentinel guarding one of the Triad's critical energy nexuses. If the Umbralox strengthens its presence there, it could destabilize not only Earth but also Tanzlora and Arcmyrin."

Draven, the overseer of Tanzloran warriors, leaned forward, his sharp gaze fixed on Keelee. "You are correct, Keelee. Sage Manor must not fall, and those left behind must be protected. We are preparing to send Callum and his team of warriors to Sage Manor."

Keelee's glow brightened slightly. "I propose that they be sent to Earth prior to the family leaving for Tanzlora. Lincoln and Bethany will be put at ease if they can visually see the sentinels who will be guarding the young children during their absence. They can be assured that a strong presence of protection will deter further shadow incursions, ensuring the safety of the ancestral home."

Draven's stern face softened slightly, his respect for Keelee evident in his tone. "Your suggestion is wise. I will see to it that Callum and six of our finest warriors are sent to Earth immediately. Callum has proven himself as a leader, and his connection to the Beaumonts through his mother, Marellis, will ensure trust between them."

Thaloria, the youngest and most clairvoyant elder, added softly, "The shadows will test the sentinels, but Callum and his warriors are prepared for such challenges. They will hold the line."

Brakar nodded firmly. "It is decided. Callum and his team will depart for Earth within hours to take their place at Sage Manor."

Keelee inclined his head in gratitude. "Thank you, Elders. Knowing Sage Manor is protected will allow the Beaumonts to focus fully on the mission at hand."

Draven's deep voice cut through the discussion again, his gaze sharp and commanding. "And once Keelee and the Beaumont family arrive on Tanzlora, I will instruct Pazlun to assemble his warriors. He and his army will escort you and the Beaumonts to the ruins of Erevelle. The path to Erevelle is treacherous, and the Umbralox will do everything in its power to stop you from reaching the Triadorne. You will need all the support you can get."

Keelee's glow flickered faintly, the enormity of the task ahead sinking in. "Pazlun's assistance will be invaluable. The Beaumont family is strong, but with Tanzlora's warriors and the elemental spirits at their side, their chances of success will increase exponentially."

Lumorith, the keeper of Tanzlora's history, stroked his shimmering beard as he spoke. "The ruins of Erevelle hold more than the Triadorne—they hold echoes of our ancestors' sacrifices and wisdom. The shadows will twist those memories against you if given the chance. Warn the Beaumonts to remain steadfast, for only purity of purpose will allow them to claim the weapon."

Brakar's tone turned resolute as she addressed Keelee. "You have your directives. Ensure the protection of Sage Manor, and then lead the Beaumonts to Erevelle. The Triadorne is our only hope against the Umbralox's onslaught. Without it, the Triad will fall."

Keelee bowed slightly, his form flickering in acknowledgment. "I will see it done, Elder Brakar."

As the holographic forms of the council began to fade, Draven spoke one last time, his voice a deep rumble. "Callum will ensure the safety of Earth, and Pazlun will ensure your success on Tanzlora. The warriors of Tanzlora stand ready."

When the connection severed, the chamber fell silent, save for the steady hum of the portal. Keelee turned toward the shimmering energy of the gate, his thoughts focused. The safety of Sage Manor and the success of the mission to recover the Triadorne were now entwined, and the path ahead was fraught with danger.

As the portal's glow reflected off the smooth stone walls, Keelee resolved that no matter the cost, he would see the mission through. The Triad's survival—and the hope of three worlds—depended on it.

The sound of a struggling engine echoed up the long, winding driveway of Sage Manor, accompanied by the unmistakable pop-pop of backfiring. Ridge, who had been pacing near the library window, glanced out and let out a low chuckle.

"She's still driving that old clunker?" he said, shaking his head. "You'd think with all her brilliance, Francis would just buy a car that can handle a hill without sounding like it's falling apart."

The others turned toward the window as the vintage car came into view, its worn but lovingly polished exterior glinting in the sunlight. The car lurched forward, chugging up the incline before sputtering to a stop in front of the manor.

"Ridge," Waverly said with a pointed glare, "maybe keep that thought to yourself."

Before Ridge could respond, Gran Celia entered the library, her sharp ears catching the tail end of his comment. "Ridge Beaumont," she said, her tone cool but firm, "that car happens to be very special to Francis."

Ridge turned toward her, his brow furrowing. "Special? It's ancient."

Gran Celia folded her hands in front of her and fixed him with a patient yet reprimanding look. "That car was a gift from Francis's husband. He bought it for her shortly before he passed away, far too young, and far too suddenly. To her, it's not just a car—it's a connection to him. She'll never let it go."

Ridge's face fell, and he looked down, his voice softer. "I didn't know that."

"You didn't think to ask," Waverly said with a sharp glance. "You should feel bad."

"I do," Ridge muttered, running a hand through his hair.

The room fell silent as the heavy oak front door creaked open, followed by the sound of purposeful footsteps. Moments later, Francis Roller appeared in the doorway of the library. She was a very graceful woman with sharp eyes that seemed to take in everything at once, her graying hair pulled into a neat bun.

"Well," she said with a faint smile, setting her bag down on the nearest table, "I'm here. What's the emergency this time?"

"Francis, thank you for coming," Waverly said, stepping forward. "We need your help with some texts we found in the archives and some symbols we found on a pendant. They're written in an ancient script we can't decipher, and it's urgent."

Francis raised an eyebrow, her curiosity piqued. "Ancient script, you say? Let me see."

She removed a pair of wire-rimmed glasses from her bag and perched them on her nose as Waverly handed her one of the wooden boxes. Francis opened it carefully, her eyes scanning the contents.

"Interesting," she murmured, tracing a finger over the symbols. "These are Tanzloran symbols, but they're much older than anything I've seen. This will take some time. Where's the pendant?"

"In the chamber," Lincoln responded, "we will need to take you down there once you are done with the journals."

Francis nodded, her eyes still fixed on the ancient text. "Very well. Let's start with these journals. I'll need some time to study them properly."

As she settled into a chair, the rest of the family gathered around, watching intently as Francis began to work. Gran Celia sat with Francis at the central table, discussing the symbols and intricate carvings that adorned the old journals.

"I assume time is of the essence?" Francis questioned.

Waverly nodded. "It is. We believe these texts and the pendant are connected to a growing threat."

Francis's expression hardened. "I see. Then I'll work as quickly as I can without compromising accuracy."

Lynx entered the library, his usual calm demeanor slightly hurried. His steps were quiet on the wooden floor, but the urgency in his voice caught everyone's attention. "Hey, everyone. I just checked in with Keelee and he says he needs to speak with all of us—now."

Lincoln straightened, closing the journal he had been studying. "Keelee must have some answers for us."

Waverly exchanged a glance with Ridge. "Let's go."

Bethany stood, smoothing her shirt. "Celia, Francis, we'll be back shortly. Can you continue working on these while we're gone?"

Gran Celia nodded, her eyes twinkling with curiosity. "Of course. Let us know what Keelee has to say."

8

The group made their way to the chamber beneath the gazebo. The soft hum of the portal greeted them as they stepped into the room, its light casting long shadows across the walls. Keelee stood in the center of the room, his expression calm but tinged with urgency.

"Keelee," Lincoln said, stepping forward. "What have you found out?"

Keelee inclined his head, his voice steady. "I bring news from the council. Elder Draven is at this moment, readying Callum and his team of warriors to journey here through the Crystal Gate with directives to protect Sage Manor. As I told you when I first arrived, they will be guarding your family and this ancestral home while you are away on Tanzlora."

Bethany nodded in understanding. "I am grateful for Elder Draven's wise decision. The disturbances near Lorinda's home and the whispers we've been hearing—it's clear that the shadows are probing for weaknesses."

Keelee continued. "It has also been decided that the contingent of seven warriors will be sent to Sage Manor prior to you leaving. We feel it best that you are able to greet Callum when he arrives here with his team of warriors. He is highly skilled and trusted by the council, and he also has a personal connection to your family."

Lincoln's eyebrows rose at this. "Yes, we do have a personal connection to Callum and his family."

Keelee nodded. "Elder Draven and I felt it was important to send someone with experience and familiarity. Callum is the son of Marellis, the healer who assisted with the twins' birth on Tanzlora. We believe his presence will put your family at ease, especially the younger ones."

Bethany smiled faintly, a glimmer of relief softening her expression. "I remember Callum well. He was always calm and steady, just like his mother. They lived in our village. Maya and Maddox will recognize him—they'll feel safe with him here."

Waverly crossed her arms, her expression thoughtful. "So, when are they arriving?"

Keelee's glow flickered slightly as he responded. "Within the next three Earth hours. As previously stated, we thought it best to acclimate the warriors to your home and your family before you depart. Callum is aware of the urgency of this mission, and the warriors are prepared to take up their duties immediately upon arrival."

Ridge let out a low whistle. "Seven Tanzloran warriors at Sage Manor. That's going to be a sight."

Lincoln placed a hand on his heart, a gesture of gratitude on Tanzlora. "Thank you, Keelee. This will give us peace of mind while we're on Tanzlora. I'll go prepare Gran Celia and the others for their arrival."

Keelee inclined his head. "Your family's safety is as important to us as the success of this mission. The warriors will ensure that Sage Manor remains secure."

Bethany stepped closer to Keelee, her expression resolute. "And the family here—they'll know what's happening?"

"We believe they will," Keelee assured her. "The warriors are trained to communicate openly while maintaining their vigilance. They understand the importance of building trust."

As the family turned to leave, Bethany glanced back at Keelee. "Callum's a good choice," she said. "If he's anything like his mother, he'll be an anchor for everyone here."

Keelee's glow brightened slightly, a flicker of warmth in his expression. "He is, Bethany. He's more than capable."

With that, the Beaumonts ascended the stairs, their minds now focused on preparing Sage Manor for the arrival of their Tanzloran allies. The portal chamber fell quiet again, its hum steady and serene, as Keelee remained, ensuring that everything was in place for what was to come.

An hour passed as Francis deciphered the text, her voice steady as she read aloud. Her tone grew more somber as she unraveled the tale written within.

"These journals document the early days of the Galactic War," she said, her voice reverent. "The Umbralox wasn't just a shadowy entity—it was a weapon. A living force that the opposition used to destabilize the Triad. Its corruption spread through all three planets, infecting their cores and turning the environment itself against their protectors."

"The Triad?" Lynx asked, leaning forward.

Francis nodded. "Yes, Lynx. Remember? It is Earth, Arcmyrin, and Tanzlora. Their alliance was the only thing keeping the war from consuming the galaxy. The Umbralox was the enemy's countermeasure. It could appear anywhere—spreading corruption, sowing fear. Shadows became battlefields."

Ridge frowned. "Why didn't the Triad destroy it back then?"

"They tried," Francis said, her voice heavy. "But the Umbralox wasn't just one entity—it was many, scattered and bound to certain artifacts. Even if one manifestation was defeated, another would emerge elsewhere. The only solution was containment and disintegration."

She paused, taking off her glasses and rubbing her temples. "It seems the Triad created powerful protections to seal the Umbralox away. But those protections were only as strong as the unity of the alliance. As the planets grew distant, the protections and seals weakened."

"And now it's loose again," Waverly said grimly.

Francis nodded. "Yes. And if it isn't stopped, it will consume the cores of all three planets, starting with Tanzlora. From what I'm reading here, the longer it feeds, the stronger it becomes. Eventually, it won't just threaten the planets—it could destabilize the fabric of the galaxy itself."

The room fell silent as the weight of her words sank in.

"What's our next move?" Lincoln asked, his voice steady but intense.

Francis looked up, her eyes sharp and determined. "I need to see that pendant you spoke about earlier, Lincoln."

"Let's go to the chamber right now," Gran Celia said as she was rising from her chair.

"Keelee is there, he can help you and Francis bring it up on the screens," Lincoln said, "the rest of us need to begin preparations to leave for Tanzlora."

The sun cast elongated shadows across the manicured lawns of Sage Manor as Gran Celia and Francis made their way toward the gazebo. The air was crisp and tinged with an earthy scent. Francis clutched a leather-bound notebook to her chest, her eyes reflecting both curiosity and a hint of apprehension.

"Are you certain Keelee doesn't mind us intruding?" Francis asked, her voice barely above a whisper.

Gran Celia offered a reassuring smile. "Keelee invited us, my dear. He understands the importance of your expertise in this matter. Besides, the more minds we have working on this puzzle, the better."

They descended the hidden staircase beneath the gazebo, the glow of the portal illuminating the stone steps with an otherworldly light. The hum of energy grew louder as they approached the chamber, a constant reminder of the vast connections between worlds that lay just beyond their reach.

Upon entering the chamber, they found Keelee awaiting them. His tall form stood beside a large, curved screen that dominated one wall of the room. The image of the shadowed figure with the crescent moon pendant was frozen on the display, the symbols faintly glowing against the silver backdrop.

"Gran Celia, Francis," Keelee greeted them with a slight bow of his head. "Thank you for coming. I believe your insights may prove invaluable."

Francis stepped forward, her gaze locked onto the pendant. "So this is the image Lincoln and Ridge mentioned," she murmured, her fingers already flipping open her notebook to a fresh page.

"Yes," Keelee confirmed. "We captured this from a vision linked to the corrupted mirror found in Lorinda's home. The figure's face remains obscured by some form of cloaking, but the pendant is clearly visible. We were hoping you might recognize the symbols or discern any clues from the surroundings."

Francis adjusted her glasses, her eyes narrowing as she scrutinized the pendant. The silver crescent moon hung on a delicate chain, its surface etched with intricate symbols that seemed to shift and change when viewed from different angles.

"These symbols..." Francis whispered, tracing them in the air with her finger. "They resemble ancient scripts I've encountered before, but not from any Earthly language. May I?" She gestured toward the control panel.

"Of course," Keelee replied, stepping aside to allow her access.

Francis manipulated the image, zooming in further on the symbols. They became larger, more defined—sharp lines intersecting with swirling patterns, each character emanating a subtle glow.

Gran Celia watched intently. "Do they match anything from the old texts in our library?"

Francis nodded slowly. "They bear a resemblance to the pre-Galactic scripts—the ones theorized to have originated from Arcmyrin. But there's something different about them. A complexity that's... layered."

She flipped through her notebook, stopping at a page filled with sketches of ancient symbols. "Here," she pointed. "This is an Arcmyrin symbol representing 'unity' or 'balance.' And this one means 'shadow' or 'veil.' But on the pendant, these symbols are combined in a way I've never seen before. It's as if they're meant to convey multiple meanings simultaneously."

Keelee's eyes flickered with interest. "What do you make of that?"

Francis tapped her pen against her chin thoughtfully. "Well, combining symbols to create new meanings isn't uncommon in ancient scripts. But the way these are intertwined suggests a duality—light and dark, creation and destruction. It's possible that the pendant is a key of sorts, capable of manipulating energies or opening pathways between realms."

Gran Celia's expression grew serious. "If that's true, then whoever possesses it could have the means to facilitate the Umbralox's passage between worlds."

Francis nodded, her gaze drifting to the rest of the image. "Can we pan out? I want to see more of the surroundings."

Keelee obliged, adjusting the image to reveal more of the figure's environment. The workspace was dimly lit, shadows pooling in the corners. Shelves lined the walls, filled with ancient tomes, vials of shimmering liquids, and peculiar artifacts. Strange symbols were etched into the stone floor, forming a complex circle around the figure.

"That circle on the floor," Francis noted, leaning in. "It's a summoning circle, but altered. See these markings? They correspond to elemental symbols—earth, water, air, fire—but they're inverted."

Gran Celia's eyes widened. "Inverted elemental symbols... that could signify corruption or a perversion of natural energies."

"Exactly," Francis agreed. "Whoever this is, they're manipulating the fundamental forces, twisting them for their own purposes."

Keelee sighed deeply, reflecting the gravity of the situation. "This supports our theory that the figure is attempting to destabilize the elemental balance, possibly to weaken the barriers between realms and allow the Umbralox to spread."

Francis took a deep breath, her mind racing. "We need to find out who this is. If we can identify them, perhaps we can anticipate their next move or find a way to counteract their efforts."

Gran Celia placed a comforting hand on Francis's shoulder. "Your insights have already brought us closer to understanding this threat. Perhaps cross-referencing these symbols with the oldest records in our library might yield more information."

Keelee interjected gently. "Time is of the essence. The Beaumonts and I are preparing to journey to Tanzlora to confront this evil. Any information we can gather before we depart could prove crucial."

Francis closed her notebook, determination shining in her eyes. "Then I won't waste another moment. I'll return to the library and begin cross-referencing immediately. If these symbols are connected to ancient Arcmyrin scripts, there's a chance we'll find something in the untranslated texts."

"Thank you, Francis," Keelee said sincerely. "Your expertise is a beacon in these uncertain times."

Gran Celia smiled warmly at Keelee and Francis. "We'll work together, as we always have. The strength of our family—and those we trust—has seen us through many trials."

As they turned to leave the chamber, Francis paused, casting one last glance at the shadowed figure on the screen. "Whoever you are," she whispered, "we'll uncover your secrets."

The hum of the portal followed them up the staircase, a reminder of the connections that bound their worlds together—and the shadows that threatened to unravel them. With renewed purpose, Gran Celia and Francis emerged into the daylight, ready to delve into the mysteries of the past to safeguard the future.

9

"Your first priority must be Tanzlora," Francis declared. "These texts suggest that the Umbralox's power is strongest where it originally manifested. If you can cut off its source there, you might weaken its influence elsewhere."

"And these journals?" Waverly asked.

"I'll keep working on them," Francis said. "They may hold more clues—rituals, artifacts, something the Triad used to fight the Umbralox. But you'll have to move fast. Tanzlora can't wait."

The family had reconvened in the library to hear what Francis had discovered about the pendant.

Lincoln stood, his expression resolute. "Then we leave as soon as possible after the Tanzloran warriors arrive."

Waverly nodded, glancing at the journals. "Please keep us updated as we prepare to leave, Francis. Anything you find could make all the difference."

Francis leaned back, adjusting her glasses. "Don't worry about me. You just focus on getting ready to go."

Francis leaned forward, her glasses perched precariously on the tip of her nose as she pored over the journal's intricate script.

Lynx asked, "Why is it always the core of the planets that gets attacked? Why is that the target?"

She traced a finger along a passage, her expression thoughtful. "It's about the life force," she began. "The core of a planet isn't just molten rock or energy. It's the heart—the source of its frequencies and vitality. Life forms, ecosystems, even the atmosphere—they all draw from this energy, directly or indirectly. It's what makes a planet more than just a mass of matter floating in space."

Francis glanced at the family, her tone growing more animated. "The core resonates at specific frequencies. Those frequencies dictate the type of life a planet can support and the kind of energy it radiates. When that resonance is corrupted—when shadows like the Umbralox take hold—it destabilizes everything. The environment collapses, lifeforms weaken or mutate, and eventually, the planet itself dies."

Waverly frowned. "So the Umbralox isn't just destroying planets. It's feeding on their essence, like a parasite."

"Exactly," Francis confirmed, flipping through more pages. "And the planets in the Triad—Earth, Arcmyrin, and Tanzlora—are particularly vulnerable because of their connection to the elemental spirits."

Lincoln leaned forward. "The spirits? Mistara, Ambreela, Terraveta, and Ignissa?"

Francis nodded. "The journals mention them explicitly. They are the personifications of the elements—air, water, earth, and fire—that sustain life on these planets. Each spirit is intertwined with each planet's core, amplifying its frequencies and keeping the balance."

"Remember," Francis clarified. "Your abilities are your own, but they're amplified by your attunement to the elements. Think of the spirits as an undercurrent of energy that you've learned to tap into. Mistara lends you agility and foresight, Lincoln. Waverly, Ambreela's influence sharpens your mind and technological intuition. Ridge, Terraveta strengthens your resilience and grounding, and Lynx, Ignissa fuels your courage and intensity."

Bethany, who had entered the room earlier and been silent, spoke up. "And the twins? Maya and Maddox?"

Francis sighed, her gaze softening. "They're still young, but their connection is undeniable. Maddox's sensitivity to higher frequencies? That's Mistara's touch. Maya's nurturing instincts? Terraveta's gift. The twins are already displaying signs of their alignment with the elemental forces."

Lincoln crossed his arms, his voice skeptical but intrigued. "So what does this mean for the Umbralox? How do the spirits factor into stopping it?"

Francis returned her attention to the journal, flipping to a page marked with a large, glowing symbol. "During the Galactic War, the Triad forces used the elemental spirits to fight back against the shadows. They created amplifiers—rituals, artifacts, even structures—that channeled the spirits' power into the planet's core to stabilize it and repel the Umbralox."

"Like the protections Keelee mentioned," Waverly said.

Francis nodded. "Exactly. But the texts suggest that the spirits themselves were weakened by the war. Their connection to the cores was strained, and without the unity of the Triad, those amplifiers began to fail."

Ridge leaned back, his expression grim. "And now we're back to square one. Weak spirits, broken amplifiers, and a shadow that's spreading like wildfire."

"But we have one advantage," Francis said, her eyes gleaming with determination. "You. The Beaumonts. You're more than just descendants of the Triad's protectors. You're connected to these spirits in ways that make you uniquely qualified to fix what's broken."

Waverly exchanged a glance with Lincoln, their shared understanding unspoken but clear.

Francis closed the journal with a decisive snap. "The Umbralox targets the cores because that's where the life force is strongest. If you can reach the core of Tanzlora, if you can find a way to amplify the spirits' energy and restore the balance, you might have a chance to stop it."

Bethany's voice was steady but heavy with concern. "And if we fail?"

Francis's gaze was unwavering. "If you fail, Tanzlora will fall. And Earth won't be far behind."

The room fell silent, the weight of the revelation pressing down on them. Waverly stood, her resolve firm.

"Then we don't fail," she said. "We can't."

Lincoln nodded. "Let's finish preparing. The sooner we leave for Tanzlora, the better."

As the family dispersed to gather the needed provisions, Francis remained at the table, her fingers brushing the glowing symbols on the journal's cover. She whispered softly, almost to herself.

"May the spirits guide you. You're going to need them."

Keelee's luminous presence filled the room with a soft, cool glow. His solemn expression immediately set the tone for the conversation as the family filed into the room next to the Crystal Gate. Lincoln, Ridge, Bethany, Waverly, and Lynx gathered around the table, their faces etched with worry. They had all felt the weight of Tanzlora's plight since Keelee had first contacted them, but the gravity of what they were about to hear and see was evident in Keelee's somber demeanor.

Keelee inclined his head slightly, a gesture of both greeting and gravity. "Thank you for gathering while we wait for Callum and the others to arrive. I felt it necessary to show that the situation on Tanzlora is becoming dire. The Umbralox's corruption is spreading faster than we anticipated, and the toll it has taken is far greater than we feared."

The four screens in the room that normally displayed the elemental spirits of air, water, earth and fire flickered, and images of Tanzlora began to appear. The once-vibrant forests, iridescent rivers, and crystalline cities had been replaced with scenes of devastation. The land was scorched and barren, the trees twisted into lifeless husks. Rivers ran gray and stagnant, their sparkling beauty replaced with lifeless sludge. Villages were in ruins, their prismatic structures shattered and darkened with shadow.

The Beaumonts stared at the screens in stunned silence. Waverly's sharp eyes darted across the images, her jaw tightening. Lynx's fists clenched at his sides, and Ridge muttered a low curse under his breath. Bethany, standing closest to Lincoln, paled as she recognized one of the destroyed villages.

Keelee's voice was calm but heavy as he narrated the destruction. "This is the village where you and Bethany lived, Lincoln. The place where your twins were born. It was one of the first to fall when the Umbralox's shadows began to spread."

Bethany gasped, her hand flying to her mouth. The screen showed the village they had once called home, now unrecognizable. The glowing streets where they had walked with their children were now cracked and broken. The nursery that had housed Maya and Maddox was reduced to ash. Even the communal gardens, once lush and vibrant, were gray and lifeless.

"I can't believe this," Bethany whispered, tears streaming down her face. "It was so beautiful... so full of life."

Lincoln wrapped an arm around her, his own face pale with grief. "We knew it could get bad," he said quietly, "but seeing this... it's worse than I imagined."

Keelee's expression softened as he addressed Bethany. "I am deeply sorry, Bethany. I know what this village meant to you. To all of us. Its loss is a wound that will not heal easily."

The screens shifted, showing images of fleeing Tanzlorans, their faces filled with terror as they escaped the encroaching shadows. Keelee's voice grew quieter. "Many were able to flee to safer regions, but not all were so fortunate. The Umbralox is relentless, quick in their attack and its corruption spreads faster than can be contained."

Bethany's tears came harder as the screen showed familiar faces—faces of people she and Lincoln had known well. Marellis, the healer who had helped her through the difficult birth of the twins, was among them, her kind eyes now frozen in a still image. Fetrin, the governess who had watched over the village's children, was another. Their names were spoken softly by Keelee, each one a blow to the family.

"I wish I could bring you better news," Keelee said, his voice heavy with sorrow. "But these are the lives we have lost thus far. These were good Tanzlorans, brave and selfless. They stayed to help others escape, but the shadows consumed them before they could flee."

Bethany broke into quiet sobs, and Waverly moved to her side, wrapping an arm around her shoulders. "We'll make this right, mom" Waverly said firmly, her voice tinged with anger. "We'll stop this."

Ridge's jaw tightened as he stared at the images on the screen. "This isn't just an attack—it's annihilation. The Umbralox isn't just destroying villages; it's erasing everything that makes Tanzlora what it is."

Keelee nodded solemnly. "You are correct, Ridge. The Umbralox thrives on destruction and despair. Its goal is to consume, to corrupt, to leave nothing but devastation and sorrow in its wake. And it will not stop with Tanzlora. We know its influence is already here on Earth, it will soon turn its attention to Arcmyrin."

Lynx took a step closer to the table, his expression dark. "Then we stop it on Tanzlora and don't let it spread any further here on Earth."

Keelee gestured, and the images on the screen shifted again, showing the Shadowed Expanse. The land was unrecognizable, a sprawling wasteland of darkness and corruption. Tendrils of shadow crept across the landscape, twisting and writhing as if alive.

"This is where the Umbralox is strongest," Keelee said. "The Shadowed Expanse is its domain, a place it has claimed as its own. And at its heart lies the ruins of Erevelle."

Lincoln's brow furrowed. "Erevelle... the ruins that are rumored to be where Tanzlorans go missing? Beth and I heard horror stories about that place when we were living on Tanzlora."

Keelee nodded. "Yes. I have always heard those same terrible rumors. Unfortunately this is where we will need to journey to once you arrive on Tanzlora. Reaching it will not be easy. The corruption there is deeper than anywhere else on Tanzlora. The shadows are more aggressive, more dangerous."

The family exchanged glances, their resolve hardening. Ridge stepped forward, his voice steady. "Then we go there. We face whatever's waiting for us if it's the only way to stop this."

Keelee's luminous eyes met Ridge's, his expression unreadable. "You must understand the risks. The Shadowed Expanse is a place that tests even the strongest of wills. The shadows will exploit your fears, your doubts. Only those who are united in purpose and pure of heart can navigate it."

Waverly's gaze sharpened. "We've faced worse. On Arcmyrin. We did not let that evil win and we're not letting this thing win either. Not on our watch!"

Bethany, wiping her tears, stepped closer to the table. Her voice was quiet but firm. "We have to do this. For Marellis, for Fetrin, for every Tanzloran lost."

Lincoln placed a hand on her shoulder, his jaw set. "We will. Together."

Keelee nodded, his expression softening. "The Elders will prepare you for the journey once you arrive on Tanzlora. The spirits will guide you, but you must trust in one another. The task ahead will not be easy, but it is necessary."

The screens faded, leaving the room in silence. The family stood together, their resolve stronger than ever. The images of destruction and loss burned in their minds, fueling their determination.

"But before we can begin, we must ensure the safety of those you leave behind. Callum and the six Tanzloran warriors accompanying him are preparing to come through the portal. You need to go up to the house and prepare to greet them."

10

The playroom on the top floor of Sage Manor was usually a cheerful place, with sunlight streaming through wide windows and toys scattered across colorful rugs. Today, however, it was unrecognizable.

Waverly was the first to arrive, drawn by the unmistakable sound of screaming. She froze in the doorway, her eyes widening in horror. The entire room was a muddy disaster. Puddles of water gleamed on the hardwood floor, streaked with footprints leading in chaotic circles. Maddox stood on one side, his hair matted with dirt, while Maya was soaked head to toe, her clothes dripping onto the floor. In the corner, Monica huddled, her arms wrapped around her knees, trembling and tear-streaked.

"What in the—" Waverly started, her voice trailing off as her brain tried to process the scene.

Maya, her cheeks flushed with defiance, pointed an accusing finger at her brother. "He started it! He soaked me first!"

"I didn't mean to!" Maddox shot back, his lower lip trembling. "I was just trying to show Monica how my powers work!"

"And then I showed him mine," Maya snapped, smirking faintly as she gestured to the dirt smeared across Maddox's shirt. "I didn't think he'd chase us!"

"You didn't have to throw dirt at me!" Maddox wailed.

Before Waverly could intervene, other family members arrived. Lincoln and Bethany were the first through the door, followed closely by Gran Celia and Lorinda. Everyone stopped short, taking in the chaos.

"What is going on in here?" Lincoln barked, his gaze darting between his children and the wreckage.

"Your son decided to flood the playroom!" Bethany snapped, throwing her hands in the air.

"My son?" Lincoln shot back. "This is why I said it was a bad idea to let them nurture their powers on Tanzlora. They're too young to control it!"

Bethany glared at him. "Don't put this on me! They got those powers from your side of the family!"

Ridge, who had walked in just in time to hear Bethany's accusation, scowled. "Really, Beth? That's low—even for you."

"It's not low; it's a fact!" Bethany shot back, her voice rising.

The tension in the room thickened, but before it could escalate further, Lynx entered, taking one look at the scene and bursting out laughing.

"Now this is what I call using your gifts," he said, doubling over with laughter. "Good work, kiddos!"

Gran Celia silenced him with a piercing glare, her stern expression enough to stop his laughter mid-chuckle.

Lorinda, who had been hovering near the door, pushed past the arguing family members and went straight to Monica. The girl was still cowering in the corner, her wide eyes darting nervously between the Beaumonts.

"Oh, sweetie," Lorinda murmured, kneeling down and pulling Monica into a hug. "You're okay. You're safe."

Monica buried her face in her mother's shoulder, her small frame trembling.

Ridge, watching the scene unfold, ran a hand through his hair, his earlier frustration softening. He walked over to Lorinda and Monica, crouching down to their level. "You two deserve an explanation," he said gently. "Let's go for a walk."

Lorinda nodded, still cradling Monica protectively, and stood. Ridge led them out the door of the playroom, leaving the rest of the family behind in the mud-covered chaos.

As they walked through the manor's gardens, the air was cool and fresh, a stark contrast to the tense atmosphere of the playroom. Monica clung to Lorinda's hand, her steps hesitant. Ridge walked beside them, his usual swagger replaced by a quiet, thoughtful demeanor.

"I'm sorry about all of that," Ridge said finally, breaking the silence. "This probably feels like a lot to take in."

Lorinda nodded. "That's an understatement. I knew you all were... different. But this? The powers? The mud? I didn't expect anything like this."

"It's complicated," Ridge admitted. "The kids—Maya and Maddox—they're still figuring things out. Their gifts are part of who they are, and sometimes they lose control. It's not easy, even for adults."

Monica looked up at him, her voice small. "What are they?"

Ridge crouched down to meet her gaze, his expression serious but kind. "They're just kids—kids with abilities that make them special. But being special comes with challenges, and sometimes things get messy."

Monica hesitated, then nodded slowly.

Lorinda squeezed her daughter's hand. "Thank you for explaining," she said softly. "This is all so overwhelming, but I appreciate you being honest."

Ridge stood, his usual grin returning faintly. "Honesty is the least I can do. Come on, let's keep walking. The garden's got a way of making everything feel a little less crazy."

As they continued their stroll through the garden, the tension began to ease and Lorinda couldn't help but ask, "Ridge, what about you? What's your... special power? How does it all work?"

Ridge smirked, shoving his hands into his jacket pockets. "You could say I've got a solid foundation—literally. My gift's tied to Terraveta, the elemental spirit of earth. It's not just about moving rocks or making the ground shake, though. Terraveta represents resilience, strength, and the unshakable determination to stand firm for what matters."

"That sounds... steady," Lorinda said, her brow furrowed.

"It is," Ridge admitted. "The power's always there, rooted deep. Learning to wield it without letting it weigh me down—that's the challenge. But the connection to Terraveta isn't just about strength—it's about balance. Earth can withstand and nurture, but it can also crumble under the wrong pressure. It's about knowing when to hold steady and when to give way."

Lorinda tilted her head, intrigued. "And the others? Waverly, Lynx, and the rest of your family?"

Ridge stopped walking and turned to face her. "It's all tied to the elemental spirits. Mistara, Ambreela, Terraveta, and Ignissa—they're the forces that make life on our worlds possible. Air, water, earth, fire. Each of us is connected to one of them in some way. It's a gift passed down through the Beaumont bloodline, a gift from Origin. The spirits amplify who we are, not just what we can do."

"That sounds... massive," Lorinda said. "How do you keep it all straight?"

Ridge chuckled. "It helps to have a good visual. Come on, I'll show you."

He led Lorinda and Monica back inside the manor, guiding them toward the parlor. The room was warm and inviting, with soft lighting and a roaring fire in the hearth. Above the mantel hung a beautiful and unique painting.

It depicted the four elemental spirits of air, water, fire and earth. An iridescent pool of pure crystal clear water with beautiful blue ridge mountains surrounding it. The sky above them was magnificently painted in pink and purple hues with swirling wisps of clouds. The most unique part was the bright flame of fire, appearing to flicker and spread its warmth over the entire scene, negating the need for a sun that normally graces landscape canvases.

Francis Roller was seated in one of the armchairs, a book open on her lap. She glanced up as they entered, raising an eyebrow. "What's all the hullabaloo about? I heard screaming and something about a pipe bursting and flooding a room?

Ridge smirked, rubbing the back of his neck. "Sort of. The twins had a little... elemental disagreement upstairs. Turned the playroom into a mud wrestling ring."

Francis sighed, closing the book with a thud. "Children with gifts and no restraint. A classic recipe for chaos."

"Exactly," Ridge said. "And since we're already diving into the deep end of explaining all this, maybe you could help me out. You're better at giving the big-picture spiel about the spirits and the gift from Origin."

Francis looked at the painting thoughtfully, then nodded. "All right, but only because I love a good lecture."

She rose from her seat, gesturing to the painting. "This," she began, her voice taking on a professorial tone, "is a depiction of the four elemental spirits: Mistara, the spirit of water; Ambreela, the spirit of air; Terraveta, the spirit of earth; and Ignissa, the spirit of fire. These spirits aren't just metaphors—they are the embodiment of the forces that sustain life on Earth, Tanzlora, and Arcmyrin. Without them, life as we know it wouldn't exist."

She pointed to Ambreela, represented by swirling clouds. "Ambreela represents the flow of thought, creativity, and intuition. Those connected to her often have heightened awareness or abilities tied to the mind and the unseen."

Moving to Mistara, represented by the serene, iridescent pond, Francis continued, "Mistara governs water, emotion, and adaptability. Her influence is felt in those who are deeply empathetic or have a strong connection to healing and movement."

Terraveta, represented by the majestic mountains in the painting, was next. "Terraveta is earth, strength, and stability. Those connected to her are often resilient, practical, and deeply rooted in the natural world."

Finally, Francis gestured to Ignissa, the flame of fire representing radiant heat and energy. "Ignissa embodies fire, passion, and transformation. Her influence brings intensity, courage, and the ability to create or destroy with equal force."

She turned to Lorinda and Monica. "The Beaumont family is unique because their bloodline was gifted this connection by Origin—the Creator source that first aligned the spirits to protect life. Their gifts aren't just abilities; they are extensions of the elemental spirits themselves. That connection comes with great power—and great responsibility."

Lorinda looked between Francis and Ridge, her expression a mixture of awe and apprehension. "And the twins? They're just kids. How do they handle all of this?"

Francis softened. "It's not easy, but they're learning. It's why the family is so protective of them—they're still discovering who they are and how to control their gifts. What happened upstairs was an accident, but it shows the importance of balance. Without it, the power can spiral out of control."

Monica, who had been quietly staring at the painting, finally spoke. "So... they're not bad?"

Francis knelt to her level, her tone gentle. "No, sweetheart. They're not bad. They're just learning—just like you're learning how to be brave in a world that feels scary sometimes. It's okay to be scared, but it's also okay to forgive."

Monica nodded slowly, her gaze flickering to Ridge. He smiled faintly and said, "And I promise, no more mud in the playroom. Deal?"

Monica gave a small smile, finally relaxing.

Francis straightened and turned back to the painting. "The challenge ahead is steep, but with the spirits' guidance—and the family's connection to them—you have a fighting chance to set things right."

Ridge clapped his hands together. "Well, there you have it. The Beaumont family crash course in elemental spirits. Ready to stick around and see how it all plays out?"

Lorinda laughed softly. "I think we've come too far to turn back now."

Francis smirked. "Good. Then buckle up. The real journey's just beginning."

After a conversation with Maya and Maddox about their powers, Gran Celia, Lincoln and Bethany left Waverly and Lynx in charge of helping the twins clean up their muddy mess. The three of them made their way back outside to the gazebo. The portal had stopped glowing, its energies now still, and they could see the tall, imposing forms of the Tanzloran warriors gathered on the grounds around the pond.

The warriors were an awe-inspiring sight, their shimmering blue-violet skin and intricate armor catching the sunlight. At the center of the group stood Callum, a head taller than most of the others, his sharp features calm but commanding.

Bethany's face softened as she stepped forward. "Callum," she said, her voice warm despite the tension in the air. "It's been so long. I am deeply sorry to hear about your mother and the other villagers."

Callum inclined his head slightly, his deep, resonant voice carrying across the space. "Bethany. Lincoln. It's an honor to be here, though I wish it were under better circumstances."

Meanwhile, back inside Sage Manor, Ridge was finishing up the conversation with Francis, Lorinda, and Monica in the parlor. Monica sat on the couch, her hands wrapped around a cup of cocoa, her wide eyes fixed on the gazebo area visible from the parlor window. Suddenly, her gaze shifted, and her cup clattered onto the side table.

"Mom," Monica whispered, her voice trembling. "They're here."

Lorinda followed her daughter's gaze, her own breath catching as she saw the massive warriors gathered outside. "Oh my," she murmured, her grip tightening on the armrest. "They're... much larger than I expected."

Francis, usually composed, let out a nervous laugh. "I've read about Tanzloran warriors, but seeing them in person is something else entirely."

Ridge turned to Monica, his voice calm and reassuring. "Monica, they're here to protect you. To protect all of us. Those shadows you saw at your house? They don't stand a chance against these Tanzloran warriors."

Monica swallowed hard, nodding but still clutching her mother's arm. "I knew they were coming," she said softly. "But I've never seen anyone from another planet before."

Ridge smiled faintly. "It's a lot to take in, but I promise—they're good. They're here to keep you safe."

Lorinda glanced at Ridge, her own unease still evident. "And you trust them completely?"

"I do," Ridge said without hesitation. "The Tanzlorans are our allies, and Callum, their leader, is someone Lincoln and Bethany knows personally. You couldn't be in better hands."

As Monica and Lorinda slowly relaxed, Ridge turned back to the window, his expression resolute. The presence of the Tanzloran warriors brought a new sense of realness and urgency to their mission, but also a measure of relief. Sage Manor—and those who called it home—were no longer defenseless against the shadows lurking in the darkness.

11

The soft afternoon light streamed through the windows of Sage Manor as Lincoln and Bethany knelt in front of Maya and Maddox in the foyer. The twins stood close together, their small hands clasped tightly as they looked up at their parents with wide, questioning eyes.

"Maya, Maddox," Lincoln began, his voice steady but warm, "your mom and I are going to be gone for a little while. It's important, but we'll be back before you know it."

"Where are you going?" Maddox asked, his brow furrowed. "Why can't we come with you?"

Bethany brushed a strand of hair from Maya's face, her emerald eyes soft. "It's something we have to handle as grown-ups. But while we're gone, we need you two to be on your best behavior, okay? Gran Celia's going to need your help keeping Sage Manor in tip-top shape."

Maya's lips quirked into a small smile. "Like a team?"

"Exactly," Bethany said, tapping the tip of her daughter's nose. "You're part of the Sage Manor team now."

Maddox crossed his arms, his expression skeptical. "But what if something happens?"

Lincoln placed a firm but reassuring hand on his son's shoulder. "Gran Celia and Francis will be here. So will Lorinda and Monica plus the warriors are here. They will all keep you safe. And you've got each other, too. You're stronger than you think."

Bethany leaned in and kissed the top of Maddox's head, then Maya's. "We love you both more than anything. Remember that, okay?"

"Okay," the twins said in unison, though their voices were tinged with reluctance.

"Good," Lincoln said, standing and ruffling Maddox's hair. "Now give us a hug before we go."

The twins rushed forward, wrapping their small arms around their parents in a tight embrace. Gran Celia stood nearby, her calm presence anchoring the moment. As the twins let go, she stepped forward, placing a hand on each of their shoulders.

"They'll be in good hands," Gran Celia said firmly.

Lincoln and Bethany exchanged a glance, their silent gratitude evident, before turning to join the others in the chamber below the gazebo.

The chamber was alive with an otherworldly hum. The Crystal Gate, a shimmering circle of light and energy, with its surface rippling like liquid starlight covered one entire wall. The family gathered in front of it, their expressions a mix of determination and trepidation. Lincoln adjusted the strap of the satchel slung over his shoulder, his eyes fixed on the portal. Beside him, Bethany was securing her gloves, her fingers trembling slightly but her jaw set with resolve.

Waverly, Lynx, and Ridge stood close together, each holding a small vial of the herbal mixture Francis and Gran Celia had prepared. The sharp, earthy scent of the concoction lingered in the cool air.

Francis approached with Lorinda and Monica in tow. Monica's wide eyes darted between the family and the glowing portal, her small hand gripping her mother's tightly.

"I wish there were a more graceful way to travel," Francis said, adjusting her glasses as she handed out the remaining vials. "But I suppose this is the only reliable method of interplanetary travel. The herbal mixture will keep you steady during the transport."

"Reliable doesn't always mean comfortable," Ridge muttered, eyeing the swirling energy of the portal with mild skepticism.

Lincoln shot him a reproachful look. "Enough, Ridge. Focus on what's important and trust the process. The last thing we need is your doubts adding to the tension."

Ridge smirked but didn't respond, his attention drawn to Lorinda and Monica. "Guess you're getting the full Beaumont experience," he said.

Lorinda managed a small smile. "I'm not sure 'experience' is the word I'd use. But I appreciate being here to see it."

Monica, her voice small, asked, "Will it hurt?"

Waverly knelt to her level, her voice gentle. "No, it won't hurt. It's like walking through a door, but... brighter. A little strange, but not scary."

Monica nodded, though her grip on Lorinda didn't loosen.

The portal flickered, and Keelee's holographic image appeared in the center of the chamber. He had returned to Tanzlora right after the warriors had arrived on Earth. His tall, elegant figure a faint violet-blue with shimmering skin glowing in the dim light. His voice carried a calm authority as he addressed the group.

"The portal system is ready for your transport. The Elders and I are waiting for you on the other side." He turned to Francis. "Francis, you and your guests will need to return to the house. The energy released during the portal's activation is too unstable for those not crossing through."

Francis nodded. "Understood. We'll clear the area. Lorinda, Monica, come with me."

Monica hesitated, looking back at the Beaumonts. "Will they be okay?"

"They'll be fine," Francis said firmly. "Come on, sweetheart. Let's go join Celia and the children in the parlor. We'll talk more about all of this at the house."

Lorinda gave Ridge a lingering glance before following Francis out of the chamber, Monica's hand still clutched in hers.

As the chamber door closed behind them, Keelee's hologram flickered slightly, his gaze shifting to the family. "The transport will take only moments, but the energy release will be intense. Drink the herbal mixture now to stabilize your internal frequencies—it's necessary for safe passage."

Waverly held up her vial, nodding to the others. "You heard him. Bottoms up."

Each family member uncapped their vial, the potent aroma filling the chamber as they downed the mixture in unison. It was bitter, with a faintly metallic aftertaste, but the warmth that spread through their bodies was immediate and grounding.

Keelee extended his arm toward the portal, his hologram shimmering with urgency. "Clasp hands and step through when I give the signal. The Elders and I will meet you on Tanzlora."

The family linked hands, forming a tight circle around the portal. Lincoln took a deep breath, his voice steady as he addressed them. "Whatever happens, we stick together. Tanzlora needs us, and we need each other."

Ridge grinned faintly. "Nice pep talk, Coach. Let's get this over with."

Keelee raised his hand. "Now. Go."

With a shared glance of determination, the family stepped forward in unison, the portal's light swallowing them whole.

The moment they crossed, the chamber was flooded with a dazzling burst of energy, the hum of the portal crescendoing into a deafening roar before fading into silence. The chamber stood empty, the shimmering circle now dormant, as though it had never been active.

Above ground, Francis paused on the manor's lawn, her gaze lifting toward the sky. She placed a hand over her heart and whispered softly, "Safe travels, dear friends. I know you will be fine," she glanced over at Lorinda and smiled, "They've got the spirits on their side."

Lorinda nodded, her lips curving into a faint smile, though her eyes betrayed the lingering unease that hadn't left her since the events at her home. Monica stood close to her mother, still clutching her hand tightly, her gaze darting nervously between the towering Tanzloran warriors visible in the distance and the sprawling manor ahead.

Francis motioned toward the house, her tone light. "Come on. Let's get inside. I think we could all use a bit of warmth and normalcy after everything that's happened today."

The group made their way into the manor, the comforting aroma of freshly brewed tea and cookies greeting them as they entered the grand foyer. Gran Celia stood waiting in the parlor doorway, her expression a mixture of warmth and concern. Maya and Maddox were seated on the plush rug in front of the fireplace, flipping through a book of fairy tales while chatting animatedly.

Francis knelt beside them, her tone playful. "How would you two—and Monica—like to watch a movie in the media room? Something fun and adventurous, maybe?"

The twins' faces lit up instantly. "Yes, please!" Maya exclaimed, bouncing to her feet. Maddox nodded enthusiastically, tugging Monica's hand. "Come on, Monica! The media room is awesome."

Monica hesitated, glancing up at her mother for approval. Lorinda smiled gently, brushing a hand over her daughter's hair. "Go ahead, sweetheart. I think you could use a little fun."

Francis straightened, her eyes meeting Gran Celia's. "I'll keep them entertained for a while. You two could probably use some time to talk." Her voice was soft, but the understanding in her gaze was unmistakable.

Gran Celia placed a hand on Francis's arm, gratitude shining in her expression. "Thank you, Francis. You're always so thoughtful."

The group dispersed, the children following Francis eagerly down the hall, their excitement palpable. As the sound of their chatter faded, Gran Celia turned to Lorinda, motioning for her to take a seat on the comfortable sofa in the parlor.

"Tea?" Celia offered, lifting a delicate porcelain teapot.

"Yes, please," Lorinda replied, settling into the plush cushions. She watched as Gran Celia poured the tea, her movements calm and practiced. When Celia handed her a cup, Lorinda held it tightly, the warmth grounding her as she finally spoke.

"Is it always like this?" Lorinda asked, her voice quiet. "Your family... the warriors, the powers, the portal... It's all so much to take in."

Gran Celia settled into her chair across from Lorinda, her gaze steady and reassuring. "Not always," she said gently. "But Sage Manor has always been a place where extraordinary things happen. Our family's connection to the elemental spirits, the portal, and the other planets—it's not something most people are prepared to understand. And I imagine for someone who has already endured so much, it feels overwhelming."

Lorinda nodded, her fingers tightening around the teacup. "Overwhelming is one word for it. I mean, I knew there was something... unique about your family. Everyone in town talks about how kind and generous you all are, but there are always whispers—rumors about strange things happening here. I never put much stock in them, but now..." She trailed off, her eyes distant.

Gran Celia leaned forward slightly, her voice soft. "Now, you've seen for yourself. And it's not easy to reconcile what you've experienced with what you've always known. That's understandable, Lorinda. Take your time to process it. Ask whatever you need to ask. I'm here."

Lorinda hesitated for a moment before speaking again. "The twins... Maya and Maddox. Their powers—are they... dangerous?"

Celia's expression softened. "Not dangerous, no. Maya and Maddox are gifted, like many members of our family. But they're still children, learning to understand and control their abilities. What you saw today was an outburst of emotion and energy—nothing more."

Lorinda exhaled slowly. "And the warriors? They're here to protect the house, right? Because of what happened at my home?"

"Yes," Gran Celia confirmed. "The Tanzloran warriors are here to ensure that you, Monica, and everyone at Sage Manor remains safe while the rest of the family is away. Callum and his team are skilled protectors, and they understand the importance of this mission."

Lorinda sipped her tea, the warmth steadying her nerves. "And the portal... It's a gateway to another world. That's how they traveled to Tanzlora?"

Gran Celia nodded. "Exactly. It connects our world to Tanzlora and Arcmyrin, the sister planets in the Triad. The portal has existed for generations, serving as both a link and a safeguard."

Lorinda set her teacup down, her hands trembling slightly. "This is all so much, Celia. Just a few days ago, Monica and I were living normal lives. Now, our house is unlivable, we're staying here, and I'm being told that shadows, warriors, and other planets are all real. I don't even know where to begin processing it."

Gran Celia reached across the table, placing a comforting hand over Lorinda's. "You've been through a great deal, Lorinda. And you've handled it with strength and grace. But you're not alone in this. We're here for you—our family, the warriors, and even the spirits themselves. You don't have to carry this burden by yourself."

Lorinda looked up, her eyes glistening. "Thank you, Celia. That means more than I can say."

Gran Celia smiled warmly. "You're part of this now, Lorinda, whether by chance or fate. And I believe that together, we'll find a way to face whatever comes next."

As the fire crackled softly in the hearth, the weight of the conversation began to lift, replaced by a shared sense of understanding. Though the path ahead was uncertain, they both knew they would not walk it alone.

12

The moment the Beaumonts stepped into the portal, the world dissolved into a maelstrom of light and sound. It was as though they were being pulled through a tunnel of shimmering energy, the air vibrating with a strange, harmonic frequency. Time felt fluid—both fleeting and infinite—as streaks of gold, blue, and violet swirled around them.

Lincoln instinctively tightened his grip on Bethany's hand, his other hand still holding Lynx's. Despite his own calm resolve, he couldn't ignore the sensation of weightlessness that sent a jolt of unease through his chest. Beside him, Bethany's face was a mixture of determination and awe as she clutched Waverly's hand.

"This is wild," Ridge said, his voice carried oddly through the pulsating space. He was gripping Lynx's arm like an anchor, his usual bravado tinged with amazement. "Like riding through a starry kaleidoscope."

The swirling vortex intensified, and for a fleeting moment, they felt a deep resonance in their chests—a connection to something vast and ancient. The glowing energy of the portal shimmered around the Beaumont family, pulling them through the interdimensional pathway toward Tanzlora.

The journey was unlike anything else—swirls of light and energy cascaded around them, a kaleidoscope of vibrant colors blending seamlessly into the infinite expanse. Ridge, Lincoln, Bethany, Waverly, and Lynx moved cautiously, their weapons and wits ready for anything.

"This place feels... different," Waverly said, her sharp eyes scanning the glowing void around them. The energy seemed heavier than usual, the vibrant colors dimming slightly.

Lynx nodded, narrowing his eyes. "It's like something's off—"

Before he could finish, the swirling light around them flickered, then darkened. The once-vibrant colors gave way to an oppressive blackness that seeped into the portal like smoke. Shadows began to form, writhing and twisting into long, snake-like tendrils. The air grew cold and heavy, the whispers of the Umbralox echoing around them.

"It's here!" Ridge shouted, stepping forward as a shadow lashed toward them. "It's in the portal!"

The shadows lunged, their tendrils reaching for the family with unnatural speed. Lincoln reacted first, summoning water from the energy around him and hurling it at the advancing darkness. The liquid burst through the tendrils, but they re-formed instantly, unaffected by the attack.

"It's not working!" Lincoln yelled, his voice tense as more shadows surrounded him.

Ridge summoned large stones of matter from the energy surrounding him and hurled them at the shadows. But like the water, the stones passed straight through the shadows, falling harmlessly into the void.

The shadows coiled around Ridge and Lincoln, wrapping their legs, pulling them down as they struggled against the darkness. "They're too strong!" Ridge grunted, trying to wrestle free.

Bethany screamed as a tendril lashed toward her. Lynx grabbed her arm, pulling her behind him as flames erupted from his palms. He hurled fire at the shadows, the light pushing them back momentarily. "Stay behind me!" he shouted, throwing another fiery blast at an advancing tendril.

Though Lynx's flames kept the shadows at bay, it wasn't enough to turn the tide. The shadows regrouped quickly, encircling Lincoln and Ridge tighter, cutting off their movements. Lynx glanced back at his mother, fear in his eyes. "I can't hold them off much longer!"

Meanwhile, Waverly stood apart, her focus sharp as she summoned a swirling wind around herself. The air whipped into a tight funnel, creating a protective vortex that kept the shadows from reaching her. Every time a tendril tried to pierce the wind, it was flung out, twisted, and torn apart by the spinning currents.

"Waverly!" Lynx called, his voice filled with urgency. "They're trapped—I can't get to them!"

Waverly's heart raced as she glanced toward her family. She could see the tendrils squeezing the life from Ridge and Lincoln, but she couldn't extend her protection without risking her own safety. The tornadic funnel around her hummed with energy, the winds whipping dangerously fast.

Then her eyes met Lynx's. In an instant, an understanding passed between them—a plan formed without a single word. Waverly twisted her body, driving her funnel forward as fast as possible. As she neared Lynx, she broke the vortex's outer edge, pushing through the protective wind.

"Now!" she shouted.

Lynx turned, his hands blazing with fire as he hurled a massive burst at the shadows surrounding them. The flames created a temporary gap, and in that moment, Waverly reached him and Bethany, pulling them into the funnel. The swirling air closed around them, creating a protective barrier.

Inside the funnel, Lynx kept the fire alive, casting a faint, warm glow that lit their faces. "We're safe for now," he said, panting. "But Dad and Ridge—"

"We'll get to them," Waverly interrupted. She spun the vortex, moving it toward Ridge and Lincoln, who were still entangled by the shadows. "Ridge! Dad! Use your knives!"

The two men, struggling against the suffocating grip of the Umbralox, heard her cry. Lincoln, his breath shallow, reached for the knife at his side. Ridge, pinned to the ground, clawed at his belt until his hand found his blade. Both men pulled their weapons free, their thoughts filled with desperate prayers that their knives would work.

As the knives cleared their sheaths, Ridge and Lincoln started slicing away at the tendrils wrapped tight around their legs. The tendrils loosened, recoiling from the relentless blades slicing through them. Freeing from their grip, the two men managed to stagger to their feet, clutching their weapons tightly.

"Get to us!" Waverly shouted, twisting the funnel toward them. The spinning air reached Ridge and Lincoln, pulling them into the protective barrier just as the shadows regrouped.

Inside the vortex, the family huddled together, their breathing ragged. The shadows swarmed outside, but Waverly's winds held firm, spinning faster as she channeled every ounce of her energy into maintaining the barrier.

"We need to get out of here—now!" Bethany cried, clutching Lynx's arm.

"The portal!" Lincoln shouted. "We're close—I can feel it!"

Waverly gritted her teeth, her focus sharp as she twisted the vortex forward. The swirling air pushed them toward the end of the portal, where a faint light marked the exit to Tanzlora. The shadows lashed out one final time, but Lynx's flames and Waverly's winds kept them at bay.

The family burst through the portal's exit in a rush of wind and energy, tumbling onto the vibrant surface of Tanzlora. The portal behind them sealed with a final shimmer, cutting off the shadows' pursuit.

For a moment, they lay on the ground, catching their breath. The vibrant colors of Tanzlora's landscape surrounded them, a stark contrast to the darkness they had just escaped. The air was warm, filled with the hum of life that seemed to rejuvenate them instantly.

Lincoln was the first to sit up, still gripping his knife. He placed it in the sheath at his waist. "That was too close."

Ridge groaned, pushing himself to his feet. "Next time, let's skip the death trap in the middle of the portal."

Bethany wrapped her arms around Lynx, her voice trembling. "You saved us, Lynx. All of you did."

Waverly knelt beside them, her breathing steadying as she looked at her family. "We made it," she said.

The family stood together, their resolve hardening. The battle in the portal was just the beginning, but they had survived—and they were ready for whatever came next.

The world around them was breathtaking. Tanzlora stretched out in all its glory, a vibrant and ethereal landscape that shimmered with life. Towering crystalline trees sparkled in the sunlight, their translucent leaves refracting rainbows across the lush, mossy ground. Rivers of silvery water wound through the land, their surfaces glinting like liquid diamonds. The air was crisp and clean, humming faintly with the energy of the planet itself.

The Beaumont family stood in a small clearing, catching their breath after their harrowing escape from the portal. The beauty of Tanzlora all around them, its colors bright and alive, but the tension from their encounter with the Umbralox still hung heavy in the air.

The soft hum of approaching energy caught their attention, and moments later, Keelee materialized before them. His silver-blue form shimmered faintly in the Tanzloran light, his luminous eyes scanning the group with relief and concern.

"You made it," Keelee said, his melodic voice carrying a weight of gratitude and tension. "I was monitoring your journey through the portal. When I felt the presence of the Umbralox, I feared the worst."

Lincoln stepped forward, his posture still taut with the adrenaline of the fight. "It was close, Keelee. Too close. The shadows... they were stronger than anything we've faced before."

Keelee inclined his head solemnly. "The Umbralox is growing bolder. Its ability to infiltrate the portal is troubling—it means its corruption is spreading even faster than we anticipated." His gaze softened as it moved to Bethany. "But you are here, alive and well, and for that, we are grateful."

Keelee took a step closer, his expression shifting to one of warmth. "Lincoln, Bethany," he said, addressing them directly, "welcome back to Tanzlora. It has been far too long since we last stood together on this soil."

Bethany smiled faintly, brushing a stray lock of hair from her face. "It feels like a lifetime ago. The landscape is just as beautiful as I remember... though it feels heavier now. Like the shadows have reached even here."

"They have," Keelee admitted, his voice tinged with sorrow. "But your return is a light in this darkness. Tanzlora has missed you both."

Keelee then turned his attention to Waverly, Lynx, and Ridge, his expression shifting to one of curiosity and respect. "And to you, Waverly, Lynx, Ridge—welcome to Tanzlora for the first time. I wish it were under better circumstances, but your presence here is no less important. You are the descendants of Galen Beaumont, and your arrival brings hope to our planet."

Waverly stepped forward, her sharp eyes studying Keelee. "Tanzlora is... incredible. It's unlike anything I imagined. But I can feel the weight here, the tension. This isn't just a planet under attack—it's a planet fighting for its life."

"You see clearly," Keelee said, his tone appreciative. "Tanzlora has always been a place of balance and vitality, but the shadows have upset that harmony. The people are fighting, but they cannot do it alone. Your family's connection to the spirits and the Origin Gift is the key to turning the tide."

Ridge smirked faintly, though his voice carried sincerity. "Well, I didn't plan on a vacation, anyway. If we're here, it's to fight."

Keelee offered a small smile. "Your determination will serve you well, Ridge. And Lynx," he said, turning to the youngest sibling, "your fire in the portal—both literal and figurative—may have saved your family's lives. The courage you displayed is rare."

Lynx rubbed the back of his neck, his face reddening slightly. "I just did what I had to do. We all did."

Keelee stepped back, his gaze sweeping over the family as a whole. "You have already faced much, and your journey is only beginning. But Tanzlora stands with you. The Elders are prepared to aid you in every way they can, and the spirits will guide you."

Lincoln nodded, his voice resolute. "We're ready. Whatever it takes, we'll fight to protect Tanzlora—and Earth."

Keelee placed his hand over his heart and inclined his head in respect. "Then let us waste no time. The council awaits your arrival. They have much to discuss with you about the task ahead."

The family exchanged glances, their expressions a mix of exhaustion and determination. Together, they began the trek toward the council chambers, the crystalline ground beneath their feet glowing faintly with each step. Keelee led the way, his presence a steadying force as they walked into the unknown.

The crystalline halls of the Tanzloran Elders council chambers shimmered with an ethereal glow, the light refracting off the smooth surfaces like sunlight through a prism. The Beaumont family followed Keelee in awed silence, their footsteps echoing faintly in the grand corridor. The structure felt alive, pulsing softly with the energy of the planet itself. The air was charged, both welcoming and solemn, as if the chambers knew the gravity of the moment.

"This is incredible," Waverly murmured, her sharp eyes tracing the intricate designs carved into the crystal walls. Each etching seemed to tell a story—of life, growth, and resilience.

Keelee glanced back at her, his expression soft but serious. "The council chambers are the heart of Tanzlora's governance and wisdom. They have witnessed the triumphs and tribulations of our people for generations. It is fitting that you stand here now, as your family's legacy becomes entwined with ours once again."

They entered a vast circular chamber, the walls lined with crystalline panels that pulsed faintly with colors never before seen by Ridge, Waverly and Lynx. The panels looked like living conduits of energy. In the center of the chamber stood five imposing looking figures, each radiating an aura of authority and wisdom. Keelee gestured for the family to step forward.

"May I present the Elders of Tanzlora," Keelee announced, his voice carrying a reverence that was impossible to miss. "Brakar, our leader and guide; Draven, the overseer of our warriors; Sylvaris, our visionary; Thaloria, the youngest and most clairvoyant among us; and Lumorith, the keeper of our history and archives."

Brakar stepped forward first. Her presence was commanding, her tall figure shimmering with an inner light that reflected her strength. Her voice was deep, rich and resonant as she spoke. "Beaumont family, we welcome you to Tanzlora. Your arrival brings hope to our people in these dark times. We thank you for coming to the aid of your sister planet."

Draven, a stoic figure with sharp silver eyes and a warrior's build, inclined his head. "Your reputation precedes you. The courage your family has shown on Earth is known to us, and we are grateful for your willingness to fight alongside us."

Sylvaris, with his violet eyes and serene expression, stepped forward next. "The bond between our worlds runs deep, and your presence here reaffirms that connection. I have seen glimpses of what lies ahead, and while the path is treacherous, I believe you are the ones who can help turn the tide."

Thaloria, her youthful features glowing with an otherworldly wisdom, smiled softly. "The spirits speak highly of you. They believe in your potential, and so do we."

Finally, Lumorith, the oldest of the council, his silvery skin glistening faintly, addressed the family. "Your ancestor, Galen Beaumont, stood with us during the Galactic War. Now, his descendants have returned to continue that fight. You carry his strength, and through you, his legacy endures."

13

B rakar motioned toward the walls, and the crystalline panels shifted, displaying vivid images of Tanzlora's devastation. The vibrant forests, once teeming with life, were shown scorched and barren. Villages lay in ruins, their glowing structures reduced to dark, jagged remains. Rivers that had once sparkled like liquid starlight were now gray and lifeless.

"This is what the Umbralox has done to our world," Brakar said, her voice steady but heavy with sorrow. "What you see here is only a fraction of the destruction. As Keelee showed you before you left Earth, entire villages have been abandoned, their people forced to flee with nothing but what they could carry. Many did not survive."

Brakar turned to face them, her expression solemn. "The Umbralox is not a single enemy but a pervasive force. It has entrenched itself in The Shadowed Expanse, a region so corrupted that it is unrecognizable from the Tanzlora we once knew. It is there that you must begin."

Sylvaris stepped forward, his voice calm but urgent. "The spirits will guide you, but you must remain vigilant. The Shadowed Expanse is dangerous, and the Umbralox will not relent in its attempts to stop you."

Draven added, his tone serious, "You will not be alone. Our warriors will provide what aid they can, but the battle ahead will test you in ways no one can prepare for."

Bethany wiped her tears, standing taller despite the grief in her heart. "We'll do whatever it takes," she said, her voice steady. "For Tanzlora, for Earth, for everyone who has been hurt by this."

Lincoln nodded, his gaze locked on Brakar. "We're ready. Just tell us what we need to do."

The council exchanged glances, a silent agreement passing between them. Sylvaris gestured to the wall behind him, where the crystalline surface shifted to display an image of a tall man with piercing eyes and a commanding presence. Galen Beaumont. His likeness shimmered, surrounded by symbols and inscriptions that pulsed faintly with energy.

"Galen was not just your ancestor," Sylvaris explained. "He was a warrior of the Triad during the Galactic War. He was one of the few gifted by Origin to wield elemental power. His connection to Terraveta gave him unmatched resilience and strength, and he used it to defend the cores of Tanzlora, Earth, and Arcmyrin from the Umbralox."

Brakar picked up the story, her voice grave. "But the Umbralox was not just an enemy to the planets. It was drawn to Galen himself. His connection to the elemental spirits made him both a threat and a target. The Umbralox sought to corrupt him, to turn him into a weapon against the Triad."

Bethany's voice was sharp with disbelief. "You're saying the Umbralox wanted to use him? How?"

Draven's silver eyes glinted. "By breaking him. Galen was subjected to relentless attacks—shadows that whispered to him, visions of despair, and corruption that tried to infiltrate his very essence. But he resisted. He fought back, and with the help of the Triad, he drove the Umbralox into dormancy. However, it came at a cost."

Sylvaris nodded solemnly. "The battle scarred him deeply, both physically and spiritually. His connection to the spirits was never the same. But his victory came with a promise: that the Umbralox would never stop seeking to destroy his bloodline. The Origin Gift, passed down through your family, has always been a beacon to the Umbralox—a light it seeks to extinguish."

Waverly's voice was quiet but firm. "So, this isn't just about Tanzlora, Arcmyrin or Earth. It's personal. The Umbralox is coming for us."

Keelee stepped forward, his luminous gaze steady. "It has always been personal. Your family's resilience has kept the balance intact for generations. But now the Umbralox sees an opportunity—with Tanzlora weakened, the barriers between worlds are fragile."

Bethany's hands tightened into fists. "We've spent years trying to protect our family and our worlds, and now we learn this has been brewing since Galen's time?"

"It is a heavy burden," Brakar said, her voice tinged with regret. "But you are not alone. The Triad stands with you. The Arcmyrins stand ready to assist if needed."

Sylvaris nodded. "And your connection to the spirits will be stronger now than it has ever been. Galen's legacy lives on in you, and it may yet be the key to defeating the Umbralox once and for all."

The Beaumonts exchanged glances, their expressions a mixture of resolve and uncertainty. Lincoln broke the silence, his voice steady. "We've always fought for what matters—our family, our home, and our worlds. If this is what we were meant to face, then we'll see it through."

Waverly's voice was steel. "The Umbralox won't win."

Draven's gaze softened slightly. "Your ancestor would be proud. But the road ahead is perilous. We must strike decisively, or everything we've fought for will fall."

The family nodded, their determination solidified. The shadows of their past might have returned, but the Beaumonts would not face them alone—and they would not falter.

Lumorith raised a hand, his expression grave. "The time for action is now. The Umbralox feeds on despair and division. You must stand united, as your ancestors did during the Galactic War."

Lumorith's silvery blue skin shimmered faintly as he stepped forward. His deep, resonant voice filled the chamber. "There is something we have kept hidden, even from our closest allies. A weapon forged long ago during the Galactic War—a weapon of immense power that could turn the tide against the Umbralox."

Lincoln exchanged a glance with Bethany, his expression growing serious. "Why haven't we heard of this before?"

Keelee stepped forward, his luminous eyes filled with urgency. "Because its existence has been a closely guarded secret. Only the Elders have known of its location, and for good reason. The weapon is so powerful that, in the wrong hands, it could bring destruction as great as the shadows themselves."

Lumorith nodded. "This weapon, known as Triadorne, was forged by a collaboration of Tanzloran, Arcmyrin, and Earth's greatest minds. Galen Beaumont himself played a crucial role in its creation, but when the war ended, it was deemed too dangerous to remain whole."

Sylvaris, his violet eyes glowing faintly, took up the explanation. "To prevent it from being used by the wrong forces, the weapon was divided. Its core remained here on Tanzlora, hidden in the ruins of Erevelle, while its keys—pieces integral to its activation—was taken to Earth by Galen."

Waverly frowned, her sharp gaze locked on Sylvaris. "Why Earth? Wouldn't that have made it harder to protect?"

Draven, his silver eyes piercing, answered, "It was a calculated risk. Galen believed that splitting the weapon across worlds would make it nearly impossible for anyone to reunite it. The pieces he took to Earth was hidden in a location only he knew, its power disguised to deter even the most determined entities."

Lynx shifted uneasily, his brow furrowing. "So what's changed? Why tell us this now?"

Keelee's voice softened. "Because we believe the time has come to reunite the Triadorne. The shadows are growing stronger, and the Umbralox is more determined than ever. The weapon's power may be the only way to tip the balance in our favor."

Terraveta, the spirit of earth, materialized beside Ridge, her towering crystalline form shimmering with resolve. "The Triadorne is not just a tool of destruction," she said, her voice rumbling like distant thunder. "It was designed to cleanse and restore, to sever the connection between the Umbralox and the life forces it corrupts."

Mistara, the spirit of water, flowed gracefully around Lincoln, her voice like a gentle stream. "But it is also discerning. The weapon will not yield its power to those with selfish or harmful intent. It must sense unity, purpose, and purity of heart."

Keelee nodded. "That is why you, the Beaumonts, are essential. Your connection to the Origin Gift and the elemental spirits gives you the ability to locate and activate the weapon—if your intent is pure."

The room fell into thoughtful silence as the gravity of their mission sank in. Bethany finally broke the silence, her voice steady. "Where are these ruins? How do we find this core?"

Thaloria, the youngest elder, stepped forward, her azure eyes filled with quiet determination. "The ruins of Erevelle lie deep within The Shadowed Expanse, a region heavily corrupted by the Umbralox. The journey will be perilous, but your elemental connections will guide you. The spirits will help you navigate the corrupted lands."

Waverly folded her arms, her sharp mind already piecing things together. "And the keys? The part Galen took to Earth?"

"Those pieces are now here on Tanzlora, I brought them back with me per the Elder's directive," Keelee said. "Celia, as the matriarch of the family, had been given the knowledge of their existence and location. As the Tanzloran warriors were journeying through the Crystal Gate to Sage Manor, the Elders felt it was a safe opportunity for the warriors and myself to transport the keys."

"More family secrets," Waverly sighed, "I wonder how much more Gran knows and can't or won't tell. It's incredible"

"Quite a lot," Brakar responded, "but you need to understand that as the matriarch of your family, the responsibilites fall on her. She can't risk the protections that are in place for her family, Sage Manor, Earth and the Triad by telling you all she knows until the right moment."

"One day, you will know it all, Waverly, but that will come at a great cost for you because it will mean you have survived your grandmother and father," Thaloria pointed at Lincoln as she spoke to Waverly.

Waverly dropped her head, her understanding of their words clearly impacting her. Ambreela, the spirit of air, floated toward Waverly, her translucent form moving like a breeze. "Your connection to the spirits will help you now and in the future. If your heart is pure and your intentions just, the Triadorne will reveal itself to you. If that comes to pass, together we will wield the key."

Waverly raised her head and nodded, wiping away a tear. The thoughts of losing Gran Celia and her father, Lincoln had made her emotional.

Ignissa, the spirit of fire, appeared beside Lynx, her radiant form glowing warmly. "Beware. The Umbralox will sense your movements. They will do everything in their power to stop you."

Lynx clenched his fists, the memory of their battle on Arcmyrin fresh in his mind. "Let them try. We're not backing down."

Sylvaris inclined his head, his expression serious. "Courage will serve you well, Lynx. But caution is equally important. The ruins of Erevelle are ancient and treacherous. The dangers there are more potent than anywhere else on Tanzlora."

The Elders moved toward the center of the chamber, their hands raised as they channeled energy into a crystalline table. A holographic map of Tanzlora appeared, highlighting the path to The Shadowed Expanse and the ruins of Erevelle. The glowing lines pulsed faintly, as though responding to the family's presence.

Lumorith gestured to the map. "This is your path. The journey will not be easy, but it is necessary. The fate of Tanzlora, and perhaps the Triad, rests on your shoulders."

Lincoln studied the map, his jaw set with determination. "We'll do whatever it takes."

Pazlun stepped forward, a faint smile breaking through his stern demeanor. "Good. Then let's show these shadows what happens when they try to consume our world."

"The people will stand with you," Keelee assured Lincoln. "They may be afraid, but they are not broken. They will fight for their homes, their families, and their future."

Brakar stepped forward, her eyes meeting Lincoln's. "Then let us prepare you for the journey. The path to The Shadowed Expanse will be treacherous, but it is the first step toward reclaiming our world."

The family stood together, their resolve stronger than ever. The images of destruction burned in their minds, fueling their determination. They knew the battle ahead would be the greatest challenge they had ever faced, but they also knew they would face it together.

Keelee gestured for them to follow him. "First, you must attune yourselves to Tanzlora. The journey here and the battle you endured in the portal can disrupt your alignment with the planet's energy. Without that connection, you'll struggle to wield your gifts. You must be rested and prepared for the challenges to come. Tanzlora will provide what aid it can."

As the family exited the council chambers, Keelee said, "We have arranged for you to stay in one of our Reficiat Haven facilities, a place designed to restore and fortify both body and mind. It is essential that you take this time to acclimate to Tanzlora's unique energy fields and prepare yourselves for the journey ahead."

14

Keelee escorted the family toward the haven, explaining its purpose along the way. "The Reficiat Havens are sanctuaries where travelers and warriors can recover and recalibrate. They are equipped with everything you will need, from healing mixtures to specialized clothing that will help you adapt to Tanzlora's environment."

The path to the haven wound through a sparkling cityscape, its streets glowing faintly beneath their feet. The buildings around them shimmered with translucent walls, their interiors visible as vibrant hues of light danced within. Despite the beauty, the energy in the air felt heavy, a reminder of the darkness that loomed over the planet.

As they approached the haven, the building came into view, its structure appearing both elegant and organic, as though it had naturally sprung from the ground. The walls glowed a soft blue, radiating a calming energy that seemed to ease the tension in their shoulders.

The interior of the Reficiat Haven was even more breathtaking. The main atrium was spacious, filled with glowing, plant-like structures that emitted a soothing light. The floor was covered in soft moss-like material, cool and springy underfoot. A faint, melodic hum resonated through the space, blending with the gentle trickle of water from a nearby fountain.

Sanodia, a Tanzloran healer and the daughter of Marellis, greeted them as they entered. Her blue-violet skin shimmered faintly, and her luminous eyes were filled with warmth and recognition as they landed on Lincoln and Bethany. "It is good to see you both again," she said, her voice soft but firm. "Though I wish it were under better circumstances."

Bethany stepped forward, her voice filled with emotion. "Sanodia... I can't believe it's you. After everything that happened, I thought—"

Sanodia placed a gentle hand on Bethany's shoulder. "Callum and I survived, though our mother did not. She was lost when our village fell to the Umbralox. Both Callum and I are honored to be able to serve your family here on Tanzlora and also on Earth where my brother is guarding your family."

Bethany's eyes welled with tears. "Your mother... she was there when Maya and Maddox were born. I don't know how we would have managed without her. She was... she was incredible."

Sanodia smiled faintly, though sadness shadowed her expression. "She spoke of that often—how strong you were, Bethany, and how much light your twins brought to the village. It gave her joy to help bring them into the world."

Lincoln stepped closer, his voice heavy. "We're so sorry, Sanodia. Your mother's kindness will never be forgotten. Neither will we ever forget what you and your brother are doing for our family now."

Sanodia nodded, her gaze steady. "She would have been proud to see you here, standing against the darkness that took her and so many others. And I will do everything I can to ensure you are ready for what lies ahead."

The family followed Sanodia through the haven as she showed them the accommodations. The guest quarters were simple yet elegant, with walls that glowed faintly and adjusted their light to the occupants' preferences. Each room was equipped with a soft, hammock-like bed suspended above a glowing mossy floor, providing both comfort and a subtle energy boost.

In a central area, there was a communal space filled with cushioned seating and tables carved from luminous crystal. Nearby, an open-air balcony overlooked the Tanzloran landscape, offering a view of the crystalline forests and glowing rivers in the distance. Despite the beauty, faint traces of corruption could be seen creeping along the edges of the horizon.

Sanodia led them to a smaller chamber filled with shelves of jars and vials, each containing mixtures of glowing herbs and liquids. "These are healing infusions," she explained. "They will help you recover and strengthen your connection to Tanzlora's energy fields. The Elders have instructed me to prepare specific blends for each of you, tailored to your unique connections to the elemental spirits."

She handed each family member a small vial filled with a faintly glowing liquid. "Drink this tonight," she instructed. "It will help your body attune to the planet's energy and prepare you for the tasks ahead."

The family thanked her and took the vials, though their thoughts remained heavy with the weight of the day's revelations.

As the family settled into the communal space, the atmosphere began to relax slightly. Ridge leaned back in one of the cushioned chairs, letting out a low whistle. "I've gotta hand it to Tanzlora—this place knows how to do hospitality."

Waverly smirked faintly. "Don't get too comfortable. This is probably the calm before the storm."

Lynx, holding his vial up to the light, watched the glowing liquid swirl. "These mixtures... they're incredible. Do you think they'll really help us connect to the spirits more?"

"They will," Sanodia said, re-entering the area. "Tanzlora's herbs are deeply connected to the ley lines of the planet. They amplify the energy within you, strengthening your bond to the spirits and enhancing your resilience."

Sanodia perched gracefully on a low stool nearby. A table beside her held small vials of colorful liquids, pouches of dried herbs, and an assortment of tools she had been using to prepare their supplies.

Sanodia worked methodically, her long, nimble fingers deftly mixing an herbal infusion in a shallow bowl. Her presence was calm and grounding, a stark contrast to the anticipation buzzing through the room.

Lynx leaned forward, his eyes narrowing as he watched her pour a shimmering green liquid into the bowl. "Sanodia," he began, his voice curious, "earlier, you mentioned something about ley lines helping guide us on the way to Erevelle. What exactly are ley lines?"

Sanodia glanced up, a soft smile gracing her serene features. "Ley lines are natural pathways of energy that crisscross a planet, connecting places of power and significance. On Tanzlora, they are particularly strong, flowing through the land like rivers of life. They carry the planet's energy, and when one is attuned to them, they can serve as guides—or even sources of strength."

Waverly tilted her head thoughtfully. "So, they're kind of like veins in the planet's body?"

Sanodia nodded. "Precisely. Ley lines are tied to the harmony of the world. They amplify the energy of places like Erevelle, where the nexus of ley lines once supported a thriving city. But when such places fall to corruption, the ley lines themselves can become unstable—or dangerous."

Ridge leaned back, a skeptical look crossing his face. "And these ley lines... we're supposed to use them to guide us? What if we run into one of those corrupted spots?"

Sanodia's expression grew serious. "That is why you must remain attuned to your elemental spirits. Their connection to Tanzlora's energy will help you navigate safely. They will sense instability and guide you around it."

Lynx frowned slightly, leaning his elbows on his knees. "So, we're walking a tightrope of energy, with only our spirits to keep us balanced. Got it."

Bethany reached over and gently touched his shoulder. "Lynx, the spirits haven't let us down yet. Trust them."

Sanodia's smile returned as she placed the bowl she had been mixing onto the table. "Which brings me to the reason I am here tonight—to ensure you are all prepared for the journey. The infusions I am creating will help sustain your energy and protect you from the effects of the corrupted terrain."

Ridge leaned forward, inspecting the colorful vials and herbs with curiosity. "What exactly are in these infusions? I've been meaning to ask—what kind of herbs and liquids are we drinking?"

Sanodia chuckled softly, her eyes sparkling with amusement. "A fair question, Ridge. The base of each infusion is derived from the glimmer-berry plant, a common Tanzloran herb known for its energizing prop-erties. Combined with the nectar of the luminaris flower, it strengthens your body's ability to adapt to Tanzlora's atmosphere and resist fa-tigue."

She picked up a pouch of finely ground powder, holding it out for them to see. "This is spiritroot, a rare plant that grows near the ley lines. It enhances your connection to the elemental spirits, allowing you to draw on their guidance more clearly."

Ridge sniffed the air above the pouch, raising an eyebrow. "Smells earthy... and kind of spicy."

Sanodia laughed. "Yes, it has a potent aroma, but its effects are in-valuable. And lastly, there are drops of purified crystwater, which carries the essence of Tanzlora's energy. It helps stabilize your own energy, es-pecially in areas where the ley lines are disrupted."

Waverly picked up one of the vials, tilting it to watch the liquid swirl. "So, basically, these are lifelines in a bottle."

Sanodia nodded. "In a sense, yes. They will not solve every challenge you face, but they will support you when the journey becomes diffi-cult."

Lincoln, who had been listening intently, reached for one of the vials and held it up. "Sanodia, thank you. I know these preparations take time, and I want you to know how much we appreciate your care."

Sanodia inclined her head gracefully. "It is my honor, Lincoln. Tanzlora owes your family a great debt, and I will do all I can to ensure your success."

"This place..." Bethany said softly, gazing out at the landscape. "It feels like a different world from the one we left. The village we called home is gone, but this... this is still so beautiful."

Sanodia nodded, her expression contemplative. "Tanzlora's beauty endures, even in the face of the Umbralox. It is a reminder of what we are fighting for."

Lincoln, who had moved to the balcony and stood gazing out over the landscape, asked. "Do you think we'll ever see it restored? The village, the forests... everything that's been lost?"

Sanodia's voice was firm. "If anyone can bring that restoration, it is you and your family. Your connection to the spirits, to Tanzlora's very essence, is stronger than you realize."

As the evening wore on, Sanodia continued her work, answering the family's questions and sharing stories of Tanzlora's history. By the time the preparations were complete, the Beaumonts felt a renewed sense of purpose. The journey to Erevelle would be perilous, but with the infusions, the guidance of their spirits, and Sanodia's wisdom, they knew they were as ready as they could be.

As the night deepened, they retired to their rooms, the glow of the haven casting a soothing light over their thoughts. Though their hearts were heavy with grief for what had been lost, there was also a spark of hope—a belief that their efforts could make a difference.

The haven was a place of refuge, a brief respite before the trials ahead. And as the Beaumonts rested, they felt the planet's energy beginning to flow through them, preparing them for the journey to come. Tanzlora was counting on them, and they would not let it down.

15

The council chambers were transformed into a place of solemn beauty. The crystalline walls glowed with vibrant hues of green, blue, red, and clear, representing the four elemental spirits—Terraveta, Mistara, Ignissa, and Ambreela. In the center of the chamber, five ornate chairs of honor were arranged in a semicircle, each crafted from shimmering Tanzloran crystal and attuned to one of the spirits.

Keelee stood at the head of the chamber alongside the five Elders of Tanzlora—Brakar, Sylvaris, Draven, Thaloria, and Lumorith. The air thrummed with energy as the Beaumont family entered, their footsteps echoing softly on the glowing floor. Each family member wore the ceremonial garments gifted by the Elders, designed to harmonize with their elemental connections.

"This ceremony," Brakar began, her voice resonating through the chamber, "is a sacred tradition of Tanzlora. It is a bond between those who dedicate their lives to the protection of our people and the spirits who guide and empower us. Today, we honor the Beaumonts for their courage, their sacrifice, and their commitment to fighting for the Triad."

The family approached the chairs, their faces reflecting a mixture of solemnity and resolve. Each chair was adorned with intricate carvings and glowed faintly with the color of the spirit it represented. Ridge was drawn to the green chair of Terraveta, its luminous patterns resembling vines and leaves. Lincoln moved toward the blue chair of Mistara, its surface rippling like water. Lynx took the red chair of Ignissa, its design evoking flames. Waverly approached the clear chair of Ambreela, its carvings swirling like currents of wind. Bethany, though not directly tied to the spirits, was honored with a central chair that glowed softly with the combined energy of all four elements, signifying her integral role in the family's unity.

As they sat, a quiet hum filled the chamber, and the elemental spirits began to materialize. Mistara, the water spirit, flowed gracefully toward Lincoln, her liquid form shimmering with silvery-blue light. Terraveta, the earth spirit, rose from the ground beside Ridge, her crystalline body solid and grounding. Ignissa, the fire spirit, appeared in a radiant burst of flame beside Lynx, her fiery eyes burning with intensity. Ambreela, the air spirit, descended lightly next to Waverly, her translucent form swirling like a breeze.

Thaloria stepped forward, her clairvoyant gaze fixed on the family. "The spirits have chosen you, as they did your ancestor, Galen Beaumont. Today, you reaffirm your bond with them and dedicate your lives to the protection of Tanzlora and the Triad."

Lumorith raised a hand, and the room dimmed as a circle of light surrounded the chairs. "This is a sacred commitment," he said, his voice deep and steady. "One that transcends time and space. By forging this bond, you become not only protectors of Tanzlora but guardians of the balance that sustains our worlds."

Keelee approached, holding a crystalline orb that pulsed with energy. "Each of you will speak your vow," he said, his gaze moving to Lincoln first. "Begin when you are ready."

Lincoln stood, the chair behind him glowing brighter as Mistara moved closer, her liquid form swirling gently around him. He took a deep breath, his voice steady as he spoke. "I, Lincoln Beaumont, dedicate my life to the fight against the Umbralox and any force that threatens the Triad. I vow to uphold the balance of the elements and to protect Tanzlora, Earth, and Arcmyrin with all my strength."

Mistara flowed upward, her shimmering hand touching Lincoln's chest. A ripple of energy passed through him, cool and invigorating, as she spoke. "Your vow is heard, and your bond with water is strengthened. May you find clarity and resilience in your path."

Lincoln returned to his chair, and Mistara remained by his side, her glow a reassuring presence.

Ridge rose next, his green chair glowing as Terraveta's towering form solidified beside him. Ridge's voice was firm and clear. "I, Ridge Beaumont, pledge my life to protect Tanzlora and the Triad. I will honor the strength and patience of the earth, using its power to rebuild and defend what has been lost."

Terraveta extended a crystalline hand, placing it gently on Ridge's shoulder. A grounding energy coursed through him, steady and unyielding. "Your vow is heard, and your bond with earth is deepened. May you stand firm and provide stability to those who depend on you."

Ridge returned to his chair, his connection to Terraveta radiating through him.

Lynx stood next, the red chair behind him flickering like embers as Ignissa's fiery form flared beside him. His voice was intense but resolute. "I, Lynx Beaumont, commit myself to the fight for Tanzlora and the Triad. I will wield the fire within me to protect, to renew, and to destroy what threatens our worlds."

Ignissa stepped closer, her fiery eyes locking onto Lynx as she placed a glowing hand over his heart. Heat surged through him, fierce but invigorating. "Your vow is heard, and your bond with fire is strengthened. May you burn brightly, protecting and renewing the life around you."

Lynx returned to his chair, the warmth of Ignissa's presence emboldening him.

Waverly rose, the clear chair beneath her glowing with shifting currents of light as Ambreela swirled beside her. Her voice was quiet but filled with conviction. "I, Waverly Beaumont, dedicate my life to the defense of Tanzlora and the Triad. I will harness the freedom and precision of the air to guide and protect those who cannot fight for themselves."

Ambreela floated closer, her translucent form wrapping gently around Waverly. A rush of cool, exhilarating energy flowed through her as she whispered, "Your vow is heard, and your bond with air is renewed. May you find clarity and swiftness in all you do."

Waverly returned to her chair, her connection to Ambreela like a breeze at her back.

Finally, Bethany stood, her central chair glowing with a soft, harmonious light. Though not directly tied to an elemental spirit, her presence radiated unity and strength. "I, Bethany Beaumont, vow to stand by my family, to protect the bond between us, and to support the fight for Tanzlora and the Triad. My strength is in our unity, and I will not falter."

The spirits moved closer, their combined energy flowing toward her. Sanodia, who had been standing near the edge of the chamber, stepped forward and placed her hands on Bethany's shoulders. "Your vow is heard," Sanodia said softly. "Though you are not bound to a single element, you are bound to all through your family. May their strength be yours, and yours be theirs."

As Bethany returned to her chair, the chamber filled with a brilliant light as the spirits fully manifested. The air vibrated with energy as the spirits encircled the family, their voices blending into a harmonious hum.

Brakar stepped forward, her voice resonating above the energy. "Your vows have been heard, your bonds strengthened. You are now bound to Tanzlora, its people, and its spirits. May your courage and unity guide you in the battles ahead."

The light gradually dimmed, and the spirits retreated to their ethereal forms, their presence lingering as a reminder of the family's connection. The Beaumonts sat in silence for a moment, the weight of their commitment settling over them.

The air in the council chamber was thick with anticipation as Keelee stepped forward, carrying the silver box encrusted with gemstones that shimmered under the crystalline light. The vibrant stones—green, red, blue, and clear—glinted like stars, casting faint patterns of color on the polished floor.

Brakar, the leader of the council, stood at the center of the chamber, her commanding presence drawing all eyes. The other council members flanked her: Sylvaris, Draven, Thaloria, and Lumorith. Each exuded an aura of solemnity, aware of the gravity of the moment.

Keelee stopped before the council and lowered the box onto the central pedestal. His calm but resolute expression reflected his faith in the Beaumonts and the elemental spirits guiding them. He looked to Brakar and inclined his head. "Elder Brakar, as requested, I present the weapons forged to aid in the fight against the Umbralox—the daggers safeguarded by Galen Beaumont and his descendants on Earth."

Brakar stepped forward, her hands resting lightly on the edge of the box. "These daggers are more than mere weapons. They are instruments of balance and harmony, tied to the elemental spirits and the energy of the Triad. Forged during the age of Galen, they were hidden on Earth to ensure they would be ready for the time when they were most needed."

She gestured to Keelee, who opened the box. The chamber filled with a faint hum as the daggers were revealed, their intricate designs and luminous stones captivating everyone present. The hilt of each dagger was crafted from a wood unknown to the Beaumonts, its texture smooth yet sturdy, as if imbued with the strength of the elements themselves. The gemstones embedded in the hilts seemed to glow from within, as though alive with power.

Brakar turned her attention to the Beaumont family, who now stood together in awe. "These daggers are not mere tools. They are extensions of the spirits that guide you, symbols of the connection between your family and the forces of this universe. Each dagger corresponds to the elemental spirit bonded to you."

She carefully lifted the dagger with the blue gemstone and held it out to Lincoln. "Lincoln Beaumont, Mistara, the spirit of water, has chosen you. This dagger embodies the fluidity, adaptability, and strength of water. Use it wisely."

Lincoln stepped forward, reverently accepting the dagger. The gemstone pulsed softly in his hand, as if acknowledging its rightful bearer. He nodded to Brakar, his voice steady. "I will."

Brakar then picked up the dagger with the green gemstone and extended it to Ridge. "Ridge Beaumont, Terraveta, the spirit of earth, has chosen you. This dagger represents resilience, stability, and the power to shape the world around you."

Ridge approached, his jaw set in determination as he took the dagger. The weight felt familiar, grounding him. He nodded once. "I'll honor this gift."

Next, Brakar selected the dagger with the red gemstone, the glow reflecting the fiery passion it symbolized. She turned to Lynx. "Lynx Beaumont, Ignissa, the spirit of fire, has chosen you. This dagger channels the intensity, creativity, and strength of flame. Wield it with purpose."

Lynx stepped forward, his eyes locked on the dagger. When he took it, the warmth of the hilt seemed to flow through him, filling him with newfound resolve. "I'll make it count," he said firmly.

Finally, Brakar lifted the dagger with the clear gemstone and faced Waverly. "Waverly Beaumont, Ambreela, the spirit of air, has chosen you. This dagger embodies freedom, agility, and the unseen power of the winds. Trust in it."

Waverly accepted the dagger, her fingers brushing over the hilt's smooth surface. A faint breeze seemed to swirl around her as the gemstone sparkled brilliantly. "Thank you," she said softly, her voice filled with resolve.

As the family held their respective daggers, the council members stepped forward, each one placing a hand on the pedestal where the silver box now rested empty. Lumorith spoke, his voice a deep, resonant echo. "These weapons have waited generations for this moment. They are tied not only to the spirits but to the destiny of your family. Together, with the Triadorne, they will be the key to restoring balance."

Draven's tone was firm as he added, "The journey ahead will test your strength, your unity, and your faith. But know this—the warriors of Tanzlora and the spirits of the Triad stand with you."

Keelee stepped forward once more, his gaze sweeping across the Beaumonts. "You are the hope of the Triad. The spirits have chosen you for a reason, and the council has entrusted you with these weapons. Together, we will face the Umbralox and ensure the survival of our worlds."

The chamber was silent, the weight of the moment pressing on everyone present. Then Lincoln stepped forward, holding his dagger aloft. "We will not fail," he said, his voice steady and filled with conviction. "For the Triad, for Tanzlora, for Earth, and for all those who believe in balance—we will see this through."

One by one, Ridge, Lynx, and Waverly raised their daggers, the gemstones glowing brighter in unison as the spirits swirled faintly around them. The council members bowed their heads in acknowledgment, their confidence in the family unwavering.

The path ahead was perilous, but in that moment, the unity of the Beaumonts, the spirits, and the Tanzloran council was undeniable. Together, they would stand against the shadows—and fight for the light.

16

The first light of Tanzlora's twin suns illuminated the crystalline city as the Beaumont family gathered with Keelee and the Tanzloran warriors in a courtyard near the Reficiat Haven. The air buzzed with anticipation and the faint hum of energy that always seemed to accompany the planet.

Pazlun, the leader of the Tanzloran warriors, stood before them, his tall and commanding figure clad in light but durable armor made of shimmering Tanzloran materials. The warriors behind him were similarly dressed, their movements quiet but purposeful as they adjusted their equipment and prepared for the journey.

The family wore garments identical in design, made of the same lightweight yet resilient material. The outfits were tailored to fit them perfectly and infused with a faint glow that seemed to harmonize with the wearers' energy. The fabric felt cool against their skin but adjusted instantly to their body temperature, a testament to Tanzloran ingenuity.

Each member of the Beaumont family also wore a finely crafted belt, designed with elegant yet sturdy sheaths that securely held their respective daggers. The belts, made from the same resilient material as their garments, were adorned with subtle engravings that mirrored the symbolic patterns on the daggers' hilts. The sheaths were positioned for easy access, the gemstones of the daggers gleaming faintly as if responding to their proximity to their bearers. The belts fit comfortably, neither too heavy nor restrictive, a perfect balance of practicality and craftsmanship.

The daggers felt like extensions of themselves, both protective and empowering, ready for whatever challenges lay ahead.

"Your clothing serves more than one purpose," Pazlun explained, his voice firm but calm as he addressed the family. "It will protect you from the elements and the shifting energies of The Shadowed Expanse. It will also help you blend in with the warriors and avoid drawing unnecessary attention from anything—or anyone—that may be watching."

Keelee stepped forward, his luminous presence softening the tension in the air. "The journey to Erevelle will not be easy," he said, his voice melodic but serious. "The terrain grows more treacherous the closer we get to the ruins. The land itself has been twisted by the corruption of the Umbralox."

Pazlun nodded. "We will move as one unit. The warriors are trained for this terrain and will ensure your safety, but you must stay alert. The Shadowed Expanse is not just physically challenging; it is a place where fear and doubt can take hold. Trust in your spirits and in each other."

The family exchanged glances, their expressions a mix of determination and unease. Ridge adjusted the straps on his gear, his lips pressing into a thin line. "Sounds like we're heading into a real vacation spot," he muttered.

Waverly shot him a look. "Focus, Ridge. This isn't a joke."

"I'm focused," Ridge replied, his tone softening as he met her gaze. "I just hope this gear is as good as they say."

Lynx ran a hand over the fabric of his sleeve, noting its lightweight feel. "If it's anything like the rest of Tanzloran tech, it'll hold up. Let's just make sure we do the same."

Bethany adjusted her own garments, her fingers brushing against the knife at her side, a gift from Sanodia. "We'll stay together," she said firmly. "That's the most important thing."

Pazlun turned to the group, his silver eyes scanning them with a sharp but reassuring gaze. "The plan is simple, but it requires precision. The journey to Erevelle will take us through a variety of terrains—dense forests, rocky outcroppings, and eventually the corrupted lands of The Shadowed Expanse. Each environment presents its own challenges, and we must be prepared for anything."

He gestured toward the map projected in front of him, a glowing hologram that displayed their route. "As we near the ruins, the corruption will intensify. The land there is unstable, and the energy of the Umbralox is strongest. We will navigate carefully, keeping close to the spirits for guidance."

Keelee added, "Once we reach Erevelle, the spirits will help you locate the Triadorne. No one knows exactly how it will reveal itself, but it is tied to your family and your connection to the elements. You must be vigilant, open to any signs or sensations."

The warriors finished their preparations, their movements swift and efficient as they adjusted their packs and secured their weapons. Pazlun moved to the front of the group, his voice rising above the quiet hum of activity. "We leave now. The journey will test all of us, but together, we will succeed."

The family fell in line behind Keelee and Pazlun, with the warriors surrounding them in a protective formation. The group moved out of the city, the crystalline structures fading into the distance as they entered a lush forest. The air was filled with the sound of vibrant wildlife and the faint hum of Tanzloran energy coursing through the trees.

As they walked, Pazlun moved back to walk alongside Lincoln. "You and Bethany lived near this region once," Pazlun said, his tone conversational but laced with curiosity. "Do you remember any of the terrain ahead?"

Lincoln glanced at Bethany, then back at Pazlun. "I remember parts of it," he said. "But the land has changed since we were here. The corruption... it's warped everything."

Bethany nodded, her voice quiet. "It's like the land has been stripped of its soul. The beauty we once knew is gone."

Pazlun's expression hardened. "That is the work of the Umbralox. It consumes not just life, but the essence of the land itself. That is why we must act swiftly."

They had been trekking all day as the suns dipped low on the horizon. The group approached a small Tanzloran village nestled within a sheltered valley. The village seemed untouched by the corruption of the Umbralox, its crystalline structures glowing faintly with a soft, golden light. The sight was a welcome reprieve after hours of traveling through increasingly rugged terrain.

Pazlun raised a hand, signaling the group to stop. "We'll rest here for the night," he said, his voice calm but firm. "The Beaumonts need to replenish their strength, and the villagers have prepared accommodations for us."

Lincoln exhaled heavily, wiping sweat from his brow. The journey had been taxing, the unfamiliar climate and thinner atmosphere of Tanzlora taking a toll on their Earth-adapted bodies. Beside him, Bethany nodded, her face pale with fatigue. The couple's memories of their time on Tanzlora rushed back to them as they entered the village, its peaceful ambiance a sharp contrast to the destruction they had seen elsewhere.

The villagers, tall and elegant with shimmering blue-violet skin, greeted the group warmly. Their leader, a gentle woman named Jarentha, stepped forward and bowed slightly. "Welcome, travelers," she said, her voice soft and melodic. "We've prepared cabins for you and your companions. Please, rest and regain your strength. We are honored to aid you on your journey."

Jarentha led them to the cabins, small but sturdy structures built from crystalline wood that shimmered faintly in the fading light. Each cabin was equipped with soft, moss-like bedding and a small hearth that radiated warmth. The interiors were simple yet comfortable, designed to provide a restful space for weary travelers.

As the family settled into one of the cabins, Lincoln and Bethany reminisced about their time living on Tanzlora. Lincoln sat by the hearth, his gaze distant as he spoke. "Do you remember how we always had to keep the herbal mixture with us? The atmosphere here is beautiful, but it's draining if you're not used to it."

Bethany nodded, smiling faintly. "I remember. It was second nature after a while—making sure we had a vial tucked away somewhere. Marellis used to scold us if we forgot, saying we were too stubborn to admit we needed it."

Lincoln chuckled, though his expression darkened slightly as he thought of Marellis and the other villagers they had lost. "She always looked out for us. I wish she could see us now, fighting for the planet she loved."

Waverly entered the cabin, holding a tray with vials of the glowing herbal mixture provided by the villagers. "I ran into one of the healers—they said these are freshly prepared. They should help with the fatigue."

Bethany took a vial and examined it, the liquid inside shimmering faintly. "Just like I remember," she murmured before taking a sip. The mixture was cool and refreshing, spreading a soothing warmth through her body almost immediately.

Ridge leaned against the doorway, his expression skeptical as he held up one of the vials. "This stuff better work. I feel like I've been hauling rocks all day."

"It works," Lincoln assured him, nodding toward the tray. "Drink it. You'll feel better."

Outside, the warriors and villagers worked together to prepare a meal for the group. The scent of roasted roots and spiced grains filled the air, mingling with the faint hum of Tanzloran energy that seemed to resonate in every part of the village. Keelee stood with Pazlun near the edge of the village, discussing their next steps as the suns disappeared completely, leaving the village bathed in the glow of its crystalline structures.

After dinner, the group retired to their cabins, their bodies weary but their spirits bolstered by the kindness of the villagers. Lincoln and Bethany sat by the hearth for a while longer, speaking quietly about the challenges ahead. Waverly, Ridge, and Lynx each found a moment of solitude, reflecting on the journey and the weight of their mission.

As the village settled into quiet, a faint sound began to drift through the air. It was soft at first, like the rustling of leaves in a distant forest. But as the night deepened, the sound grew more distinct—whispers, faint but insistent, carried on the wind. The shadows were near.

In their cabin, Waverly stirred, her sharp instincts waking her instantly. She sat up, listening intently to the sound outside. The whispers weren't close enough to be a direct threat, but they were a reminder of what lay ahead.

Across the village, Pazlun and Keelee stood on the perimeter, their expressions grim as they listened to the whispers. Keelee's luminous eyes scanned the horizon, his voice quiet. "They know we are coming. This is their warning."

Pazlun nodded, his hand resting on the hilt of his weapon. "Let them warn us. It changes nothing. We will press forward."

The next morning, the village was alive with activity as the travelers prepared to continue their journey. The villagers worked efficiently, providing the group with supplies, including freshly prepared herbal mixtures and food that would sustain them in the harsher terrain ahead.

Jarentha approached the family as they gathered in the courtyard. "The path ahead is steep and treacherous," she said. "You will face thin air and sharp winds as you ascend. Take these mixtures with you—they will help you adapt."

Bethany accepted the vials with gratitude. "Thank you. Your kindness means more than you know."

Jarentha smiled softly. "It is we who are grateful. You fight for all of us. We only wish we could do more."

As the group prepared to depart, Pazlun addressed them, his voice firm. "The terrain ahead will test your endurance. Stay close to the warriors and follow their lead. The shadows will try to disorient you, but you must remain focused. Trust in the spirits and in each other."

Keelee added, his tone calm but urgent, "The spirits will help guide you, but their presence does not make you invulnerable. Be vigilant. The closer we get to Erevelle, the more aggressive the shadows will become."

The family nodded, their resolve solidified by the reminders of their mission. As they left the village, the whispers from the night before echoed faintly in their minds—a chilling reminder of the darkness they faced. But they moved forward, their spirits united and their determination unshaken.

Ahead lay the ruins of Erevelle, the heart of The Shadowed Expanse, and the key to saving Tanzlora and the Triad.

17

The journey grew more challenging as the day wore on. The dense forest gave way to rocky terrain, the ground uneven and covered in jagged stones. The warriors moved with practiced ease, their steps sure and steady. The family, though less experienced, followed their lead, relying on their sturdy boots and the guidance of the spirits.

Terraveta, the earth spirit, appeared beside Ridge, her crystalline form blending seamlessly with the rocky landscape. "The ground here is restless," she said, her voice rumbling like distant thunder. "Feel its movements, and it will guide your steps."

Ridge nodded, his focus sharpening as he attuned himself to the spirit's guidance. The rocks seemed less treacherous as he moved, his steps becoming more confident.

As the group ascended a steep incline, Ignissa, the fire spirit, appeared beside Lynx. Her fiery form flickered like a flame caught in a breeze. "The path ahead is grueling," she said, her voice crackling softly. "But your fire is your strength. Use it to push forward."

Lynx smiled faintly, his resolve hardening. "Thanks. I'm trying my best, this is a difficult climb."

Further back, Mistara flowed beside Lincoln, her liquid form shimmering as she spoke. "The journey tests not just the body, but the mind. Let water's clarity guide your thoughts and keep you focused."

By the time they reached the edge of The Shadowed Expanse, the air had grown heavier, and the light dimmer. The land ahead was starkly different—barren and twisted, with dark tendrils of shadow creeping across the ground. The once-vibrant energy of Tanzlora was muted, replaced by a suffocating stillness.

Pazlun raised a hand, signaling the group to halt. "This is the boundary of the Expanse," he said. "From here, we must move with even greater caution. The land is unstable, and the shadows will sense our presence."

Keelee stepped forward, his luminous form casting a faint glow. "The spirits will guide us, but we must remain vigilant. Stay close to one another and to the warriors. The Triadorne is near, but so is the enemy."

The family exchanged glances, their determination outweighing their fear. Ridge tightened his grip on his weapon, his gaze fixed on the horizon. "Let's do this," he said.

Waverly nodded, her green eyes sharp. "Together."

As they stepped into The Shadowed Expanse, the corruption seemed to pulse around them, a living force that watched and waited. But the spirits were with them, their presence a guiding light in the darkness. The journey to Erevelle had truly begun, and the Beaumonts knew that the fate of Tanzlora—and perhaps the Triad—rested on their shoulders.

The group stood at the edge of the mountain ridge, gazing down into the ravine that stretched before them. The ruins of Erevelle lay at the bottom, shrouded in shadow and mystery. The faint outlines of once-majestic structures were barely visible beneath a creeping darkness, their crystalline surfaces dulled by centuries of abandonment. Cutting through the ravine was a narrow river, its waters shimmering faintly in the dim light, a stark reminder of a bygone era.

Keelee's luminous form stood near the edge, his gaze fixed on the river below. "What you see was once an aqueduct," he said, his voice tinged with sorrow. "Built by our ancestors, it brought water from the mountain streams to Erevelle, a city that once thrived with life and prosperity. But when the city was attacked and abandoned, the aqueduct fell into disrepair. The flowing waters carved away at the structure over time, transforming it into the river you see now."

Waverly stepped closer to Keelee, her sharp green eyes scanning the terrain. "It's beautiful in a way," she said softly. "But also haunting. It's like the land itself remembers what was lost."

Pazlun, standing nearby, folded his arms as he studied the ravine. His silver eyes narrowed with concern. "The river complicates things," he said. "If the weapon is hidden beneath the ruins, the water may have damaged or obscured its location. Finding the Triadorne could be more difficult than we anticipated."

Terraveta, the earth spirit, rose beside Ridge, her crystalline form gleaming faintly. "Do not fear the water's path," she said, her voice rumbling like distant thunder. "The land remembers. The elements will guide us to what we seek."

Mistara, the water spirit, appeared beside Lincoln, her flowing form shimmering as she spoke. "The river may conceal, but trust in its currents—they may lead you to the truth."

Lynx glanced down at the steep, rocky descent. "Well, whatever's waiting for us down there, we're not going to find it standing up here."

Pazlun turned to the group, his tone firm. "The descent will be treacherous. The path is narrow and unstable, and the shadows are likely to grow stronger as we near the ruins. Stay close to the warriors and follow their lead."

Ridge adjusted the straps of his pack, his gaze steady. "Let's get moving, then. The sooner we get down there, the sooner we can figure out what's waiting for us."

The group began their descent, moving single file down the rocky slope. The path was narrow, barely wide enough for one person at a time, with sheer drops on either side. The air grew cooler as they descended, the faint sound of rushing water growing louder with each step.

Terraveta moved alongside Ridge, her presence a steadying force. "Feel the ground beneath you," she said, her voice calm. "Trust its strength, and it will support you."

Ridge nodded, his focus sharpening as he attuned himself to the spirit's guidance. Each step felt more secure, the shifting rocks beneath his feet seeming to stabilize as he moved.

Further back, Ignissa's fiery form flickered beside Lynx, her tone brisk. "Keep your focus," she said. "The mountain tests your resolve, but your fire burns brighter. Let it fuel you."

Lynx nodded, his steps growing more confident. "Noted."

The path grew steeper as they descended, forcing them to slow their pace. Pazlun led the way, his movements sure and deliberate as he guided the group. Keelee stayed near the middle, his luminous form casting a soft glow that illuminated the treacherous terrain.

As they neared the bottom of the ravine, the ruins of Erevelle came into clearer view. The city's skeletal remains were a haunting sight, its once-grand structures reduced to crumbling walls and toppled spires. The river wound through the heart of the ruins, its waters glinting faintly in the dim light.

Bethany paused to catch her breath, her hand resting on Lincoln's arm. "It's hard to believe this was once a thriving city," she said softly. "It feels... forgotten."

Lincoln's gaze remained fixed on the ruins. "Not forgotten," he said quietly. "Just waiting."

Mistara flowed closer, her voice gentle. "The water carries the memories of this place. It remembers its purpose, just as the land does. Trust in the currents—they will guide you."

The group reached the base of the ravine, the ground leveling out as they stepped into the outskirts of the ruins. The air was heavy, filled with an unnatural stillness that pressed against them like a weight. The river flowed silently nearby, its waters dark and swift.

Pazlun motioned for the group to stop, his gaze scanning the surroundings. "This is where we must be most vigilant," he said. "The shadows will not allow us to move freely here. Stay close and be ready for anything."

Ambreela, the air spirit, appeared beside Waverly, her translucent form swirling like a breeze. "The shadows are watching," she said, her voice soft but firm. "They sense your presence, but they do not understand your purpose. Let the winds guide you—they will shield you from their grasp."

Keelee stood near the center of the group, his luminous eyes fixed on the ruins. "The Triadorne is here," he said, his voice filled with quiet certainty. "The spirits will lead you to it. Trust in their guidance and in your connection to them."

The family exchanged glances, their determination solidifying as they prepared to enter the heart of Erevelle. The ruins stretched before them, a labyrinth of crumbling walls and darkened corridors. The shadows pressed closer, their presence a chilling reminder of the enemy they faced.

Waverly looked around at the surroundings, her gaze steady. "Let's find this thing," she said. "It's time to end this."

With the spirits at their side and their resolve unshaken, the group moved forward into the ruins, their every step drawing them closer to the Triadorne—and the battle that awaited them.

The ruins of Erevelle loomed around the group as they stepped cautiously through its crumbled streets. The city was a haunting mix of decay and resilience; though much of it had been claimed by time and shadow, fragments of its past still lingered—crystalline walls that shimmered faintly in the dim light, intricate carvings barely visible beneath layers of debris, and pathways worn smooth by generations long gone.

Pazlun moved at the front, his sharp gaze scanning the ruins. "Erevelle was once the heart of this region," he began, his voice carrying in the still air. "It was not just a city, but a center of culture and innovation. The Tanzloran ancestors who lived here were among the most skilled artisans, architects, and healers of their time."

Keelee walked beside him, his luminous form casting a soft glow. "The aqueduct that now serves as the river was a marvel of engineering, bringing fresh mountain water to sustain the city. It nourished not only the people but the land itself. Erevelle thrived because it was in harmony with its surroundings."

The group moved deeper into the ruins, their footsteps crunching softly on the worn ground. Waverly ran her fingers along the remnants of a carved wall, tracing the faint outlines of geometric patterns and symbols. "You can feel it," she murmured. "The energy of this place—it's still here, even after all this time."

Terraveta, the earth spirit, materialized beside her, her crystalline form blending seamlessly with the ruins. "The land remembers," she said. "It holds the echoes of what once was, waiting for those who can listen."

Bethany paused as they entered what appeared to be a communal area. Broken tables and benches lay scattered, but their design hinted at gatherings once held here. She touched one of the tables, imagining the laughter and conversations that must have filled the space. "It's like you can almost hear them," she said softly. "The people who lived here—they were vibrant, alive."

Pazlun gestured toward a larger structure, its walls partially intact. "This was likely a gathering hall," he said. "A place where the community came together to share meals, discuss matters, and celebrate life. It was a symbol of unity."

As they explored further, Bethany's attention was drawn to a terraced area just beyond the hall. The steps were overgrown with resilient plants, their roots twisting through the stone. She knelt, examining the space with interest. "This must have been a garden," she said, her voice tinged with awe. "Look at the way the terraces are designed—perfect for growing food and medicinal plants."

Keelee stooped down beside her, nodding. "You are correct. The people of Erevelle valued self-sufficiency and harmony with nature. This garden would have been essential to their way of life."

Bethany smiled faintly, running her fingers over one of the plants. "It's incredible how much they accomplished. Even now, their legacy endures."

Lynx, meanwhile, had wandered further ahead, drawn by a faint sound that seemed to echo through the ruins. It was a low hum, steady and rhythmic, growing stronger as he moved closer. He followed it to a narrow opening in the ground, where a jagged stone staircase descended into darkness. The humming intensified, resonating in his chest like a heartbeat.

"Guys," Lynx called, his voice steady but urgent. "I think I found something."

The group quickly gathered around him, their curiosity piqued. Pazlun and Keelee exchanged a glance before turning to Lynx. "What is it?" Keelee asked.

"There's something down there," Lynx said, pointing to the opening. "It feels... familiar. Like the portal in the gazebo back home. That same energy, that same hum."

Lincoln stepped forward, his expression sharpening. "Are you sure?"

"Positive," Lynx replied, his voice unwavering. "It's strong—stronger than anything I've felt so far."

Mistara, the water spirit, materialized beside Lincoln, her shimmering form flowing gracefully. "The energy you feel is ancient," she said. "It is tied to the lifeblood of Tanzlora. If you sense its call, it may be the path we seek."

Ignissa, the fire spirit, flared to life beside Lynx, her fiery form flickering with intensity. "Then let us follow it," she said. "The answers lie below."

18

The dining room of Sage Manor was warm and inviting, the soft glow of candles casting flickering shadows across the elegantly set table. Gran Celia sat at the head, her serene presence anchoring the group. Francis was to her right, idly spinning her glass of water as she listened to Lorinda's questions with a faint smile. Monica sat beside her mother, quietly munching on a piece of bread, her wide eyes darting between the adults as they spoke. The twins had eaten earlier and were sound asleep in their beds.

"I still can't believe it," Lorinda said, setting down her fork. "The things you've told me about the Beaumonts, about the portal, and about these sister planets—Tanzlora and Arcmyrin. It's... overwhelming."

Gran Celia offered her a kind smile. "It is a lot to take in, especially when it's your first time hearing about it. But it's all true. Our worlds are more connected than most people realize."

Lorinda leaned forward, her brow furrowed. "But why didn't I know? Why don't any of us know? This isn't taught in schools. History books don't say a word about other planets or the galactic war. Why is it all hidden?"

Francis sighed, setting her glass down and adjusting her glasses. "That's a fair question, and the answer isn't simple. After the Galactic

War, Earth's leaders at the time made a decision to keep the existence of the sister planets and the war itself a secret."

"Why?" Lorinda pressed. "Surely people had the right to know about something that huge."

Gran Celia nodded thoughtfully. "They did. But the leaders were afraid—afraid of what knowledge like that might do to society. They feared mass panic, political instability, and the potential for another war. If the wrong people learned about the portals or the resources of Tanzlora and Arcmyrin, they could exploit them."

Francis picked up the tale. "And so, the story of the Galactic War and the sister planets became what they call 'classified history.' Only certain families—like the Beaumonts—maintained their ties and responsibilities because of their connection to the gifts from Origin, the elemental spirits."

Monica, who had been quiet until now, looked up at her mother. "Does that mean we're not supposed to know, Mama? Are we breaking the rules?"

Gran Celia smiled gently. "Sometimes, Monica, the truth is too important to stay hidden. You and your mother are part of this story now, whether you realize it or not. Knowing the truth can help protect both our world and the others."

Lorinda shook her head, disbelief etched across her face. "But keeping it a secret? That doesn't seem fair. We're all connected to this, even if most people don't realize it. Why should only a handful of families carry that burden?"

Francis gave a wry smile. "Because the burden is heavy, and most people wouldn't be able to carry it. The knowledge of sister planets and interplanetary wars isn't just history—it comes with responsibility. Imagine if an evil entity and its followers—or even just corrupt, ambitious world leaders—got hold of the portal technology. They'd see Tanzlora and Arcmyrin not as allies, but as resources to conquer."

"That's horrible," Lorinda murmured. "And the Beaumonts—your family—they've been guarding this all along?"

Gran Celia inclined her head. "For generations. It's why the portal is hidden at Sage Manor. It's why the family has kept their connection to the elemental spirits alive. Protecting the balance of the Triad—Earth, Tanzlora, and Arcmyrin—is our legacy."

Monica tilted her head. "Does that mean the twins—Maya and Maddox—will have to do it too?"

Gran Celia's expression softened. "One day, yes. But not until they're ready. For now, they're just children. Their time will come, but it's our job to protect them until then."

Lorinda leaned back in her chair, her eyes distant as she absorbed this. "So, the Beaumonts are fighting this war again, and the rest of us... we're just living our lives, oblivious. It feels so strange to think about."

Francis's gaze grew sharp. "It may feel strange, but you and Monica aren't bystanders anymore. By stepping into Sage Manor, you've become part of this story. Whether you like it or not, the choices you make now will ripple far beyond what you see in front of you."

Monica reached for her mother's hand. "I'm not scared anymore, Mama. Not really. I just want to help now."

Lorinda looked at her daughter, then at Gran Celia and Francis. "I don't know how we can help, but I want to try. I just... I wish the rest of the world could understand."

Gran Celia smiled, her voice filled with quiet strength. "Perhaps one day, Lorinda. But for now, the fight remains with those who are willing to bear it. You're here, and that means more than you realize."

The conversation shifted to lighter topics as they finished their meal, but the weight of Lorinda's questions lingered in the air. The truth of the hidden histories and the Beaumonts' legacy was out, and though it was overwhelming, it also felt like the beginning of something important—something that Lorinda and Monica would come to play a larger role in than they could yet imagine.

The stillness of the night was shattered by piercing screams echoing through the halls of Sage Manor. Gran Celia sat upright in bed, her heart pounding. The cries were coming from the twins' bedroom. She scrambled out of bed, throwing a shawl around her shoulders as she hurried toward the source of the commotion.

In the hallway, she nearly collided with Francis, who was clutching her robe closed, her face pale. Behind them, Lorinda emerged from her room, holding a trembling Monica by the hand. "What's happening?" Lorinda asked, her voice shaky.

Before anyone could respond, the sound of heavy footsteps thundered up the staircase. Callum and two Tanzloran warriors burst onto the landing, their luminous skin faintly glowing in the dim light. Callum's sharp gaze swept over the group before he gestured for the other two to follow him. "Stay behind us," he commanded, his voice firm but calm.

The group entered the twins' bedroom to find Maya sitting on the edge of her bed, her arms wrapped tightly around Maddox. He was sobbing uncontrollably, his small body trembling with fear. Maya's face was pale but composed as she whispered soothing words to her brother.

Gran Celia rushed forward, kneeling beside Maddox. "It's all right, sweetheart," she said softly, stroking his hair. "You're safe now. Tell me what happened."

Maddox clung to her, his breaths coming in short, panicked bursts. Between sobs, he managed to choke out, "Th-the shadows... they... they attacked me in my sleep!"

Everyone in the room exchanged uneasy glances. Callum's expression darkened, and he stepped closer to the bed. "Shadows?" he repeated. "Did you see them, Maddox?"

Maddox nodded, burying his face in Gran Celia's shoulder. "They were... whispering and wrapping around me. I couldn't move. I couldn't breathe."

Francis placed a comforting hand on Monica's shoulder, her face etched with worry. "This is worse than we thought," she murmured. "If the shadows are attacking Maddox here, inside the manor..."

Callum straightened, his presence commanding. "Celia, we need to take immediate action to ensure everyone's safety. I suggest finding a single room where all of you can sleep together. It will be easier to protect everyone that way."

Gran Celia nodded, her mind racing. "You're right, Callum. My bedroom suite would be the best option. It's large enough to accommodate all of us, and the sitting room has ample space for additional sleeping arrangements."

Callum turned to the other warriors. "Secure the route from this room to Celia's suite. Ensure the area is clear." The warriors nodded and moved swiftly to obey.

As the group began gathering the essentials to relocate, Gran Celia turned to Lorinda. "I think you should sleep in the bed with the children. You're petite enough to fit comfortably with them, and they'll feel safer having you close."

Lorinda hesitated, glancing at Monica, who clung to her side. "Are you sure? What about you and Francis?"

Francis chimed in with a wry smile, attempting to lighten the mood. "Oh, don't worry about us. Celia and I are perfectly suited for the chaise lounges in her sitting room. They're wide enough—or at least I hope they are. Our matronly figures might test their limits."

The unexpected humor broke the tension momentarily, and the three women dissolved into a fit of giggles. But their laughter quickly subsided when they noticed the warriors and others in the room weren't joining in. Gran Celia cleared her throat, regaining her composure. "Well, let's not delay. Let's get settled."

Callum took charge, ensuring that the twins, Lorinda, Monica, and the older women were escorted safely to the suite. Once they arrived, Gran Celia directed everyone on where to settle. She turned to Callum as the others began arranging blankets and pillows. "Would you or one of your warriors mind lighting a fire in the sitting room's fireplace? I think the warmth and light will help everyone feel more secure."

Callum nodded. "Of course. I'll see to it." He gestured to the other two warriors. "Tend to the fire and secure the French doors between the sitting room and the bedroom. They should remain open, but ensure they cannot be shut unintentionally."

The warriors moved efficiently, one igniting a fire that quickly filled the sitting room with a soft, comforting glow while the other adjusted the French doors. The warm light spilled into the bedroom, casting dancing shadows across the walls, though none of them carried the menace of the ones Maddox had described.

As everyone settled, Lorinda climbed into the grand king-size bed with Maya, Maddox, and Monica, arranging herself so that the children felt cocooned by her presence. Gran Celia and Francis each claimed a chaise lounge, draping themselves in blankets provided by one of the warriors.

Francis sighed as she adjusted her position. "Well, here's to hoping these chaises are as sturdy as they look."

Gran Celia smiled faintly, her concern for the children outweighing her own discomfort. She glanced toward Callum, who stood at the doorway, his imposing figure silhouetted against the soft firelight. "Thank you, Callum," she said sincerely. "Your presence brings great comfort."

Callum inclined his head, his expression resolute. "It is my duty, Celia. I will remain just outside the door. If you need anything, do not hesitate to call for me."

As the room grew quiet, the soft crackle of the fire providing a sooth-ing backdrop, Gran Celia whispered a silent prayer for the safety of her family on Tanzlora and those under her care. Though the threat of the shadows loomed large, she took solace in the knowledge that they were not alone in this fight.

With everyone finally settled, the glow of the fire and the watchful presence of Callum offered a small measure of peace. But even as sleep began to claim them, the lingering unease in the room was a stark re-minder that the battle against the shadows was far from over.

19

Pazlun nodded, gesturing to the warriors to secure the area Lynx had discovered. "We will descend," he said. "But cautiously. The shadows are strong here, and we do not know what lies ahead."

Lynx led the way down the narrow staircase, the hum growing louder with each step. Lincoln followed closely behind, with Mistara and Ignissa flanking them, their presence illuminating the dark passage. The air grew cooler as they descended, and the walls began to shimmer faintly with a crystalline glow.

At the bottom of the staircase, the group entered a cavernous space that seemed to pulse with energy. The walls were lined with intricate carvings that glowed faintly, their patterns reminiscent of the designs on the daggers. In the center of the chamber stood a massive crystalline structure, its surface smooth and reflective, radiating a faint light.

Lincoln approached the structure cautiously, his hand resting on the hilt of his dagger. "This must be it," he said, his voice low. "The source of the energy."

Mistara flowed closer, her voice soft but firm. "It is more than a source—it is a conduit. The energy of Tanzlora flows through this place, connecting it to the ley lines of the planet."

Ignissa's fiery form crackled as she examined the structure. "This is ancient, crafted with purpose. It is tied to the Triadorne—we are certain of it."

Lynx stepped forward, his eyes wide with wonder as he placed a hand on the crystalline surface. A surge of warmth and energy coursed through him, making him gasp. "It's alive," he said, his voice trembling with awe. "It's like it's waiting for us."

Lincoln placed his own hand on the structure, feeling the energy pulse beneath his touch. "Then we need to figure out what it's trying to tell us," he said.

Keelee moved closer. "The spirits will guide you," he said. "This place is a nexus of energy, a connection point for the Triadorne. It will reveal itself when the time is right."

The group stood in the cavern, their senses heightened as they felt the energy around them. The ruins of Erevelle, once a bustling city of innovation and culture, had become a resting place for the weapon that could save Tanzlora. And now, the Beaumonts were one step closer to uncovering its secrets.

The cavern hummed with energy, the air heavy with anticipation as Ridge and Waverly entered to join Lincoln, Lynx, and the elemental spirits. Terraveta and Ambreela flanked the newcomers, their luminous forms shimmering faintly in the crystalline light that emanated from the chamber walls.

"What's going on?" Ridge asked, his sharp gaze moving between his family and the glowing crystalline structure in the center of the room.

"There's something here," Lynx said, his voice filled with awe. "Something powerful."

Mistara and Ignissa hovered near Lincoln, their energies pulsing in time with the increasing hum that filled the space. Keelee moved near the cavern's entrance, observing the scene.

The ground beneath their feet began to vibrate, a low rumble that grew steadily louder. Ridge stepped back instinctively, his hand going to the hilt of his dagger. "What now?"

Before anyone could answer, the floor beneath them began to crack, a jagged line splitting the ancient stone. The rumbling intensified, and pieces of the floor began to shift and crumble. Pazlun, standing just outside the cavern, heard the noise and immediately summoned the warriors.

"The Umbralox must be attacking!" Pazlun barked, unsheathing his weapon as the warriors moved swiftly toward the entrance.

"Wait!" Keelee's voice cut through the tension, his luminous eyes fixed on the elemental spirits. He raised a hand, signaling the warriors to hold back. "This is not the work of the Umbralox."

Inside the cavern, the elemental spirits began to swirl around the Beaumonts, their movements synchronized as if responding to an unseen force. Mistara's liquid form glided gracefully around Lincoln, while Ignissa's fiery presence flickered protectively near Lynx. Terraveta's crystalline body emitted a low, resonant hum as she encircled Ridge, and Ambreela's translucent figure spiraled gently around Waverly.

"Step back," Mistara instructed, her voice calm but firm. "Stand against the wall."

The Beaumonts hesitated only a moment before obeying, moving to the edge of the chamber as the spirits continued their protective dance. The rumbling beneath the floor grew louder, and the crack widened, revealing an abyss below.

As the group watched, a faint light began to emerge from the darkness. It was small at first, like the flicker of a distant star, but it grew steadily brighter. The humming in the cavern intensified, resonating through their bodies like a deep, rhythmic pulse.

"What is that?" Waverly whispered, her eyes fixed on the light.

"It does not feel malevolent," Ambreela said, her voice soft and steady. "It is... ancient."

The crack in the floor widened further, and the edges of the stone began to crumble, falling into the abyss. The sound of the falling debris echoed back up to them, but instead of disappearing into the depths, the stones seemed to bounce back as if striking something solid below.

"I have to see this," Lincoln said, stepping forward despite the protests of the others. He approached the edge cautiously, leaning slightly to peer into the crack. His breath caught in his throat, and he gasped.

"What is it?" Ridge asked, moving closer but keeping his distance from the crumbling edge.

Lincoln backed away slowly, his face a mixture of awe and disbelief. "There's a pillar... a massive stone pillar, and it's rising."

As if on cue, the rumbling grew louder, and the light from the abyss intensified. The pillar emerged slowly, its surface carved with intricate patterns that glowed faintly with the same crystalline energy that permeated the cavern. Atop the pillar sat a golden vessel, its surface etched with symbols that seemed to shift and shimmer in the light.

The Beaumonts and the others stood frozen, their eyes fixed on the rising pillar. The elemental spirits remained in motion, their energy focused on the pillar as if sensing its importance.

"It's beautiful," Waverly murmured, her voice filled with wonder.

The golden vessel atop the pillar gleamed with an otherworldly light. It was cylindrical, with delicate handles on either side, and the carvings that adorned its surface seemed to pulse faintly, as if alive. The pillar came to a halt, its base settling firmly into the fractured floor as the rumbling ceased.

Keelee stepped forward cautiously, his luminous blue-violet hued form shimmering with a mix of curiosity and reverence. "This is no ordinary artifact," he said softly. "It is ancient, crafted by hands long forgotten. Its presence here is... intentional."

Lincoln approached the pillar slowly, his movements deliberate. He felt a pull toward the vessel, an almost magnetic draw that he couldn't ignore. "Do you think this is the Triadorne?" he asked, his voice barely above a whisper.

Mistara's shimmering form glided closer to him. "It is connected," she said. "But its purpose is not yet clear."

Pazlun and the warriors entered the cavern cautiously, their weapons drawn but lowered as they took in the scene. "What is this?" Pazlun asked, his sharp gaze fixed on the vessel.

"We're not sure yet," Ridge said, his tone uncharacteristically subdued. "But whatever it is, it's powerful."

Lynx stepped forward, his eyes locked on the vessel. "It feels alive," he said. "Like it's waiting for something."

Terraveta's crystalline form hummed softly. "The vessel holds a memory—a purpose. It has awaited this moment for centuries."

Waverly tilted her head, her sharp eyes narrowing as she studied the vessel. "If it's connected to the Triadorne, then we need to figure out how to use it."

Keelee hovered near the pillar, his expression thoughtful. "The vessel's markings are Tanzloran in origin," he said. "They tell a story, but it is incomplete. The spirits may hold the key to understanding its purpose."

The elemental spirits moved closer to the pillar, their energy resonating with the light that emanated from the vessel. The humming in the cavern shifted, growing softer but more harmonious, as if the spirits and the artifact were communicating.

"Stand together," Ignissa instructed, her fiery form flickering brightly. "The vessel will reveal its purpose when the time is right."

The Beaumonts exchanged glances before moving closer, standing side by side before the pillar. The elemental spirits encircled them, their energy forming a protective barrier as they faced the golden vessel.

As they stood there, the cavern seemed to hold its breath, the air heavy with anticipation. The Triadorne's secrets were close, and the Beaumonts were ready to uncover them.

The cavern was silent, the hum of energy around the pillar fading into an almost imperceptible vibration. The Beaumonts stood transfixed, their eyes darting between the golden vessel atop the rising pillar and the elemental spirits that continued to swirl protectively around them.

"What now?" Ridge muttered, his voice breaking the heavy silence. He glanced at Keelee, Pazlun, and the others, hoping for guidance, but even the usually composed Keelee appeared uncertain.

Before anyone could respond, a faint creaking sound echoed through the chamber. The noise grew louder, and everyone instinctively looked up. High above, the ceiling of the cavern began to shift, its smooth crystalline surface splitting apart in intricate patterns. The movement revealed a hidden mechanism, the fragments of stone sliding seamlessly into place as if moved by some ancient, unseen force.

"What's happening?" Waverly asked, her voice edged with both awe and alarm.

"I don't know," Keelee admitted, his luminous form flickering faintly. "But whatever it is, it's connected to the pillar and the vessel. Stay vigilant."

As the ceiling continued to shift, a small object began to descend. At first, it was just a faint glimmer, but as it drew closer, its form became clear—a silver box, ornate and laden with gemstones in vibrant colors:

red, green, blue, and clear. The box glowed softly, its light illuminating the cavern as it descended gracefully toward the pillar.

The group watched in stunned silence as the box came to rest beside the golden vessel. The two objects sat side by side on the smooth surface of the pillar, their radiant light casting intricate patterns across the cavern walls.

"What is that?" Lynx asked, his voice barely above a whisper.

"I don't know," Lincoln replied, stepping closer to get a better look. "But it's... beautiful."

The silver box also seemed it was alive, its gemstones pulsing faintly as if in rhythm with the energy of the cavern. The red, green, blue, and clear stones on its surface glowed brighter, their light merging with the golden hue of the other vessel.

Suddenly, a beam of light shot down from the opening in the ceiling, bathing both boxes in its radiant glow. The intensity of the light forced the group to shield their eyes, but they couldn't look away completely.

As the light enveloped the silver box, it began to hum softly, the sound resonating through the cavern. The gemstones on its surface shimmered brilliantly, their colors blending into a dazzling display of energy. With a soft click, the lid of the silver box began to open, revealing its contents.

Inside lay the Triadorne.

The weapon was breathtaking—a crystalline construct that seemed to pulse with its own life force. It was intricate yet elegant, its design both alien and familiar. The core of the Triadorne was a large, multifaceted crystal, its surface glowing with all four elemental colors. Surrounding it were intricate carvings and conduits that seemed to channel the energy of the crystal outward.

"That's it," Pazlun said, his voice filled with awe. "The Triadorne."

Waverly stepped closer, her eyes wide as she took in the sight. "It's more than I imagined," she said softly. "You can feel its power just standing here."

Terraveta's crystalline form hummed with resonance. "The Triadorne has been waiting for you," she said. "It is tied to your family, to the spirits. But its purpose is not yet complete."

The group stared at the weapon, mesmerized by its beauty and the raw energy it exuded. But their attention was soon drawn to the golden vessel beside it, which remained firmly closed.

"Why hasn't this one opened?" Lynx asked, gesturing to the golden box.

Ambreela swirled beside him, her translucent form shimmering faintly. "Its purpose is different," she said. "The Triadorne is revealed, but the vessel holds a secret that must be uncovered in time."

Lincoln stepped forward, his expression thoughtful as he examined both boxes. "It's like they're connected," he said. "Two pieces of the same puzzle."

Mistara flowed closer, her voice calm but firm. "The vessel is a key, a guide. Its contents will reveal themselves when the time is right."

Keelee, his luminous form glowing softly, moved to stand beside Lincoln. "The Triadorne is the heart of this mission," he said. "But its full power cannot be realized without understanding the connection between these artifacts. Your family must be the ones to uncover its secrets."

Pazlun and the warriors stood at the edge of the chamber, their weapons still at the ready. "This changes everything," Pazlun said, his voice steady. "The Triadorne is here, but the journey is far from over. We must protect it—and you—at all costs."

The humming in the cavern grew softer, the light from the ceiling dimming until only the glow of the Triadorne and the golden vessel remained. The elemental spirits gathered around the Beaumonts, their energy swirling in unison as if to reassure them.

"We've found it," Bethany said, her voice filled with both relief and determination. "Now we need to figure out how to use it."

Waverly nodded, her gaze fixed on the Triadorne. "And we need to protect it. Whatever the Umbralox is planning, it's not going to stop until this is destroyed—or until we use it to destroy them."

The group stood together, their resolve solidified by the revelation of the Triadorne. Though the golden vessel remained a mystery, its presence alongside the weapon was a reminder that their mission was far from over. The secrets of Erevelle were beginning to unfold, and the Beaumonts knew that the path ahead would be as treacherous as it was vital.

20

The cavern was silent except for the faint hum of energy radiating from the Triadorne. The elemental spirits gathered around the glowing weapon, their forms shimmering brighter than ever. Their movements were deliberate, synchronized, as they examined the Triadorne with a reverence that made even the Beaumonts hold their breath.

Mistara flowed gracefully around the crystalline weapon, her liquid form rippling with soft, bluish light. "The energy is pure," she said, her voice calm and resonant. "This is the true Triadorne, forged by your ancestors with the help of our kind."

Terraveta stepped closer, her crystalline body radiating a steady warmth. "The carvings are as they should be," she said, her tone grounding. "The conduit lines are intact, ready to channel the elemental energies."

Ignissa, her fiery form flickering with intensity, examined the central crystal embedded in the weapon. "The core still burns with its original light," she said, her voice crackling softly. "It is ready to be awakened when the time comes."

Ambreela circled the weapon in a spiral of air, her translucent form shimmering faintly. "The balance is perfect," she said. "Each element is represented, each thread of energy woven together. The Triadorne is complete."

As the spirits finished their inspection, they turned their attention to the golden vessel still resting on the pillar. The ornate box, etched with shifting symbols, pulsed faintly with an inner light, as if aware of their scrutiny.

Mistara was the first to approach, her shimmering form flowing around the vessel. "This holds the key to activating the Triadorne," she said. "The tools needed to channel its power."

Terraveta extended a crystalline hand, touching the golden vessel lightly. The surface responded, glowing brighter as if recognizing her presence. "Let us see what it holds," she said. "The time has come."

One by one, the elemental spirits moved to the golden vessel. With each spirit's touch, a side of the box opened. The first panel swung open under Mistara's influence, revealing a shimmering blue interior with an indentation mirroring the exact shape of the dagger Lincoln was currently in possession of.

Terraveta opened the second panel, revealing a shimmering green interior that glowed like sunlight through a forest canopy. Ignissa approached the third panel, her fiery presence causing the golden surface to flare briefly before it opened. Inside was a brilliant red interior that seemed to hold a flickering flame within.

Finally, Ambreela opened the fourth panel. The interior sparkled like a prism and had the exact indentations in it that the other three did. This was the vessel that was created to hold the daggers.

The Beaumonts watched in awe as each panel was opened. The elemental spirits turned to the family, their luminous forms glowing brighter.

"This vessel is for the energizing of the daggers," Mistara said, her voice firm but gentle. "Each one will need to be placed into its respective panel. Please come forward, Lincoln."

Lincoln approached with a deep sense of reverence. As his fingers closed around the hilt of the dagger at his side, a wave of calm energy flowed through him, steadying his breath and sharpening his focus. "This... it's like it knows me," he said, his voice soft but resolute as he removed the dagger from its sheath and placed it into the golden vessel.

Mistara watched as Lincoln gently fitted the dagger in place then she turned to him, her liquid form glowing faintly. "Lincoln, the blue dagger is yours. It carries the clarity and resilience of water, the ability to adapt and endure. Once the energizing process is completed, each dagger will be ready to activate the Triadorne."

Terraveta gestured toward Ridge, her crystalline form steady. "Come forward, Ridge. The green dagger is yours but needs to return to be energized for its purpose."

Ridge stepped forward, his eyes wide as he reached for the dagger at his side. The moment his hand touched the hilt, a pulse of energy coursed through him, strong and steady. "It's incredible," he murmured, the weight of the dagger feeling natural in his grasp as he placed it in the golden vessel. It's as if he could feel the energizing of the dagger before it was even put in its proper place.

Ignissa's fiery form flared as she turned to Lynx. "Lynx, the red dagger is yours. It holds the essence of fire—your passion, your courage, your ability to burn away what threatens those you protect."

Lynx approached with the dagger, his hand hesitating briefly before he pulled it from the sheath on his belt. A surge of heat radiated through him, invigorating and empowering. "This... this is something else," he said, a faint smile crossing his lips. He stepped forward and gently placed it into the golden vessel.

Ambreela floated toward Waverly, her voice soft and encouraging. "Waverly, the clear dagger is yours. It is light and swift, like the air itself. It will give you clarity and speed in moments of doubt."

Waverly stepped forward, her hand steady as she placed her dagger into the prismatic panel of the golden vessel. The moment she put it in its place, a cool breeze seemed to wrap around her, sharpening her senses. "It feels like it was made for me," she said, her tone filled with quiet awe. "The energy I am feeling is indescribable, like I am invincible."

As each family member stepped back from the vessels that now held the Triadorne and the daggers, the elemental spirits gathered around them, their energy swirling protectively. Keelee stepped closer, his luminous form flickering with emotion. "These daggers are more than weapons," he said. "They are keys to the Triadorne, tools to activate its power when the time comes."

Pazlun nodded, his expression solemn as he addressed the family. "The path ahead will not be easy. The Umbralox will stop at nothing to prevent you from reaching your goal. But with these weapons and the spirits at your side, you have the strength to face what lies ahead."

The Beaumonts stood together, the daggers glowing faintly as they began their energizing process. The energy of the cavern seemed to resonate with them, the Triadorne and the vessels pulsing in time with the elemental spirits.

"We're ready," Waverly said, her voice steady and strong. "Whatever comes next, we'll face it together."

The spirits swirled around them, their energy a comforting presence as the group prepared for the battles ahead. The daggers were now in their rightful place, and the Triadorne awaited its moment to fulfill its purpose. The journey was far from over, but the Beaumonts were ready to fight for the Triad and to eradicate the darkness threatening their worlds.

Keelee addressed the group. "This mission has been a success," he declared, his voice carrying a sense of calm authority. "The Triadorne and the daggers have been secured, and their power is now in the hands of those destined to wield them. But our journey is far from over. We must return to the Elders and report this immediately."

Pazlun stepped forward, his sharp silver eyes scanning the room. "Agreed. We cannot linger here. The longer we stay, the greater the risk of the Umbralox discovering what we've found." He turned to his warriors, who were stationed near the cavern's entrance. "Gather the others from around the ruins and prepare for our departure."

The warriors moved quickly, their disciplined movements showing no signs of hesitation. The Beaumont family stood together near the pillar, their expressions resolute.

Keelee moved closer to the family, his gaze softening. "The return journey will not be easy," he said. "The path back to the council chambers is long, and we must be prepared for any challenges the shadows may present. Drink the herbal mixture you received in the village. It will help sustain your energy levels for what lies ahead."

Bethany nodded, retrieving the vials from her pack and handing them to her family. "Here," she said. "We'll need every bit of strength we can get."

As the family drank the glowing liquid, a soothing warmth spread through their bodies, revitalizing their energy. Waverly flexed her fingers, feeling the difference immediately. "That's some powerful stuff," she remarked, her voice steady.

Meanwhile, Pazlun dispatched two of his warriors to scout the route they had taken to descend into Erevelle. The rest of the group busied themselves securing the vessels for travel. The Triadorne in its silver vessel was carefully wrapped in protective fabric and placed inside a reinforced case, while the golden vessel with the daggers was stowed securely in a separate pack. Pazlun assigned two warriors per case for optimal protection of the vessels.

Just as they were finishing their preparations, the two scouts returned, their faces grim. Pazlun moved to intercept them, his tone sharp. "What is it? What have you found?"

One of the scouts, a tall warrior with a deep scar across his cheek, shook his head. "The path we took to descend the mountain is no longer accessible. A rockslide has blocked the way entirely. We'll have to take another route."

Keelee slumped slightly as he processed the news. "Is there another viable path?" he asked.

The second scout, a younger warrior with bright violet eyes, nodded reluctantly. "There is, but it's far more dangerous. It winds along the edge of a steep ravine and passes through terrain heavily corrupted by the Umbralox. It's treacherous, but it's our only option."

Pazlun frowned, his jaw tightening. "We'll take it," he said firmly. "There's no time to search for alternatives."

Keelee turned to the Beaumonts, his expression grave. "You must prepare yourselves," he said. "This route will test all of us. The terrain will be harsh, and the shadows will not remain silent. Stay close to the elemental spirits, and trust in their guidance."

The group moved as one, leaving the cavern and stepping out into the open air. The ruins of Erevelle stretched behind them, a haunting reminder of what had been lost—and what they now carried with them. As they began their ascent out of the ravine, the faint sound of whispering reached their ears.

It was soft at first, barely audible above the sound of their footsteps. But as they moved further from Erevelle, the whispers grew louder, insistent, like voices carried on the wind. The words were unintelligible, but their tone was unmistakably hostile.

"What is that?" Lynx asked, his hand tightening around the hilt of his dagger.

"The shadows," Keelee said simply. "They know we are leaving with what they sought to destroy."

The warriors tightened their formation, surrounding the family and the vessels with a protective ring. Pazlun's voice was steady as he addressed them. "Stay focused. The shadows will try to distract you, to sow fear and doubt. Do not give them the chance."

The elemental spirits moved closer to the Beaumonts, their energy forming a faint barrier against the encroaching darkness. Mistara flowed gracefully around Lincoln, her liquid form glowing softly. "The shadows cannot touch you if you remain steadfast," she said. "Their whispers are nothing but lies."

Terraveta's crystalline form hummed beside Ridge, her voice grounding. "Feel the strength of the earth beneath your feet. It will support you, no matter how unstable the path may seem."

The new route was every bit as treacherous as the scouts had described. The path was narrow, with steep drops on one side and jagged rocks on the other. The air grew colder as they climbed, and the corrupted terrain around them seemed to pulse with an unnatural energy. Dark tendrils of shadow flickered at the edges of their vision, moving just out of reach.

Ignissa, her fiery form flickering protectively around Lynx, spoke with a sharp intensity. "Do not let the cold or the darkness seep into your spirit," she said. "Your fire burns brighter than their void."

Ambreela swirled around Waverly, her translucent form a calming presence. "Keep your focus on the wind," she said. "It will guide you, no matter how disorienting the shadows may become."

The group pressed on, their pace steady but cautious. The whispering continued, a constant reminder of the danger that surrounded them. But the spirits' presence gave the Beaumonts strength, their protective energy warding off the worst of the shadows' influence.

As they reached a particularly steep section of the path, Pazlun paused, his sharp eyes scanning the terrain ahead. "We're nearing the most dangerous part of the route," he said. "Stay close, and be ready for anything."

The Beaumonts nodded, they knew that the journey back to the council chambers would be anything but easy, but they also knew that the fate of Tanzlora—and the Triad—depended on their success.

With the Triadorne secured and their spirits resolute, the group continued their ascent, the shadowed whispers fading into the background as they focused on the path ahead.

21

The soft glow of the firelight cast a warmth over Gran Celia's sitting room. The rich scent of tea filled the room as Gran Celia poured a fresh pot, her hands steady and practiced. Lorinda and Francis sat across from her, their expressions a mix of curiosity and anticipation.

The previous nights events had left the household quieter than usual. Thankfully the day had passed without incident. The children had been able to play outside and get rid of nervous energy. They had ended the evening early with milk and cookies while watching a movie.

With the children now settled into Gran Celia's bed fast asleep and the rest of the Beaumont family on Tanzlora, the manor seemed both serene and eerily vast. Gran Celia settled into her chair, her sharp eyes glinting as she looked at the two women.

She couldn't help but chuckle softly to herself. The thought struck her that Victoria, with her sharp wit and mischievous humor, would likely find the current sleeping situation endlessly amusing.

After all, she and Galen had poured their hearts and souls into building this grand, sprawling manor—a house meant to stand as a testament to their family's legacy and strength.

Yet here they all were, crammed into a single bedroom and its adjoining sitting area, while the rest of the vast estate sat eerily empty. Victoria would undoubtedly quip about the irony, perhaps suggesting they could've saved themselves the trouble and just built a two room shed. Celia could almost hear her laugh, a sound that would've brought levity to even the darkest of nights.

Francis noticed the quiet chuckle that escaped Gran Celia and raised an eyebrow in curiosity. "Celia, what's so funny?" she asked, her tone light but genuinely intrigued.

Celia glanced at her friend, a small smile lingering on her lips. "I was just thinking about how Victoria would've found this whole situation hilarious. She and Galen built this grand manor, designed to hold generations of our family, and yet here we all are—piled into one bedroom and a tiny sitting area like we're camping out in a shed."

Francis let out a soft laugh, shaking her head. "She'd have plenty to say about it, I'm sure."

Lorinda looked up at Celia with curiosity. "Victoria and Galen... they're your ancestors, right? I've heard their names mentioned a few times, but I don't know much about them. Who were they?" Her question hung in the air, drawing the room's attention as Celia's expression softened with nostalgia.

"Ah, well," Celia began, her tone taking on a warm, storytelling quality, "Galen and Victoria were extraordinary—more than just ancestors, really. They were the ones who started it all."

"Galen Beaumont was much more than just an ancestor. He was a visionary, a protector, and the bridge between Earth and the sister planets—Tanzlora and Arcmyrin. What you see of our family today, all the strange and extraordinary things, began with him."

Lorinda, sitting quietly with her hands folded, finally spoke. "Was he... like the rest of your family? Connected to these elemental spirits?"

Gran Celia's expression softened. "Yes, but Galen's connection was different. He was the first to forge bonds with the elemental spirits—not just one, but all four. They chose him, sensing something unique in his heart and soul. Through him, the spirits found a way to communicate and collaborate with humanity, and eventually with the Tanzlorans and Arcmyrins."

She paused, pouring tea into their cups before continuing. "It all started centuries ago, during the early days of the Galactic War. The Abasimtrox and Umbralox—malevolent forces of shadow and corruption—had begun to spread across the Triad of planets. Its goal was to consume and destroy, leaving nothing but darkness in its wake. Galen was a young man then, but even at that age, he had a fierce determination to protect not only his own planet but the harmony of the Triad."

Francis furrowed her brow. "So, he was... what? A warrior?"

Gran Celia smiled faintly. "Not at first. Galen was a scholar, a thinker. But when the war came, he realized that knowledge alone wouldn't be enough to stop the evil. He sought the elemental spirits, who had long been silent observers of the Triad. They saw his courage, his determination, and his selflessness—and they chose him as their champion."

Lorinda's gaze was fixed on Gran Celia, her voice tinged with wonder. "How did he find them? The spirits, I mean."

"Through perseverance and faith," Gran Celia replied. "Galen traveled to places most people feared to tread—ancient forests, treacherous mountains, forgotten caverns. The spirits tested him at every turn, challenging his resolve and his intentions. But he never wavered. Eventually, they revealed themselves to him, each one offering a part of their power and wisdom."

She gestured toward a painting on the wall, one depicting a young man standing amid swirling elemental forces. "But Galen didn't work alone. When he married Victoria, he discovered she had clairvoyant abilities. It is like the spirits aligned their meeting and marrying, and perhaps they did. As the children were born, their special talents started being revealed as they grew. It became a family trait, a true gift from Origin."

Lorinda tilted her head. "Why hide it? Wouldn't it have been better to reveal these special powers to help the world? Think of what you all could've accomplished—what you still could."

Celia's expression grew thoughtful, her gaze drifting toward the fire as she considered her response. "It's a question we've wrestled with for generations," she began. "Galen and Victoria knew what a gift the elemental spirits were, but they also understood the danger of that knowledge becoming widespread. People—especially those in positions of power—don't always act with good intentions when faced with something they can't control or fully understand."

Francis, who had been quietly listening, leaned forward slightly. "Celia's right. Throughout history, we've seen what happens when people covet power they weren't meant to wield. Wars, corruption, the destruction of entire civilizations. The connection to the spirits isn't just a tool or a weapon—it's a bond, a sacred trust. If the wrong people sought to exploit it, the balance of our world—and the Triad—could be irreparably damaged."

Lorinda frowned, her hands resting on her knees. "But isn't it also selfish to keep it hidden? Couldn't you use those gifts to make the world better?"

Gran Celia met Lorinda's gaze, her voice steady but kind. "We do, in our own way. The work our family has done through Sage Manor—protecting the Cradle of Forestry, preserving the natural balance, and quietly helping those in need—may not be flashy, but it's vital. The elemental spirits don't seek recognition or fame; they seek harmony. And sometimes, the best way to maintain harmony is to work quietly, without drawing attention."

Francis added, "Think of it like a gardener tending their plants. If you uproot everything to show the world how it grows, you risk destroying the entire garden. Some things are best left to flourish in peace."

Lorinda considered this, her expression softening. "I guess I can understand that. But doesn't it ever feel... lonely? Keeping this secret, even from people who might support you?"

Gran Celia smiled gently. "It can, at times. But we've always had each other, and we've always had the spirits. The bond we share with them—and with the Triad—is more fulfilling than anything the outside world could offer. And now, Lorinda, you and Monica are part of this circle, too. That connection, that trust, extends to you."

Lorinda's eyes widened slightly, her hand instinctively going to her chest. "I... I don't know what to say."

"You don't have to say anything," Francis said, her voice soft. "Just know that you're not alone in this. You're part of something bigger now—something that's been quietly protecting this world for generations."

The room fell quiet again, the only sound the gentle crackling of the fire. Lorinda looked down at her hands, her thoughts clearly still racing, but her posture more relaxed than it had been earlier.

"I think I'm starting to understand," she said finally, her voice thoughtful. "Thank you, both of you, for trusting me enough to share this. It's... a lot to take in, but I'm glad I know."

Gran Celia reached over and placed a comforting hand on Lorinda's. "You're handling it beautifully, my dear.

Lorinda leaned forward slightly, her expression thoughtful. "Just one more thing I need clarification on," she began, her tone curious but gentle. "Francis, where did you come into the picture? How did you learn about the Beaumonts and their... special powers?"

Francis, who had been quietly sipping her tea, set her cup down with a soft clink. She glanced at Gran Celia, who gave her an encouraging nod, then turned her gaze back to Lorinda. "Well, that's quite a story," she said with a faint smile. "But if you're asking, I suppose it's time you knew."

She shifted slightly, folding her hands in her lap. "I've always been a bit of a recluse—introverted, bookish, and perfectly content to spend my time in the company of books rather than people. When I came to Galen Valley as a young newlywed with my husband, I was still adjusting to the idea of community life. My husband, bless him, was far more outgoing than I ever was."

"When the community decided to build a library, I was over the moon. Books had always been my escape, my refuge. I applied for the librarian position the moment I heard about it, and to my delight, I was chosen as the first librarian of Galen Valley." She smiled fondly at the memory. "That's how I met Celia. She was one of the library's biggest benefactors."

Gran Celia chuckled softly, her eyes twinkling. "I saw a kindred spirit in Francis right away. She was passionate about books, and I knew she'd be perfect for the library. But she was also terribly shy—too shy to make the most of her role. So, I made it my mission to drag her out of her shell."

Francis laughed quietly, shaking her head. "Drag is the right word. Celia practically forced me to go out for lunch with her and attend fundraising events for the library. She'd insist we needed a diverse collection of books and texts, which, of course, meant we had to raise the funds to get them."

"It was through those outings that we forged a real friendship," Francis continued. "Celia has a way of making people feel seen and valued. Over time, I came to trust her more than anyone else I'd ever known."

Lorinda tilted her head, intrigued. "So, when did you learn about the family's... connection?"

Francis's smile faded slightly, replaced by a look of quiet wonder. "It started with the books. As the library's collection grew, I noticed that Celia had a particular interest in texts about interstellar communications, ancient symbols, and obscure histories. At first, I thought it was just an intellectual curiosity. But as more and more of these unusual books arrived—many of them requested by Celia herself—I couldn't help but start asking questions."

Gran Celia chimed in, her voice warm. "And Francis, ever the sharp mind, was relentless. I knew she'd never stop digging, and I realized it was time to let her in on the truth."

Francis nodded. "Celia told me everything—about the family's connection to the elemental spirits, the Triad of planets, and the portal chamber under the gazebo. It was... overwhelming, to say the least. But Celia trusted me, and I swore to keep their secret."

Her expression darkened slightly as she continued. "After my husband passed away far too early in life, I shut myself away. I didn't need to work, thanks to the inheritance he left me, and I used that time to immerse myself in study. I became even more reclusive, pouring over texts and documents, diving into research about ancient symbols and interstellar lore."

Gran Celia reached over and placed a hand on Francis's arm. "But even in her isolation, Francis was still part of our circle. When Waverly and I found ancient texts that needed deciphering, I knew there was only one person who could help."

Francis smiled faintly, the memory bittersweet. "Celia and Waverly came to my house—my sanctuary—and practically dragged me out. I'd been alone for so long that I'd forgotten what it was like to feel needed, to be part of something bigger. But they reminded me. Celia knew my decades of study would be invaluable, and she was right. That's how I became more deeply involved in the Beaumont family's mission."

Lorinda sat back, her expression a mix of admiration and wonder. "So, you've been helping them all this time, behind the scenes?"

Francis nodded. "It's been one of the greatest privileges of my life. The Beaumonts are extraordinary, not just because of their powers but because of their unwavering dedication to protecting what matters most."

Gran Celia smiled warmly at her friend. "And we couldn't do it without you, Francis."

The room fell quiet for a moment, the firelight flickering softly. Lorinda looked down at her hands, her thoughts clearly racing. Finally, she spoke, her voice filled with quiet gratitude. "Thank you for sharing that, Francis. It's clear that Celia wasn't wrong to trust you. You've been a part of something truly remarkable."

Francis glanced at Celia, a hint of emotion in her eyes. "Remarkable doesn't even begin to describe it."

22

The path back to the council chambers had somehow become a wasteland of twisted trees and blackened earth. The group—Keelee, Pazlun, the Beaumonts, and Tanzloran warriors—halted as they took in the devastation. The air was thick and heavy, the faint sound of crackling energy and distant whispers filling the silence.

"We can't go this way," Pazlun said, his tone grim. "The Umbralox has claimed this ground."

Keelee nodded, his luminous eyes scanning the surroundings. "We'll have to take another detour,the wooded one. It's longer, but it's our only choice."

Lincoln exchanged a glance with Bethany. "Stay close," he murmured, gripping her hand briefly before they all started moving again.

This detour led them into a dense, shadowy forest. The trees here were still intact, their crystalline leaves shimmering faintly, but the light struggled to pierce the canopy. The group moved cautiously, every sound seeming amplified in the eerie stillness.

"I don't like this," Ridge muttered.

"You're not alone," Waverly replied, her voice tight.

Suddenly, the shadows around them deepened, and an unnatural chill swept through the forest. The whispers grew louder, shifting into guttural growls. From the darkness, tendrils of black smoke-like energy emerged, coiling and writhing as they reached for the group.

"It's the Umbralox!" Pazlun shouted, drawing his weapon.

Chaos erupted as the tendrils lashed out, targeting the Beaumonts and their Tanzloran allies. Lincoln was the first to react, his connection to Mistara sparking to life. He raised his hand, and a torrent of water surged from the air around him, slamming into the shadowy tendrils and forcing them back.

"Stick together!" Lincoln bellowed.

Ridge planted his feet firmly, summoning the strength of Terraveta. The ground beneath him rumbled and then sharp spikes of crystal erupted upward, severing the tendrils nearest to him. "You want a fight? You've got one!"

Waverly, her eyes glowing faintly, called upon Ambreela. A whirlwind swirled around her, slicing through the shadows and creating a protective barrier for Bethany and the others.

Lynx was fending off his own attack when he faltered. The tendrils wrapped around his legs, then his torso, tightening like a vice. He gasped, struggling to breathe as the dark energy constricted around him.

"Lynx!" Waverly shouted, trying to reach him, but another wave of tendrils forced her back.

Before Ignissa could appear to aid him, a piercing, screech cut through the air. From the underbrush, a massive, round creature leapt into the fray. Its body was covered in rainbow-colored crystalline spikes that shimmered like gemstones. With incredible agility, the creature launched itself at the tendrils holding Lynx, its spikes slicing through them like a blade.

The tendrils recoiled, hissing and writhing as the creature severed them one by one. Freed, Lynx fell to his knees, gasping for air as the creature positioned itself protectively in front of him, its spiked body glowing and pulsing faintly.

"A Porcufera," Keelee breathed, his voice filled with awe.

The battle raged on. Mistara appeared beside Lincoln, her ethereal form swirling with water. She guided his attacks, amplifying his power as waves of energy crashed against the shadows. Ridge fought alongside Terraveta, whose towering, earthy form smashed through the tendrils with unrelenting strength. Ambreela danced around Waverly, her air currents slicing through the darkness with precision.

Despite their combined efforts, the Umbralox was relentless. Bethany, trying to defend herself, was struck by a tendril that sent her sprawling to the ground.

"Bethany!" Lincoln shouted, rushing to her side.

Pazlun and his warriors formed a protective circle around her, driving back the tendrils as Lincoln scooped her up in his arms.

"We need to get her to the healer!" Pazlun commanded.

With the spirits aiding them and the Porcufera guarding Lynx, the group managed to fight their way out of the forest. The Umbralox, weakened but not defeated, recoiled into the shadows, its whispers fading as they reached the edge of the woods.

Arriving at the council chambers, the group hurried inside, the warriors bustling to locate Sanodia so she could tend to Bethany's injuries. Keelee, still stunned, knelt beside Lynx, who was sitting on the ground with the Porcufera at his feet.

"It saved you," Keelee said, his voice reverent. "Porcuferas are guardians of purity and light. They only appear to protect those they feel a deep connection with. For one to defend you…"

Lynx looked down at the creature, which now seemed shy and timid despite its earlier ferocity. It sat quietly, its rainbow-colored spikes glinting softly as it gazed up at him with large, crystalline eyes.

"Does it… want to stay with me?" Lynx asked, his voice filled with wonder. He had never even had a pet on Earth so this was new territory for him.

"Perhaps," Keelee said, his tone hushed. "Porcuferas rarely show themselves, even to Tanzlorans. Many of us have never seen one in our lifetime. For it to choose you… it is extraordinary."

The other Tanzlorans gathered around, murmuring in awe as they studied the creature.

"It's beautiful," Waverly said, kneeling beside her brother. "And it saved your life."

Ridge grinned faintly, though his voice carried a note of respect. "Guess you've got a little guardian now, Lynx. Better treat it right."

Lynx reached out hesitantly, his hand brushing against the Porcufera's crystalline spikes. The creature didn't flinch, instead leaning into his touch.

"Thank you," Lynx whispered.

The Porcufera gave a soft, melodic chirp, its glow pulsing faintly in response.

As the group gathered their strength and tended to Bethany's wounds, the council chambers filled with a renewed sense of hope. The spirits had appeared, the Beaumonts had fought valiantly, and a rare creature had joined their cause.

The council chamber was filled with tension as the two Tanzlorian warriors arrived carefully carrying the vessels. Pazlun had urged them to move quickly ahead of their group to ensure the safety of the weapon. Somehow they had been able to stay on the path the group had started on when they left Erevelle thus avoiding the attack from the Umbralox.

The crystalline walls shimmered faintly, reflecting the energy of the weapon as it was set on a central pedestal for examination. The council members—Brakar, Sylvaris, Draven, Thaloria, and Lumorith—gathered around, their expressions ranging from solemn curiosity to grim determination.

Lumorith, the oldest and most revered of the council, stepped forward. His tall frame moved with deliberate grace, and his silvery skin glowed faintly in the chamber's light. He watched as Keelee gently removed the Triadorne from its silver box. Lumorith studied it with a mixture of awe and nostalgia, his ancient eyes narrowing as he traced his fingers over it.

"This," Lumorith said, his voice deep and resonant, "is not just a weapon. It is a symbol of hope forged in the darkest days of the Galactic War. I remember when it was made."

The chamber fell silent, the weight of his words sinking into the room.

"You remember?" Thaloria asked, her tone laced with disbelief. She was the youngest council member, her azure eyes wide with awe. "This weapon is over a millennium old."

Lumorith nodded, his gaze fixed on the weapon. "I was but a young apprentice when this was forged. It was a collaboration between the greatest minds and hearts of Tanzlora and Earth, led by none other than Galen Beaumont and his son, George."

Lumorith turned to face the council, his expression grave. "The Umbralox was never an ordinary threat. It was a force of corruption, feeding on the cores of worlds and twisting them into its shadow. The weapon was designed not to destroy, but to trap. To bind the Umbralox and sever its connection to the life force of the Triad."

Sylvaris leaned in, his tone sharp. "Then why wasn't it used during the Galactic War?"

Lumorith sighed, the weight of centuries in his voice. "Because the war ended before the weapon could be fully tested. Galen and George hoped it would never need to be used—that Origin would guide their descendants to it if the Umbralox ever returned. They believed the future generations of the Beaumont family would possess the strength and unity needed to wield it."

Draven stepped closer, his silver eyes narrowing as he examined the carvings on the weapon's base. "There is more here than we first realized. These symbols—they contain a message."

Lumorith nodded. "Indeed, and I believe I can decipher it."

He gestured for the room to fall silent as he traced his fingers over the carvings. His voice carried the rhythm of memory as he read aloud: 'To those who stand against the shadow, the light of the Origin shall guide you. Unity binds what darkness cannot break. The Triad must stand as one, and the core shall be its anchor.'

Thaloria frowned. "The core again. The message ties the Triad's survival to the planets' cores. But how?"

"The cores are the source of life's resonance," Lumorith explained. "They are the heartbeat of the planets, and through them, the Triad is connected. The Umbralox seeks to corrupt and sever that connection. The weapon can stop it, but only if wielded by those bound to the Origin Gift—descendants of Galen himself."

Brakar's voice rumbled. "The Beaumont family."

Lumorith nodded. "Yes. It was always meant for them. The Origin's design is clear: their bloodline is uniquely suited to face this threat. Together, with the council and this weapon, we can plan a strategy to entrap and eradicate the Umbralox for good."

Sylvaris stepped forward, his tone resolute. "Then we waste no time. We must move quickly—the Umbralox will not wait for us to act."

Draven glanced at Lumorith. "And you, elder? Do you believe this weapon will work?"

Lumorith's gaze returned to the Triadorne, his expression solemn but filled with determination. "I do. It was forged with the combined wisdom of two worlds and the guidance of the spirits. But its success depends on us—and them. The Beaumont family must face their legacy and their destiny. Only then can we hope to prevail."

"The Umbralox has proven itself cunning and relentless," Lumorith continued, his voice deep and measured. "To defeat it, we must out-think it. And that begins with understanding its weaknesses."

Sylvaris nodded, his violet eyes sharp. "The weapon was designed to sever the Umbralox's connection to the life force of the Triad—Earth, Tanzlora, and Arcmyrin. But it must be activated in a place of great resonance, where the cores' energies converge."

Draven spoke, his silver gaze fixed on the Beaumonts. "Such a place exists here on Tanzlora. It is known as the Inbula Dustria, a nexus where the ley lines converge. If we can lure the Umbralox there, the weapon can be activated to entrap and sever it."

Lincoln responded. "Luring it won't be easy. The Umbralox feeds on life and corruption. It won't follow us blindly."

Keelee tilted his head, his luminous gaze steady. "It doesn't need to. The Umbralox is drawn to power—specifically, the Origin Gift. Your family is its greatest threat, but also its greatest temptation."

Waverly crossed her arms, her expression tense. "You're saying we have to use ourselves as bait?"

Lumorith nodded gravely. "Yes. The Beaumont family must draw the Umbralox to the Inbula Dustria. But you will not be alone. The spirits will aid you, as will Pazlun and his warriors."

Pazlun, standing tall at Keelee's side, rested a hand on the hilt of his blade. "My warriors and I will create a perimeter around the Inbula Dustria to ensure the Umbralox cannot escape once the trap is sprung."

Bethany, still recovering from her injuries but resolute, spoke up. "And how do we ensure the weapon works? It hasn't been used in centuries, and we only recently decoded its full message."

Thaloria, the youngest elder, gestured to the weapon. "The weapon is attuned to the cores of the Triad. It draws its energy directly from them. When the Umbralox is within range, the weapon will amplify the connection, creating a field that binds and severs its essence. However, it requires a wielder who is connected to the Origin Gift."

Lynx glanced at the weapon, then at his family. "So, one of us has to use it?"

"Not just one," Sylvaris interjected. "The weapon's power is amplified by unity. All of you must stand together, your gifts aligned. Only then will it have the strength to succeed."

Ridge ran a hand through his hair, his voice laced with skepticism. "So, let me get this straight. We bait the big bad shadow, lure it to this nexus of energies, surround it with warriors, and somehow use this ancient superweapon—all while not getting killed?"

"That is the essence of the plan," Draven said bluntly.

"Fantastic," Ridge muttered.

Keelee stepped forward, his tone calm but firm. "It is dangerous, yes. But it is also the best chance we have to end this. The Umbralox grows stronger every day. If we wait, it will be unstoppable."

Waverly's gaze swept the room, landing on the elders and finally her family. "It's risky. But we've faced worse. If this is what it takes to save Tanzlora—and Earth—then I'm in."

Lincoln nodded, his expression resolute. "We've fought to protect our worlds before. We can do it again. Together."

Pazlun's warriors exchanged determined glances, their leader addressing the group. "My warriors and I will hold the line. The Umbralox won't escape—not while we still stand."

Lumorith raised a hand, silencing the room. "Then it is decided. We move at first light.

23

After the meeting, the Beaumonts gathered back at Reficiat Haven, the weight of the plan heavy in the air. Lynx sat with the Porcufera at his feet, the tiny creature chirping softly as if sensing the tension.

"This is it," Bethany said, her voice quiet but firm. "If we pull this off, we stop the Umbralox for good."

"And if we don't?" Ridge asked, his tone unusually serious.

Waverly placed a hand on his shoulder. "We will. We have to."

Lynx looked down at the Porcufera, then back at his family. "Origin chose us for a reason. Galen left us this weapon because he believed in us. I think... it's time we believe in ourselves."

The quiet hum of the Reficiat Haven was broken only by the faint rustle of the breeze through the crystalline foliage outside. Inside, the Beaumonts sat together in the warm communal space, their exhaustion evident but their spirits still holding firm. The day had been a long one and the weight of what lay ahead pressed heavily on them.

As they settled in, the soft sound of footsteps approached. Sanodia, the healer, entered the room, her presence bringing an immediate sense of calm. She carried a tray filled with small vials of an iridescent liquid and bowls of dried herbs, the faint aroma of earth and mint wafting into the air.

"Good evening," Sanodia greeted, her voice soft but steady. "I've brought the herbal mixture for you to take before bedtime. It will help restore your energy and prepare your bodies for the challenges ahead."

The family murmured their thanks as Sanodia placed the tray on the low table at the center of the room. She began carefully measuring out doses of the liquid, mixing it with the herbs in small cups for each of them. As she worked, Lynx stood and approached her, his hands tucked into his pockets, his expression thoughtful.

"Sanodia," he began hesitantly, "do you have a moment? There's something I've been meaning to ask you."

Sanodia looked up, her serene smile encouraging. "Of course, Lynx. What's on your mind?"

He glanced toward the corner of the room where the porcufera sat quietly, its tiny, crystalline spikes glinting softly in the light. The creature had been following Lynx since it saved him during the battle in the forest, and it had become a constant, comforting presence. "It's about the porcufera," he said. "I've never seen anything like it before. Can you tell me more about it? Where it comes from, what it needs?"

Sanodia's expression grew thoughtful as she set down the cup she had been mixing. "Ah, the porcufera," she said, her tone reverent. "They are rare creatures, deeply connected to the energy of Tanzlora. It is said they are born from the crystalline veins beneath the surface, manifestations of the planet's purest essence. They are guardians of balance and harmony, appearing only to those who possess a true connection to the elemental spirits."

Lynx's eyes widened. "So it's... tied to the spirits?"

Sanodia nodded. "In a way, yes. The porcufera are attuned to the same energy that binds the spirits to our world. That is why it chose you, Lynx. It sensed your bond with Ignissa, your purity of heart, and your determination to protect."

Lynx looked over at the creature, which was now watching him with its wide, luminescent eyes. "It's incredible," he said softly. "But I don't really know how to take care of it. Is there anything I should be doing?"

Sanodia chuckled gently. "The porcufera requires very little in terms of care. It feeds on the ambient energy of the environment, drawing sustenance from the balance of the elements around it. As long as it is near you and the spirits, it will thrive."

Lynx's face clouded slightly. "But what if I go back to Earth? Can it survive there? The environment, the atmosphere—it's so different from Tanzlora."

Sanodia's expression softened, her voice taking on a more serious tone. "That is a difficult question, Lynx. The porcufera is deeply connected to Tanzlora's energy. While it may be able to adapt to Earth's environment temporarily, it would not be able to thrive there in the long term. Its connection to this planet is too strong."

Lynx's shoulders slumped slightly as he processed her words. "So... I'll have to leave it behind when we go back."

Sanodia reached out and placed a comforting hand on his arm. "I understand how difficult that must be for you. The bond you share with the porcufera is unique, and it will always remain connected to you, no matter the distance. But its place is here, on Tanzlora, where it can continue to protect and nurture the balance of this world."

Lynx nodded slowly, his gaze still fixed on the creature. "I guess I always knew that was the case. It's just... it saved my life, you know? I feel like I owe it something."

Sanodia's smile was gentle. "And you have already repaid that debt, Lynx. The porcufera does not seek anything in return. It chose you because it saw in you the strength and courage needed to face the challenges ahead. By continuing to fight for balance, for the spirits, and for the Triad, you honor its choice."

Lynx exhaled deeply, a faint smile tugging at his lips. "Thanks, Sanodia. That helps. I'll make sure I do everything I can to live up to that."

She gave his arm a reassuring squeeze before returning to her work, handing each family member their prepared herbal mixture. "Now, drink this before you rest. It will help you recover and prepare for tomorrow."

The Beaumonts each took their cups, the warmth of the mixture spreading through them as they sipped. Lynx sat back down, the porcufera waddling over to curl up at his feet. He glanced down at it, his heart heavy but filled with gratitude. He knew their time together might be limited, but he was determined to make every moment count. As the room grew quieter, Sanodia finished her preparations and stood. "Rest well, all of you. Tomorrow will bring new challenges, but I have no doubt you will face them with strength and unity."

She left the room with a graceful nod, her presence leaving behind a sense of calm. The Beaumonts settled into their spaces, the warmth of the herbal mixture lulling them into a peaceful sleep. For Lynx, the soft hum of the porcufera's presence beside him was a comfort he would carry into the battles to come.

Back at Sage Manor, Gran Celia settled deeper into her chair, a warm smile touching her lips as she prepared to answer more questions. Lorinda had become a sponge about all things Beaumont. Francis leaned forward as well, eager to hear more about Victoria. Celia did not talk about her too often yet Francis had always been fascinated by Victoria's story.

"Galen Beaumont was extraordinary in many ways," Gran Celia began, her voice soft but filled with pride. "But even someone as remarkable as Galen couldn't accomplish all he did alone. It was his partnership with Victoria that truly cemented the Beaumont legacy. She was more than his wife—she was his equal, his partner in purpose, and in many ways, his guide."

Francis tilted her head, intrigued. "Was Victoria connected to the spirits too?"

"In a manner of speaking," Gran Celia replied. "Victoria had a gift that was rare even among those attuned to the supernatural. She was clairvoyant, able to see not just glimpses of the future but the threads of connection that tied people, places, and events together. But her true gift was her connection to Origin, the very essence of creation that binds all life in the universe."

Lorinda frowned slightly. "Origin? Is that the same force your family talks about when they mention their powers?"

Gran Celia nodded. "It is. Origin is the source of all life, the wellspring from which the elemental spirits draw their power. While most people can only experience it in subtle, indirect ways, Victoria could feel it deeply. She described it as hearing a song that never ended, a melody that guided her actions and choices."

"How was it again that she met Galen?" Francis asked, "I was always under the assumption that they were connected because of their gifts."

"No, they claimed that their meeting was purely by chance—or so it seemed," Gran Celia said with a knowing smile. "Victoria was also a healer, a young woman who had devoted herself to helping those who suffered during the early days of the Galactic War. She had no idea of her connection to the spirits or Origin at first. She only knew she could feel when someone was in pain, not just physically but emotionally. Her presence alone could soothe the most troubled hearts."

She paused, her gaze distant as if envisioning the moment. "The story I have always been told is that Galen first met her when he was wounded working in the forest. He went to the local doctor who was out on a house call and Victoria tended to him instead, her touch so gentle and her presence so calming that he felt immediately healed in both body and soul."

Lorinda smiled faintly. "Sounds like he fell for her right away."

Gran Celia chuckled. "He did, though he didn't realize it at first. Galen was so focused on his conservation work, so determined to protect the forests, that he didn't think he had room in his life for love. But Victoria saw through his stoic demeanor. She saw the weight he carried and the sacrifices he was willing to make. Her clairvoyance allowed her to see glimpses of his path—and the role she was meant to play in it."

Francis said, "So, she chose him just as much as he chose her."

"Exactly," Gran Celia said. "Victoria wasn't a passive partner. She was a visionary in her own right. She understood the importance of the conservation efforts and the work he was doing before Galen fully grasped the scope of his mission. She didn't just support him—she challenged him, guided him, and stood beside him every step of the way."

Lorinda leaned forward, her expression thoughtful. "Did her connection to Origin help with Galen's special powers?"

"I believe it did," Gran Celia said, her tone reverent. "While Galen worked with the spirits prior to meeting her, it was Victoria who understood the deeper purpose. She saw beyond the physical, sensing the intricate balance spiritually between the elemental energies and not succumbing to corruption. Her insights ensured that Galen was not tricked or trapped into becoming a tool of destruction but a means of purification, a way to restore harmony to the Triad."

Francis was enthralled with the story. "It sounds like they were perfectly matched."

"They were," Gran Celia agreed. "But their relationship wasn't without challenges. Both of them were fiercely independent and headstrong, and they often clashed over how to approach things and the responsibilities they carried. But those disagreements only strengthened their bond. They respected each other's strength and relied on each other's wisdom."

The warmth in Gran Celia's voice grew as she spoke of their legacy. "Galen and Victoria weren't just partners in battle—they were partners in life. They had children, and through those children, the Beaumont line continued. Victoria's clairvoyance and her connection to Origin were passed down, weaving through the generations and manifesting in different ways. The elemental spirits remained close to the family, recognizing that the bond Galen and Victoria forged with them was meant to last forever."

Lorinda's eyes glimmered with admiration. "They must have been incredible people."

"They were," Gran Celia said with a nod. "But they were also human. They had doubts, fears, and moments of weakness. What made them extraordinary wasn't that they were perfect—it was that they never stopped striving to protect what they loved, no matter how difficult the path."

Francis set down her cup of tea. "Hearing about them... it makes everything your family is going through now feel even more meaningful. They're not just fighting for this moment—they're continuing a legacy that began with Galen and Victoria."

Gran Celia smiled, her eyes sparkling with quiet pride. "Exactly. And as much as we miss them while they're away, I know they're doing exactly what Galen and Victoria would have done. They're standing for the Triad, for balance, and for the future."

24

The next morning dawned with a pale, silvery light that barely penetrated the swirling mists surrounding the Reficiat Haven. The air was heavy with anticipation as the Beaumont family, Keelee, Pazlun, and the Tanzloran warriors prepared for the arduous journey to the Inbula Dustria, the planet's core nexus where the ley lines converged. It was a place of immense power, where they hoped to entrap and sever the Umbralox's connection to the Triad once and for all.

The Porcufera, which had become an unshakable companion to Lynx, chirped softly as it nestled against his leg. Its rainbow-colored crystalline spikes shimmered faintly in the early light, drawing the occasional glance of awe from the Tanzloran warriors. Despite the creature's small size and timid demeanor, its presence radiated a calming energy that seemed to ground Lynx in the midst of the tension.

"I think it's decided you're its favorite person," Waverly teased, watching as the Porcufera trotted alongside Lynx while he adjusted the straps of his pack.

"Seems like it," Lynx replied, glancing down at the creature. He crouched briefly to pat its head, its tiny eyes blinking up at him with unwavering trust. "I don't mind. It's kind of nice, actually."

Pazlun approached, his expression stern but respectful. "The Porcufera's loyalty is a rare blessing. Its presence speaks to your connection with Tanzlora's life force. Many warriors have fought for decades without ever seeing one."

Lynx offered a faint smile. "Well, I'll do my best not to let it down."

As the group set off, the elemental spirits materialized beside the Beaumonts, their forms shifting gracefully as they moved. Ambreela, the spirit of air, swirled around Waverly, her translucent, ethereal figure creating gentle breezes that pushed away the lingering fog. Terraveta, the embodiment of earth, walked solidly beside Ridge, her towering form leaving faint trails of life in her wake as the corrupted ground beneath their feet slowly healed. Mistara, the water spirit, flowed like liquid light around Lincoln, her calming presence steadying the team's resolve. Ignissa, fiery and radiant, glided beside Lynx, her energy fierce yet protective, casting a warm glow over the group.

The spirits' combined presence seemed to bolster everyone's determination, their energies blending seamlessly with the natural rhythms of Tanzlora. Even Pazlun and his warriors, seasoned and battle-hardened, appeared humbled by the spirits' silent, powerful support.

"The Inbula Dustria lies far to the southeast," Keelee said as they moved through the dense forest. His luminous eyes scanned the horizon, his voice steady. "It will take us a full day's journey to reach the outer perimeter. The closer we get, the stronger the Umbralox's influence will become. Stay vigilant."

"Any idea what we'll face along the way?" Ridge asked, his voice carrying a note of both curiosity and caution.

Keelee glanced at him. "The Umbralox's tendrils may lash out to stop us. It knows we're moving against it. But its true power will be concentrated at the nexus. That is where the final confrontation will take place."

"Perfect," Ridge muttered, tightening his grip on his backpack. "Nothing like a leisurely stroll toward impending doom."

Waverly rolled her eyes. "Try to keep your cynicism in check, Ridge. We need focus, not sarcasm."

"Focus is my middle name," Ridge replied with a faint grin, though his eyes betrayed his unease.

The forest grew denser as they traveled, the air thickening with a faint hum that resonated in their bones. The warriors moved in formation, their weapons glowing faintly with Tanzloran energy. Pazlun led the way, his presence a beacon of calm amidst the growing tension.

As they pressed on, the landscape began to change. The trees became more crystalline, their branches refracting light in dazzling patterns. The ground beneath their feet hummed faintly, and the group could feel the energy of the ley lines converging as they drew closer to the Inbula Dustria.

"This place feels alive," Bethany murmured, her voice tinged with awe. "More than anywhere else we've been."

"It is," Keelee replied. "The nexus is the heartbeat of Tanzlora. Its energy sustains the planet, and through it, the Triad."

The Porcufera chirped, trotting ahead of Lynx as though it sensed something important. Lynx watched it curiously, noting how its rainbow spikes seemed to glow brighter the closer they got to their destination.

"Looks like our little friend knows where we're headed," Lynx said.

Keelee's gaze softened. "The Porcufera is deeply attuned to the nexus. It may guide us better than I can."

As night began to fall, the group reached a high ridge overlooking a vast, glowing expanse. In the distance, the Inbula Dustria shimmered like a giant, radiant crystal, its light casting long shadows across the surrounding terrain. The energy here was palpable, vibrating through the air with a strength that made it hard to breathe.

"We'll set up camp here," Pazlun announced, gesturing to a sheltered clearing just off the ridge. "The final stretch will require all of our strength."

As they prepared for the night, the Beaumonts gathered near the edge of the ridge, staring out at the nexus that awaited them. The spirits stood silently beside them, their forms blending into the luminous landscape.

"This is it," Lincoln said quietly. "Everything we've fought for, everything our family has stood for—it all comes down to this."

Waverly nodded, her gaze resolute. "Then we don't stop. Not until the Umbralox is gone for good."

Ridge exhaled, his usual bravado giving way to a rare moment of seriousness. "Guess it's time to prove we're as strong as Galen and George believed we'd be."

Lynx crouched down, stroking the Porcufera's head as it chirped softly. "We'll finish this. For Tanzlora. For Earth. For everything."

As the group settled in for the night, the nexus pulsed in the distance, a constant reminder of the battle to come. The spirits stood watch, their energy a protective shield as the team prepared for the final confrontation.

The night was unnervingly still, save for the faint hum of the nexus in the distance. The group had settled into their makeshift camp near the ridge, the flickering light of their small fire doing little to dispel the growing tension. The Porcufera sat curled at Lynx's feet, its iridescent spikes casting faint rainbow patterns on the ground. The elemental spirits lingered near their respective Beaumonts, silent sentinels in the dark.

Ridge poked at the fire, his jaw tight. "I don't like this quiet. Feels like the calm before a storm."

"It is," Pazlun said, his voice low but steady. He stood at the edge of the camp, scanning the horizon. "The Umbralox won't let us reach the nexus without a fight. It knows we're coming."

Bethany, still weary from her earlier injury, shifted uncomfortably beside Lincoln. "If it attacks before we're ready, will we even stand a chance?"

"We have more than a chance," Lincoln said, his voice firm. "We have each other, the spirits, and the weapon. That's more than most people ever get when facing something like this."

Keelee nodded, his luminous eyes reflecting the firelight. "Your unity is your greatest strength. The Umbralox thrives on division and fear. Together, you can resist its corruption."

As the group began to drift into uneasy rest, Waverly stayed awake, sitting cross-legged a short distance from the fire. Ambreela hovered near her, the air around the spirit swirling gently. Waverly closed her eyes, trying to quiet her mind, but the weight of their mission pressed heavily on her.

"What if we're not enough?" she murmured, almost to herself.

"You are," Ambreela's voice answered, soft and melodic, resonating in her mind. "Origin chose you not for what you are, but for what you will become. Trust in that."

Waverly opened her eyes, the spirit's words giving her a flicker of hope.

The attack came just before dawn.

A sharp, guttural whisper cut through the air, sending a shiver down everyone's spines. The ground trembled faintly as shadowy tendrils began to slither out of the forest, their forms writhing unnaturally against the dim light of the nexus.

"Everyone up!" Pazlun bellowed, drawing his weapon. His warriors moved instantly, forming a protective circle around the camp.

The Beaumonts sprang into action, the elemental spirits flaring brightly as they stepped forward. Ridge slammed his hands into the ground, summoning jagged crystal barriers to block the advancing tendrils. Waverly called upon Ambreela, the spirit's winds slicing through the shadows with precision. Lincoln stood beside Mistara, torrents of water surging from the ground to force the tendrils back.

Lynx tried to stay close to the Porcufera, which chirped nervously, its spikes glowing fiercely as it stood protectively in front of him and Bethany. He used his connection to Ignissa to create a protective ring of fire around himself and a group of warriors, keeping the shadows at bay.

"They're stronger than before!" Keelee shouted, dodging a tendril that lashed out toward him. "The nexus's energy must be amplifying them!"

"We're stronger, too," Waverly called back, her voice firm. "Don't let them push us back!"

Amid the chaos, a towering, amorphous form began to take shape in the distance—a mass of swirling darkness with faint, glowing eyes that radiated malice. The presence of the Umbralox itself sent a wave of fear rippling through the group.

"It's here," Pazlun said grimly, his grip tightening on his blade.

The Umbralox's form stretched and twisted, its tendrils striking out in every direction. One shot straight toward Lynx, who had turned to protect the Porcufera. Before he could react, the tendril wrapped around his torso, lifting him off the ground as it began to tighten.

"Lynx!" Ridge shouted, but he was too far away to reach him.

The Porcufera, however, was not. With a sudden, piercing cry, the tiny creature leapt into the air, its crystalline spikes glowing brightly as it collided with the tendril. The impact sent a shockwave of light through the shadow, severing it instantly and freeing Lynx.

Lynx hit the ground hard, gasping for air, as the Porcufera landed beside him, chirping angrily at the retreating tendril. He looked at the creature in awe. "You... you saved me."

The Porcufera nudged him gently, its spikes pulsing with light as if to reassure him.

As the battle raged on, the Beaumonts fought with everything they had, their powers blending seamlessly with the elemental spirits. Ambreela's winds carried Mistara's water, creating blades of ice that shattered the tendrils. Terraveta's crystal barriers channeled Ignissa's flames, turning the shadows into ash.

The Umbralox's form began to waver, its tendrils retreating slightly as if testing their defenses. Keelee stepped forward, his voice ringing out. "It knows it can't defeat us here. We're too close to the nexus. Keep pushing!"

With a final, combined effort, the group drove the shadows back into the forest. The Umbralox's towering form melted into the darkness, its guttural whispers fading into silence. For now, it had retreated—but everyone knew it was only a temporary victory.

As the first light of dawn broke over the horizon, the group gathered themselves, their breaths heavy but their resolve unshaken. The Porcufera chirped softly as it nestled against Lynx, who stroked its head with a faint smile.

"We're almost there," Keelee said, his tone both reassuring and urgent. "The nexus is just beyond the next ridge."

Lincoln looked at his family, their faces marked with exhaustion but also determination. "Then let's finish this."

The elemental spirits swirled gracefully around the group, their luminous forms glowing with a vibrant energy that seemed to resonate with the very air. One by one, they moved toward the silver and golden vessels, their ethereal hands carefully unlocking the intricate mechanisms that held them closed. As the lids of the vessels opened, the Triadorne was revealed in all its glory—a magnificent weapon of pure crystalline energy, pulsating with a rhythm that mirrored the heartbeat of Tanzlora itself.

Mistara, the spirit of water, turned to Keelee, her voice serene yet commanding. "Keelee, the Triadorne must be carried with care to the nexus at the Inbula Dustria. You are entrusted with its safekeeping until the moment of activation." Keelee stepped forward, his form resolute as he carefully lifted the weapon from its resting place, cradling it as though it were the most precious treasure in the universe.

Meanwhile, the golden vessel now gleamed with the light of the four energized daggers, their gemstones shining brighter than ever before. The elemental spirits turned to the Beaumonts, nodding in unison as if signaling it was time. One by one, Lincoln, Ridge, Lynx, and Waverly approached the vessel, their expressions a mix of awe and determination. They each reached for their respective dagger—Mistara's blue for Lincoln, Terraveta's green for Ridge, Ignissa's red for Lynx, and Ambreela's clear for Waverly.

The moment their hands touched the hilts, the daggers pulsed with life, as if acknowledging their rightful bearers. The Beaumonts carefully placed the daggers into the sheaths on their belts, each weapon now fully charged and ready for its role in activating the Triadorne. The spirits swirled around them once more, their energy intertwining with that of the family, as they prepared to face the final battle to destroy the Umbralox for good.

The group pressed onward, their eyes fixed on the radiant glow of the Inbula Dustria ahead. The final confrontation with the Umbralox awaited, but together—with the spirits, the Porcufera, and each other—they felt ready to face whatever darkness lay ahead.

25

As the sun climbed higher, its light grew brighter, illuminating the landscape ahead. The nexus, known as the Inbula Dustria, shimmered in the distance, a massive crystalline structure that pulsed with the energies of Tanzlora's core.

The air buzzed with an electric charge, each step bringing the group closer to the convergence point where the ley lines intertwined.

The Beaumonts, Keelee, Pazlun, and his warriors moved with purpose, their exhaustion from the earlier battle overshadowed by the weight of what lay ahead. The elemental spirits hovered around the family, their forms shifting and glowing as if responding to the increased energy of the nexus. Even the Porcufera seemed energized, its crystalline spikes glowing brighter as it stayed close to Lynx.

"This is it," Keelee said, his voice reverent. "The Inbula Dustria is the heart of Tanzlora. It's where our planet's energy is purest—and most vulnerable."

Pazlun signaled for his warriors to spread out, forming a protective perimeter around the group. "If the Umbralox strikes here, it will throw everything it has at us. Be prepared."

The group reached the base of the nexus, where massive crystalline spires jutted out from the ground, forming a natural barrier around the central structure. The energy in the air was almost overwhelming, resonating deep within their bones.

Waverly stepped forward, her hand brushing the smooth surface of one of the spires. The touch sent a ripple of light through the crystal, as though the nexus itself recognized her.

"It's alive," she murmured, awe in her voice.

"It's connected to the core," Keelee explained, his gaze fixed on the glowing structure. "The Inbula Dustria is both a protector and a channel. It amplifies the energy of the ley lines, making it the perfect place to activate the weapon."

Lincoln stepped forward, his eyes scanning the surroundings. "And the perfect place for the Umbralox to strike."

As if on cue, a deep, guttural whisper filled the air, sending a shiver down everyone's spine. The shadows at the edge of the clearing began to writhe and twist, coalescing into a massive, swirling form that towered over the group. The Umbralox had arrived.

The elemental spirits flared brightly, taking their full forms as they moved to protect the Beaumonts. Ambreela created a swirling barrier of wind, deflecting the first wave of tendrils that lashed out. Mistara flowed forward, her liquid form striking the shadows like a tidal wave. Terraveta slammed her massive fists into the ground, creating crystalline barriers to shield the group, while Ignissa's fiery presence scorched the advancing tendrils.

Pazlun and his warriors engaged the shadows with their glowing blades, their movements precise and coordinated. Keelee stood beside

Lincoln, his hands glowing as he channeled energy into the nexus to prepare it for the Triadorne's activation.

"We need to hold it off long enough to lure it into the center!" Keelee shouted over the chaos.

Ridge nodded, his hands glowing with Terraveta's energy as he summoned jagged crystals to block the Umbralox's advance. "Consider it held off."

Waverly darted to Lynx's side, her connection to Ambreela creating a protective vortex around them. "The weapon—it's the only way to trap it. We need to get it ready!"

Lynx glanced at the Porcufera, which chirped nervously but stood its ground. "Let's do it."

As the Beaumonts moved toward the center of the nexus, Keelee's voice rang out, guiding them. "The Triadorne needs all of you. Your gifts must align. Focus on your connection to the spirits and to each other!"

The family formed a circle around the Triadorne, they removed the daggers from their sheaths and inserted them into the weapon then clasped their hands together as they channeled their elemental powers. The spirits joined them, their energies intertwining and amplifying the light starting to emanate from the Triadorne.

As the weapon was activating,the nexus responded, its crystalline spires glowing brighter with each passing second.

The Umbralox roared, its tendrils striking furiously at the barriers surrounding the nexus. The shadows began to push through, and the warriors struggled to hold the line.

"It's breaking through!" Pazlun shouted. "We can't hold it much longer!"

Lincoln's voice was steady, despite the chaos. "We don't need longer. Just a second or two!"

The weapon began to hum, its energy building as the Beaumonts' connection strengthened. A beam of light shot upward from the center of the nexus, illuminating the clearing. The Umbralox hesitated, its form wavering as the light reached it.

"This is it!" Keelee shouted. "The weapon is ready—focus everything you have!"

The family poured their energy into the Triadorne, the elemental spirits adding their power. The beam of light expanded, enveloping the Umbralox and trapping it within the nexus's energy field.

The shadows writhed and screamed, their guttural whispers turning into shrieks as the weapon's power began to sever their connection to the core.

The ground shook violently as the nexus absorbed the Umbralox's energy, its crystalline spires glowing brighter than ever before. With one final, deafening roar, the shadows imploded, disappearing into the light.

Silence fell over the clearing, broken only by the faint hum of the nexus. The Beaumonts collapsed to the ground, their breaths heavy as they tried to process what had just happened. The elemental spirits hovered nearby, their forms dim but steady.

Keelee stepped forward, his voice filled with quiet awe. "You did it. The Umbralox is gone."

The Porcufera chirped softly, nudging Lynx's hand as if to reassure him. He smiled faintly, stroking its head. "We all did it."

Pazlun and his warriors lowered their weapons, their expressions a mixture of relief and exhaustion. "The nexus is safe," Pazlun said. "Tanzlora is safe."

Lincoln looked at his family, his voice steady despite his weariness. "One battle down. But the war isn't over yet."

As the light of the nexus dimmed to a soft glow, the group knew that while they had won a great victory, their journey was far from complete. But for now, they had hope—a light to guide them in the battles yet to come.

26

The light of the nexus continued to pulse softly, a steady rhythm that seemed to echo the heartbeat of Tanzlora itself. The once-chaotic clearing now stood quiet and still, the air tinged with an odd mixture of serenity and exhaustion. The warriors began gathering their fallen weapons, their movements sluggish but purposeful.

The Beaumonts sat together near the base of the central spire, catching their breath as the elemental spirits hovered close by. Each spirit's presence had dimmed, their energy visibly spent after the battle. Still, their forms remained steady, a silent reminder of the strength they had lent to the fight.

"We did it," Waverly said softly, her voice filled with equal parts disbelief and relief. "The Umbralox is really gone."

"From here," Keelee corrected gently, stepping forward. His luminous form glimmered faintly as though he, too, were recovering from the ordeal. "But its corruption has spread to other places—most notably Earth. What you've accomplished today has weakened it, but the battle is far from over."

Bethany, sitting with her back against a crystalline pillar, winced as she adjusted her position. "We knew it wasn't going to end here. But at least Tanzlora has a chance to recover now."

Pazlun approached, his tall figure casting a long shadow in the dim light. "What you've done today is more than a victory. It's a turning point. Tanzlora owes you a debt we can never repay."

Lincoln shook his head, his voice firm. "You don't owe us anything. This is bigger than just Tanzlora. If the Umbralox had taken hold here, it would've spread to Arcmyrin. We're all in this together."

As the group began to gather themselves, Lumorith's voice filled the clearing, amplified through a communication orb that Keelee carried. His tone was steady but tinged with urgency.

"Beaumonts, Keelee, Pazlun, you must return to the council chambers immediately. There is much to discuss. While the battle here has been won, our work is not done. The Umbralox's corruption remains active on Earth, and its influence must be eradicated before it regains strength."

Keelee nodded, his expression grim as he turned to the group. "The elders are right. We've weakened the Umbralox but it's influence is still out there, so we can't let this victory blind us to the larger fight. Earth is still at risk."

Ridge, who had been unusually quiet, stood and stretched, his movements stiff from the battle. "Guess there's no rest for the weary. Let's get moving."

The others rose slowly, leaning on one another for support as they prepared to head back toward the council chambers. The path ahead was long, but the light of the nexus offered a flicker of hope in the darkness.

As they began their trek back, the Porcufera trotted alongside Lynx, its soft chirps a small comfort amidst the heavy silence. The elemental spirits, though quieter now, lingered close to their respective Beaumonts, their forms a constant reminder of the strength they had drawn upon to achieve this victory.

Waverly glanced at Lincoln as they walked. "Do you think Gran and the others are okay? With everything that's happened here, I can't stop thinking about what might be happening on Earth."

"They're strong," Lincoln said, though his voice carried a note of worry. "If anything had gone wrong, we would've felt it. We'll check in with them as soon as we get back to the council chambers."

By the time they reached the outer edges of the council chambers, the soft glow of Tanzlora's twin moons had taken over the sky. The elders were waiting for them, their expressions a mix of relief and determination. Lumorith stepped forward, his commanding presence filling the space.

"You have done well," he said, his deep voice resonating in the crystalline hall. "The nexus is safe, and Tanzlora is beginning to heal. But we cannot lose focus. The Umbralox's influence is present on Earth and must be addressed immediately. Its corruption has begun to take root there, and the longer we wait, the more difficult it will be to eradicate."

Keelee inclined his head. "We're ready to begin the next phase. With the Beaumonts' help, we can—"

Lumorith raised a hand, cutting him off. "First, you must rest. The battle has taken much from all of you, and to fight on in your current state would be unwise. Gather your strength. The fight for Earth will demand everything you have."

The group exchanged weary glances, the enormity of their task weighing heavily on them. For now, they would rest. But they knew that their journey was far from over—and that the greatest battle was yet to come.

The Porcufera chirped and nudged Lynx's hand again, drawing a small smile from him despite the tension lingering in the air. He stroked the creature's head absentmindedly, its glowing spikes casting faint rainbow patterns on the ground.

"Any idea why this little guy decided to stick with me?" Lynx asked, glancing at Keelee.

Keelee crouched beside him, his expression thoughtful. "Porcuferas are guardians of purity and connection. They only appear to those they feel a deep bond with, often in moments of great need. For one to choose you... it means you are deeply attuned to Tanzlora's energy."

Lynx raised an eyebrow. "Does that mean it's staying with me?"

Keelee's faint smile softened. "It seems you've earned its loyalty. And its presence may yet prove invaluable. Porcuferas have a way of sensing danger before it arrives."

Suddenly, a faint shimmering light appeared near the entrance. Sanodia stepped through the archway, her presence graceful yet urgent. She moved with purpose toward Keelee, her long robes trailing lightly behind her. The room fell silent as all eyes turned to her.

"Sanodia," Keelee greeted, concern flickering across his face. "What brings you here?"

Sanodia inclined her head respectfully before speaking. "I bring a message from Callum. He has requested that I inform you of an incident that occurred at Sage Manor."

Keelee's expression grew serious, and the elders leaned forward slightly, their interest piqued. "An incident? Is everyone safe?"

Sanodia nodded reassuringly. "Yes, everyone is safe and unharmed, but Callum felt it was important for you to know what transpired. Last night, young Maddox was attacked by the influence of the Umbralox while he was asleep. He described shadows wrapping around him, whispering, and attempting to paralyze him. The experience left him terrified, but Celia, the others in the house, and Callum himself were able to calm him."

Gasps of concern rippled through the chamber. Bethany began weeping and Lincoln wrapped her into a comforting hug as his own heart sank at he news. Elder Brakar's expression hardened. "The Umbralox's reach extends to Earth more than we thought. This is deeply troubling."

Sanodia continued, her tone steady. "Callum wishes to assure all of you that measures have been implemented to ensure the safety of everyone at Sage Manor. He has consolidated the Earthlings into a single room to make protection easier, and he and the Tanzloran warriors are on constant guard. He has fortified the portal chamber and established a perimeter to monitor for any further disturbances."

Elder Draven, the overseer of the Tanzloran warriors, nodded approvingly. "Callum is a wise and capable leader. His measures should be sufficient to safeguard Sage Manor and its occupants."

Keelee exhaled slowly, his glow brightening slightly as he processed the news. "Thank you, Sanodia. This information is vital. Please convey our gratitude to your brother, Callum, for his vigilance and let him know that we trust his leadership completely."

Sanodia gave a slight bow. "I will relay your message immediately, Keelee.

Waverly spoke, her voice firm. "Thank you, Sanodia. Knowing they're safe gives us peace of mind temporarily, however we really do need to go back to Earth as soon as possible."

Sanodia smiled gently and gave another slight bow. "I will return to my duties now, but should there be any further updates, Callum will send word."

As Sanodia exited the chambers, the Tanzloran elders stood from their crystalline thrones, their expressions a mix of solemnity and gratitude. Brakar, the leader of the council, stepped forward, her gaze sweeping over the weary Beaumonts.

"Beaumont family," she began, her voice strong yet warm, "on behalf of all Tanzlorans, we extend our deepest gratitude. Your courage, unity, and the bond with the elemental spirits have saved our planet. The eradication of the Umbralox from our core has restored hope and balance to Tanzlora."

The family exchanged glances, their exhaustion evident but their resolve unbroken. Lincoln stepped forward, nodding respectfully.

"Thank you, Elder Brakar. It was our honor to fight alongside you and the people of Tanzlora. But now that we know the Umbralox's influence has reached Earth, we need to leave immediately. Our home and family are at risk."

Before Brakar could respond, Thaloria, the youngest and most clairvoyant elder, raised her hand. "That would not be wise," she said gently, her luminous eyes meeting Lincoln's. "You are all weakened from the battle. Attempting to travel through the portal in your current state would be dangerous. The residual energy of the portal could exacerbate your fatigue and leave you vulnerable."

Draven nodded in agreement. "Elder Thaloria is correct. You need rest and healing before embarking on another journey. We will have Sanodia prepare herbal mixtures to replenish your strength. Stay the night here in Reficiat Haven and leave at first light."

Waverly frowned, her worry evident. "But what about Sage Manor? What about our family? We can't risk leaving them unprotected."

Brakar stepped closer, her tone reassuring. "Callum and his warriors are confident in the measures they've implemented. Your family is secure. Take this time to recover so that when you return to Earth, you can face the challenges ahead with your full strength."

Lynx leaned forward slightly, his expression thoughtful. "Speaking of challenges, I have a question about the Umbralox. What we just fought here—it was a physical manifestation of their power. But on Earth, it seems like their influence operates differently. Can you explain the difference?"

Sylvaris, the visionary elder, answered, his voice calm but grave. "The Umbralox's influence takes many forms. On Tanzlora, it manifested as tangible shadows capable of destruction because it was anchored to our core, feeding directly on our planet's energy. On Earth, its influence is subtler, more insidious. It manipulates fear, whispers doubts, and preys on the vulnerabilities of the mind. It sows discord and erodes trust, creating an environment ripe for chaos."

Ridge crossed his arms, his brow furrowing. "So, we're dealing with something more psychological on Earth. If that's the case, can we use the Triadorne to eradicate it there, just like we did here?"

Lumorith, the eldest and keeper of Tanzloran history, stepped forward, his voice resonant with wisdom. "The daggers may accompany you to Earth, as their power is tied to the elemental spirits and your family's bond with them. However, the Triadorne itself cannot be taken to Earth. Its power is too immense for a planet with a core that does not vibrate at a high frequency, like Tanzlora or Arcmyrin."

Ridge tilted his head, his gaze sharp. "Why is that? Why wouldn't Earth's core be able to handle it?"

Lumorith's expression softened, though his words carried a weight that could not be ignored. "Earth, while beautiful and abundant, remains a planet where the balance is fragile. Its leaders have not yet moved past the corruption that comes with absolute power. The elders of Tanzlora and Arcmyrin agreed long ago that the existence of the Triadorne should be hidden from Earth's governments. Such power, in the wrong hands, would lead to devastation."

Ridge stiffened, his jaw tightening as the words sank in. "So... you're saying Earth isn't worthy of the same protections as Tanzlora and Arcmyrin because of its flaws?"

Lumorith's gaze was compassionate but firm. "Not unworthy, Ridge. Simply not ready. Earth's people have the capacity for great good, but their leadership often struggles with greed and shortsightedness. To introduce the Triadorne into such an environment would be to invite disaster."

The room fell silent, the weight of Lumorith's words pressing down on them. Ridge's expression hardened, though there was a flicker of hurt in his eyes. Lincoln placed a hand on his brother's shoulder, his voice low but steady. "Ridge, it's not about us—or even Earth as a whole. It's about the bigger picture. The daggers are enough to help us fight the influence there."

Ridge exhaled sharply, his shoulders relaxing slightly. "I get it. It's just... hard to hear. Earth's my home, and knowing that it's seen as... less trustworthy, it stings."

Thaloria stepped closer, her voice soft but resolute. "Earth is not without hope, Ridge. The fact that your family exists, that you are willing to fight for your planet, is proof of that. The elemental spirits chose you because they believe in your ability to bring balance—not just to Tanzlora, but to Earth as well."

Gran Celia's voice echoed in Ridge's memory: *Balance is the key. Always.* He nodded slowly, the tension in his expression easing. "Okay. We'll work with what we have."

Lumorith placed a hand on Ridge's shoulder, his touch surprisingly gentle. "That is all anyone can do. And in your family's hands, the daggers will bring hope and strength where it is needed most."

As the conversation settled, Keelee stepped forward, his presence grounding. "For now, let us focus on the present. I will summon Sanodia to prepare the herbal mixtures, and you will all rest tonight. To-morrow, you will be ready to face what awaits you on Earth."

27

As the Beaumonts gathered their belongings and prepared for the journey back to Earth, Lynx crouched down beside the Porcufera, which chirped softly and nuzzled his hand. Its crystalline spikes glowed faintly, a reflection of the bond they had formed during their time on Tanzlora. The small creature had been his constant companion, a symbol of hope and courage when the battle seemed insurmountable.

Keelee approached quietly, his luminous gaze falling on the pair. "Lynx," he said gently, "there's something we need to discuss."

Lynx looked up, his expression wary. "What is it?"

"The Porcufera has been a loyal guardian to you, a bond that is rare and extraordinary. But it cannot accompany you to Earth."

To his surprise, Lynx immediately had to blink back tears, "Yes, I know that," he murmured quietly as he tenderly petted the creature at his side.

"Porcuferas are deeply tied to Tanzlora's energy. Their very existence depends on the life force of this planet. Earth's environment is different—its energy isn't compatible. If the Porcufera were to leave Tanzlora, it would not survive."

Lynx nodded. His shoulders sagged as he absorbed the weight of Keelee's words. He looked down at the Porcufera, which chirped softly as if it understood. "But it saved my life," Lynx said, his voice breaking. "It's been there through everything. It's hard to just... leave it behind."

The Porcufera nudged his hand, its rainbow-colored spikes shimmering faintly. Keelee knelt beside him, his voice filled with compassion. "It knows, Lynx. It knows you care deeply for it. And that bond will not disappear, even if you're apart."

Pazlun stepped forward, his eyes filled with compassion for Lynx. "The Porcufera has chosen you, but its purpose is to protect and preserve Tanzlora. Its loyalty to you doesn't end here—it will continue to guard the nexus and ensure the planet remains strong."

Lynx swallowed hard, his throat tightening as he nodded slowly. "I get it. It's just... hard to say goodbye."

The Porcufera chirped again, hopping closer to rest its glowing spikes against Lynx's chest. He wrapped his arms around it, holding it close for a moment. "Thank you," he whispered. "For everything."

As Lynx stood, the Porcufera stayed at his feet, watching him with large, crystalline eyes. Keelee raised his hand, and a faint glow surrounded the creature. "We will ensure it remains safe and honored, Lynx," he said. "Its bond with you will be remembered as a testament to the strength of this alliance."

The family, Sanodia and Pazlun stood in solemn silence, the weight of the moment palpable. Lynx turned to Keelee, his voice barely above a whisper. "Take care of it."

Keelee placed a hand on his shoulder, nodding. "I promise."

As the family moved toward the portal, Lynx took one last look at the Porcufera, which chirped softly and glowed with a faint rainbow light. The creature remained in sight, surrounded by Keelee, Pazlun and Sanodia until the portal closed for the journey to Earth.

When the light of the portal enveloped the Beaumonts, Lynx closed his eyes, the image of the Porcufera etched into his memory. Though his heart ached, he carried its spirit with him, a reminder of the bond they had shared and the hope it had given him in their darkest moments.

The sun rose lazily over Sage Manor, its golden light filtering through the ancient sycamore and oak trees surrounding the estate. The air was crisp, but there was an unusual stillness that Gran Celia couldn't ignore. She stood looking out the kitchen window, her sharp eyes scanning the sprawling grounds as if searching for a sign of what she already suspected: something wasn't right.

Behind her, Lorinda, Monica, Maddox and Maya were finishing breakfast. The usual warmth of Sage Manor felt oddly muted this morning, as if the house itself shared the weight of the Beaumonts' absence. Francis, sitting at the head of the breakfast nook with a steaming cup of herbal tea, flipped through one of the old journals Waverly had left behind. Her brow furrowed as she traced a faint diagram of the portal's pathways.

"Gran Celia?" Monica's small voice broke the silence. "Are the others okay? Will they come back soon?"

Gran Celia turned from the window, offering a reassuring smile that didn't quite reach her eyes. "They'll be fine, sweetheart. They're stronger than you can imagine. Now, how about you help me pick flowers for the dining room? It needs a little brightness today."

Monica hesitated, her small fingers clutching the edge of the table. "Okay," she said softly, sliding out of her chair.

Lorinda gave Gran Celia a questioning glance. "Is everything really okay? I've had this strange feeling all morning, like something's... off."

Francis didn't look up from the journal. "You're not the only one. The air feels heavy—different."

Gran Celia's smile faded. "I noticed it, too. Something is stirring, but until we know what it is, we keep calm. This house has weathered much worse."

Later that afternoon, Monica and Lorinda were in the garden, Monica skipping between rows of flowers with a small basket while Lorinda was helping out by pruning one of the hedges. The soft rustling of leaves and the faint hum of energy in the air felt almost alive, vibrating through her senses in a way that hadn't stopped since she'd arrived.

She felt everything more keenly now—the subtle shifts in the wind, the faint crackle of energy from the manor itself, even the way the light refracted off the crystal chandeliers in the hallways. It was as if her perception had sharpened to the point of madness. Am I losing my mind? she wondered, the thought both terrifying and oddly grounding.

Her life had turned upside down in just a few days. It seemed like a lifetime ago that she and Monica had fled their home in fear, seeking refuge at Sage Manor after hearing those sinister whispers in the walls. Since then, nothing has been normal.

She had called her boss and taken a leave of absence from work, citing a vague family emergency, and informed Monica's school that her daughter would be out for a few weeks. It wasn't technically a lie. The Beaumonts felt like family now, and they were undeniably in an emergency.

It just so happened that the crisis was bigger than anyone could imagine—an entire planet, perhaps the entire galaxy, hanging in the balance. The sheer insanity of it all was enough to make her laugh if she weren't so fearful and overwhelmed. No one else knows, she thought, shaking her head. How can Earth keep rotating like nothing's happening while we're living in the middle of a galactic battle?

As Lorinda straightened to stretch her back, a chill ran down her spine. She froze, her ears straining to catch a faint sound carried on the breeze. A low, eerie whisper seemed to weave through the air, indistinct but unmistakable. It was the same sound she had heard in her home the night she fled to Sage Manor—the sound that had haunted her dreams ever since.

"Monica," she said sharply, her voice barely above a whisper. "Get up. We need to go back to the house. Now."

Monica looked up, confused by her mother's urgent tone, but obeyed without question. Lorinda grabbed her daughter's hand and began walking briskly toward the manor, her heart pounding. As the whispers grew louder, panic set in, and her brisk walk turned into a run. Monica clutched her mother's hand tightly, her smaller legs struggling to keep up.

Inside the kitchen, Gran Celia was pouring tea when she heard the back door slam open. She turned to see Lorinda and Monica rush in, both wide-eyed and breathless.

"Lorinda?" Celia asked, setting the teapot down. "What's wrong?"

Lorinda placed the basket of flowers on the counter, her voice trembling. "The whispers, Celia. The same ones I heard the night I fled my house. They're coming from the woods."

Before Celia could respond, Callum appeared in the doorway, his expression sharp and alert. Two other Tanzloran warriors followed close behind him, their movements swift and deliberate.

"Celia," Callum said firmly, "we sensed it too. Something is in the woods. We're going to investigate."

He turned to leave but stopped, glancing back at her. "Take everyone in the house to one room and stay there. Do not leave until I come to get you. Do you understand?"

Celia nodded, her calm demeanor masking her rising worry. "Understood. Be careful, Callum."

Without another word, Callum and the warriors vanished through the back door, heading toward the woods with purposeful strides. The tension in the air was palpable as Celia turned to Lorinda, Francis, and Monica.

"We need to go upstairs," Celia said, her tone firm but gentle. "Let's gather with Maddox and Maya in the playroom. The children will be distracted there, and we'll all be together. Come quickly."

Francis grabbed a thick shawl draped over the back of a chair and threw it around her shoulders. "Let's move," she said, her usual sarcasm replaced with a rare seriousness.

Celia led the way, her steps brisk but steady as they ascended the grand staircase. Monica clung to her mother's hand, her small face pale with fear. Lorinda whispered reassurances to her daughter, though her own nerves were frayed.

As they reached the playroom, the sound of the children's laughter greeted them. Maddox and Maya were sprawled on the floor, surrounded by blocks and toy animals, their carefree giggles a stark contrast to the tension gripping the adults.

Celia crouched beside the children, her voice light and cheerful. "We thought we'd come join you for a bit. How about that?"

Maya looked up, her eyes sparkling. "You can play too, Gran Celia! We're building a zoo."

Celia smiled warmly. "That sounds wonderful, darling." She turned to Lorinda, Francis, and Monica. "Let's settle in here for a while."

Monica hesitated before sitting cross-legged on the floor beside Maya. The younger girl immediately handed her a small giraffe figurine, and Monica managed a small smile in return. Lorinda and Francis moved to the nearby armchairs, their postures tense despite the children's innocent play.

Celia glanced toward the window, her thoughts with Callum and the warriors as they investigated the woods. The whispers Lorinda had described—faint, menacing, and otherworldly—lingered in her mind. She knew they were connected to the Umbralox, its influence reaching out even across worlds.

Francis leaned toward her, keeping her voice low. "Do you think it's the same thing that attacked Maddox?"

"I'm afraid it might be," Celia replied softly, her gaze still on the children. "But Callum and his warriors will keep us safe. They're trained for this."

Lorinda, seated nearby, wrung her hands. "I just don't understand why it keeps following us. First my house, now the woods here. What does it want?"

Celia placed a comforting hand on Lorinda's arm. "It feeds on fear and chaos. But it's not going to find that here. We're together, and we're stronger than it thinks."

The room fell into a heavy silence, broken only by the sound of blocks clattering as the children built their imaginary zoo. Celia took a deep breath, drawing strength from their innocent joy. She knew the battle wasn't just in the woods—it was here too, in their hearts and minds.

"Let's keep the children calm," Celia said quietly. "If they stay happy and distracted, the whispers won't have any power over them—or us."

The adults nodded, each silently bracing themselves for whatever news Callum would bring when he returned. Until then, all they could do was wait and hope.

28

The shimmering portal pulsed with energy as the Beaumont family stepped through, their forms disappearing into the radiant light. Keelee, Pazlun, and Sanodia watched silently, their expressions a mixture of gratitude and concern.

"They'll succeed with eliminating the Umbralox influence from Earth," Keelee said, his voice heavy with certainty. "They must."

"The Umbralox's influence on Earth is troubling," Pazlun said, his voice steady but laced with concern. "It's a different kind of fight there, one of subtlety and manipulation. The Beaumonts are strong, but the task ahead of them is not an easy one."

Keelee nodded, "They have faced unimaginable challenges on Tanzlora and emerged victorious. Their bond with the elemental spirits will be their greatest weapon. I am confident they will adapt to this new battle and eradicate the influence quickly."

Sanodia let out a quiet sigh, "I know the Beaumonts are capable, but I can't help worrying about Callum and the warriors still on Earth. The whispers, the shadows—they are so insidious. What if...?" Her voice trailed off.

Keelee reached out, his expression softening. "Sanodia, Callum is one of the most capable warriors we have. He understands the dangers and has prepared for them. He will not let his guard down."

Pazlun's deep voice joined Keelee's, his tone resolute. "Callum knows how to protect not only himself but also those under his care. He and the warriors were chosen for this mission because of their skill and strength. They will keep the Beaumont family's home and those within it safe."

Sanodia nodded, though her worry lingered. "I trust in his abilities, truly. But he's my brother. I can't help feeling anxious for him, especially with the Umbralox's influence still lingering on Earth. It's hard, coming so soon after losing our mother."

The mention of their loss brought a moment of silence. Pazlun bowed his head slightly, his usually stoic face betraying a flicker of pain. "Marellis was a warrior at heart, even if her path was one of healing. She gave everything to protect Tanzlora, and her legacy lives on in you, Sanodia. Callum carries that same strength."

Keelee added, his tone gentle, "She would be proud of him, Sanodia. Just as she is proud of you. Your family has always stood for balance and protection, and Callum is continuing that tradition."

Sanodia managed a small smile, her eyes misting slightly. "I know you're both right. It's just... the absence feels so sharp sometimes. Especially now, with everything happening so quickly. I just want him to come home safely."

Pazlun reached over, placing a firm but comforting hand on her shoulder. "He will come home, Sanodia. Callum is as stubborn as he is skilled. Nothing will stop him from returning once the mission is complete."

Keelee nodded in agreement adding, "And remember, he is not alone. The warriors with him are equally capable, and the Beaumonts themselves are formidable allies. Together, they will see this through."

Sanodia exhaled deeply, some of the tension leaving her shoulders. "Thank you, both of you. It helps to hear that. I suppose I've always been the worrier of the family."

Pazlun chuckled softly, his tone lightening. "That you have. But it's a good thing. It keeps the rest of us around you grounded."

Keelee smiled faintly. "And your worry, Sanodia, is rooted in your deep care for those around you. That care is what makes you an exceptional healer, a remarkable sister and a special friend."

Sanodia's smile grew, "I'll hold on to your words, both of you. And I'll trust in Callum, just as mother always trusted in us."

The three of them stood in companionable silence for a moment. As they were preparing to leave the portal gate area and return to the council chambers, Sanodia noticed that a small, familiar presence was missing.

"Wait," she said, her eyes scanning the space. "Where is the porcufera?" Keelee and Pazlun turned sharply, their gazes following hers. The tiny creature, which had been faithfully shadowing Lynx since its miraculous intervention, was gone.

A faint shimmer in the distance, just at the edge of the forest's crystalline trees, caught Keelee's eye. The porcufera's glinting form disappeared quietly into the shadows of the woods, as if answering some unseen call. The three stood in stunned silence for a moment, a mixture of awe and concern flickering in their expressions.

"It must feel its purpose here is fulfilled," Pazlun said finally, his voice low. "Perhaps it returns to where it belongs, to protect the balance elsewhere." Sanodia frowned but nodded reluctantly. "Let us hope it remains safe. That little creature has already done so much."

Keelee exhaled, his glow dimming slightly as he stepped toward the portal gate. "The porcufera acts with purpose beyond what we can fully understand. We must trust that it knows its path, just as we know ours." With heavy hearts, they turned and left the portal gate, the absence of the porcufera lingering in their minds like the fading echoes of its silent farewell.

The journey through the portal was brief but jarring, the transition from Tanzlora's vibrant, crystalline energy to Earth's familiar yet muted atmosphere feeling almost surreal. When the light subsided, the Beaumonts found themselves standing once again in the chamber beneath Sage Manor's gazebo. The air was cool and still, the faint hum of the dormant portal the only sound.

Ridge was the first to step forward, glancing around the chamber with a faint smirk. "Feels good to be back. Tanzlora's great, but I missed Earth."

Waverly shot him a glance, "Don't get too comfortable. We have no idea what's happened while we were gone."

Lincoln led the way up the stone staircase, his hand gripping the hilt of his weapon out of instinct. As they reached the main foyer of the manor, the sound of children playing reached their ears. The family exchanged a look before heading upstairs.

Inside the playroom, Gran Celia, Francis, Lorinda, Monica and the twins were gathered waiting on Callum's return. The atmosphere was tense, a mix of exhaustion and quiet vigilance etched into their expressions. The sight of the Beaumonts walking through the door brought audible gasps of relief.

"You're back!" Monica cried, rushing forward to wrap her arms around Ridge.

"Mommy! Daddy!" The twins yelled out in unison and ran to their parents. Bethany scooped up Maddox while Lincoln caught Maya in a big bear hug.

Gran Celia rose gracefully, her eyes narrowing as she studied her family. "What happened? Did you defeat it?" She reached out to give Waverly, then Lynx a hug.

Lincoln nodded, his tone firm. "The Umbralox is gone from Tanzlora. The planet is safe."

Bethany added, "But the fight isn't over. Its corruption has started to spread here. We need to act quickly."

Francis leaned back in her chair, her sharp gaze flicking between them. "You've missed quite a lot. The shadows around the manor have grown stronger. The whispers have become louder. We've been holding vigil together in one room every night to make sure the house stays protected."

Lorinda, sitting beside her, looked pale but determined. "It's like the darkness knows you were gone. It felt...bolder, more invasive even with the Tanzloran warriors here."

Monica, still holding on to Ridge's arm and hand said, "It's been scary, but we stayed strong."

Gran Celia's lips tightened into a thin line. "It's good you're back. But I'm afraid the situation here is worse than we realized."

"What exactly is going on?" asked Ridge. "Where is Callum and the warriors?"

Monica let go of his hand and arm to go continue playing zoo with the twins.

"I was wondering about that too," said Lincoln.

"Me three," Waverly chimed in.

Gran Celia exhaled deeply, her gaze moving to the children before settling on Lincoln and Ridge. "Callum advised us to stay together," she began, her voice steady but laced with tension. "Lorinda and Monica heard something while they were in the cutting garden earlier—a sound that reminded Lorinda of the whispers she heard the night she fled her home. Callum and the Tanzloran warriors sensed it too, a disturbance in the woods. He thought it best to investigate."

Ridge raised an eyebrow. "The whispers? You're saying those shadows might be out there, right now?"

Celia nodded. "That's what Callum believes. He and the warriors went into the woods to look for any sign of them. Until they're certain the area is safe, we're to remain here, together. This room was chosen because it's secure and because the children can stay distracted while we wait."

Francis chimed in, her tone dry but tinged with unease. "Distracted is an understatement. Those two seem completely oblivious to the potential doom lurking in the woods."

Celia gave a faint smile, glancing at the children. "And that's exactly how it should be. They're children, Francis. They deserve to feel safe, no matter what's happening outside."

Ridge paced toward the window, peering out at the dimming sky. "What's the plan if they actually find something? Because if it's the Umbralox, I'm guessing it's not going to just politely leave."

Before Celia could respond, the door to the playroom opened, and Callum entered, his tall frame radiating authority. The faint glow of his skin was dimmer than usual, a sign of his exertion. The room fell silent as all eyes turned to him.

"Callum," Celia greeted, rising from her chair. "What did you find?"

Callum's expression was grim as he stepped forward, his hand resting on the hilt of his blade. "We saw something," he confirmed. "The shadows were there—faint, but visible. They were moving through the trees, and when we approached, they scattered. We tried to track them, but they vanished before we could determine their direction."

Lorinda's face paled, "So they're still out there?"

Callum nodded. "Yes. Something is out there, but it's elusive. The shadows aren't lingering—they're probing, testing the boundaries. It's as if they're trying to see how far they can go before being confronted."

Lincoln frowned, his tone sharp. "Do you think it's connected to the Umbralox's influence on Earth?"

Callum's jaw tightened. "It's possible. The energy feels similar, but weaker—more fragmented. Whatever this is, it's not the same as what we faced on Tanzlora, but it's still dangerous."

Celia gestured for everyone to sit. "Thank you, Callum. For now, we'll stay together as you advised. Do you and your warriors have any plans for how to track it further?"

Callum glanced toward the window. "We've placed sentries around the perimeter of the property. If the shadows return, we'll be ready. For now, I recommend continuing to stay indoors. I'll come for you if there's anything urgent."

Francis folded her arms, her tone cautious. "You sound like you're expecting them to come back."

Callum nodded. "I am. Shadows like these rarely act alone. They'll likely try again when they think we're unprepared."

As the group absorbed his words, Maya and Maddox looked up from their game, their attention drawn by the tension in the room. "Gran Celia," Maya asked innocently, "are we staying in here all night?"

Celia smiled, her voice calm and reassuring. "We're just spending some time together, sweetheart. It's a cozy place to be, isn't it?"

Satisfied with the answer, the twins returned to their game. Celia stood and turned to Callum. "Thank you for everything, Callum. Please, be careful."

Callum inclined his head. "Always, Celia. I'll be right outside if you need me."

As he turned to leave, a sudden chime echoed through the house—the sound of the front doorbell ringing insistently. Everyone froze, the sound jarring in the tense atmosphere.

"Who could that be?" Lorinda whispered, her eyes wide.

Lincoln's expression darkened, and his hand instinctively went to his dagger. "Stay here," he ordered, his voice sharp. "Do not leave this room until I return."

Celia moved toward the door, placing a hand on his arm. "Be careful."

Lincoln nodded, his face set with determination as he stepped out into the hall, followed closely by Ridge. The door closed behind them, leaving the group in a heavy silence. The bell rang again, its urgency sending a ripple of unease through the room.

Lincoln descended the stairs two at a time, his expression grim. "Something tells me this isn't a friendly neighbor dropping by with cookies."

Ridge utilizing the same two step method as his brother said, "Let's just hope it's not something worse."

As they reached the front door, Callum stepped out of sight just inside the parlor so he could hear but not be seen. He hoped his warriors had seen the visitor or visitors coming and made themselves scarce, if not Lincoln and Ridge will have a lot of explaining to do.

29

When Ridge opened the door, two familiar faces stood on the porch—Seth Dixon, the district ranger, and Sheriff Marshall Bowen. Both men looked haggard, their usual composed demeanor replaced with visible concern.

"Ridge," Seth said, his voice hurried. "We need your help."

Ridge stepped aside, letting the two men into the foyer. "What's going on?"

"It's the waterfalls," Seth said, glancing nervously between Ridge and Lincoln. "Something's happening to them. The water isn't flowing right, and there's this...darkness spreading through them. It doesn't feel natural."

Sheriff Bowen nodded, his tone grim. "People are starting to notice. We've had reports of strange noises, shadows moving where there shouldn't be any, even lights flickering around the falls at night. It's got folks spooked."

Lincoln's calm voice cut through the tension. "Sounds ominous, what do you think this could be?"

Seth hesitated, then nodded. "I don't know. Whatever it is, it's not normal. And I figured if anyone could make sense of it, it'd be you and Ridge."

Ridge crossed his arms, his expression thoughtful. "I guess we could help you look into it."

Sheriff Bowen looked at them curiously. "What exactly are we dealing with here? I think you may know. Your family has always been...different, but this feels more abnormal than anything I've ever seen. Surely you have some idea of what's going on here."

Lincoln exchanged a glance with Ridge. "It is abnormal. And we can explain but for now, we need to see the falls. We will meet you there."

After Lincoln closed the door behind Sheriff Bowen and Ranger Dixon, he went into the parlor to find Callum standing near the window, his arms crossed as he stared outside watching them leave. The Tanzloran warrior's glowing eyes flicked toward Lincoln as he entered, his expression unreadable but his stance tense.

"You heard all that?" Lincoln asked, walking over to the small table where a half-empty pot of coffee sat. He poured himself a cup, his hand steady despite the knot forming in his stomach.

Callum nodded. "Every word. This sounds worse than we initially thought." He turned fully toward Lincoln, his voice calm but firm. "If what the ranger and sheriff described is accurate, this is not just random disturbances. The Umbralox—or whatever remnant of it has made its way to Earth—is growing bolder. Testing boundaries."

Lincoln sat down heavily in one of the armchairs, his coffee forgotten. "That's what Ridge and I were thinking too. This isn't just whispers and shadows anymore—it's something more tangible, and it's escalating."

Ridge entered the room, his brow furrowed. "We need to go check it out, Lincoln. Sitting here and waiting for it to get worse isn't an option."

Lincoln nodded, then turned to Callum. "Would you and another warrior come with us? We could drop you off a few yards before the pull-off for the falls. You two could sneak through the woods on the opposite side and get a better look at what's happening. If this is tied to the Umbralox, we'll need your eyes on it too."

Callum considered the suggestion, his expression thoughtful. After a moment, he nodded. "Agreed. The warriors and I are trained for stealth reconnaissance. If there's anything to find, we'll see it. I'll bring one with me. The rest will remain here to protect the family."

Without another word, Callum stepped outside, the door clicking shut softly behind him. Lincoln and Ridge exchanged a look, both knowing the risks but determined to move forward.

A moment later, Callum returned, two Tanzloran warriors in tow. He gestured to one of them, a tall, lithe figure with sharp features and a confident stance. "Varstyn will come with us," he said. Turning to the other warrior, he added, "Drexel, you'll remain here. Stay upstairs outside the playroom door. Ensure nothing disturbs the family while we're gone."

Drexel nodded, his glowing eyes steady. "Understood."

As Drexel headed upstairs to guard the family, Ridge grabbed his jacket and motioned toward the stairs. "We'll meet you out front. Just need to check in upstairs and grab Lynx."

Callum inclined his head. "We'll be ready."

Upstairs, the playroom was a quiet buzz of activity. Maya and Maddox were engrossed in their game of building the imaginary zoo with blocks, while the adults spoke softly in the corner. Waverly glanced up as Lincoln and Ridge entered, her brow furrowing at their expressions.

"What's going on?" she asked.

"We're heading out to check the falls," Lincoln said, keeping his tone calm but firm. "Callum and one of his warriors are coming with us. Lynx, you're with us too."

Lynx straightened from where he was leaning against the wall, his expression shifting from curiosity to determination. "Got it. When do we leave?"

Ridge shot him a faint grin. "As soon as you grab your jacket."

Waverly crossed her arms. "And what about me? I'm just supposed to stay here and twiddle my thumbs?"

Lincoln placed a hand on her shoulder, his tone softening. "We need you here, Waverly. Callum's left warriors to guard the family, but they'll need your help if anything happens while we're gone. You're better equipped for defense than any of us. Keep the manor safe."

Her lips pressed into a thin line, but she nodded. "Fine. Just... be careful, okay?"

Ridge patted her on the back as Lynx returned, jacket in hand. "Always."

Within minutes, the group assembled on the front porch. Ridge's Jeep idled nearby, its engine humming softly. Lincoln, Lynx and Varstyn squeezed into the back, their movements precise and deliberate, while Callum slid into the passenger seat. Ridge adjusted the rearview mirror and glanced back. "Hope you like tight spaces. This is going to be a snug ride."

The drive to Looking Glass Falls was tense. Ridge gripped the steering wheel tightly, his eyes scanning the forested edges of the road for any signs of movement.

"So," Lynx said, breaking the silence, "anyone else getting the feeling this is going to be more than a sightseeing trip?"

Lincoln shot him a wry look. "I think we passed that point about five minutes ago."

Callum leaned forward slightly, his voice low but firm. "Stay focused. Whatever we find, it's imperative we assess without engaging. If it's the Umbralox's influence, we need a strategy before making any moves."

As they neared the pull-off for Looking Glass Falls, Ridge slowed the Jeep and pulled over onto the gravel shoulder. The roar of the falls was faint but audible, carried on the wind. The group exited the vehicle quietly, their breaths visible in the cool night air.

Callum motioned to Varstyn. "We'll take this side through the woods and go around behind the falls. We will stay hidden. Signal if you see anything unusual."

Lincoln nodded, gripping the flashlight he'd brought for that purpose even though it was still daylight. "Got it. Let's move."

The group split, with Callum and Varstyn disappearing into the shadows of the forest. Lincoln, Ridge, and Lynx hopped back in the Jeep and drove just a few more yards to the pull-off. Ridge parked his Jeep right behind the Sheriff.

The roar of the falls grew louder as they approached, the sound almost masking the faint whispers that seemed to dance on the edge of hearing.

Lynx paused, holding up a hand. "Do you hear that?" he whispered.

Lincoln and Ridge stopped, their ears straining. The whispers were faint but unmistakable, threading through the sound of the rushing water like an insidious melody. Ridge's jaw tightened, and he glanced toward the trees. "That's not just the wind."

The three of them exchanged a look before continuing, their senses on high alert.

Ridge, Lincoln, and Lynx stepped cautiously onto the wooden viewing deck of Looking Glass Falls. The sound of the rushing water filled the air, loud and powerful, yet somehow overshadowed by an unnatural stillness that seemed to weigh on the atmosphere.

The sheriff, Marshall Bowen, stood near the railing, his hands on his hips, looking down at the cascading water with a furrowed brow. Beside him was District Park Ranger Seth Dixon, who was speaking in low tones with two other officials—one wearing a National Park Service badge and the other a local emergency responder vest.

As the Beaumonts approached, Bowen turned to acknowledge them with a curt nod. "Glad you could make it," he said, his voice carrying an edge of tension. "We've got something... strange happening here."

"What exactly are we looking at?" Lincoln asked, his tone calm but direct as he joined them at the railing.

Seth Dixon gestured toward the falls, his expression grave. "Visitors have been reporting some pretty unusual things—whispers, shadows moving just beyond the water, and this constant sense of being watched. We thought it might be some kind of natural phenomenon spooking people, but..." He trailed off, clearly unsettled.

The official with the National Park Service, a woman with short-cropped hair and a serious demeanor, stepped forward. "We've tried to keep this quiet to avoid panic, but it's getting harder. Just this morning, a family reported seeing what they described as 'dark tendrils' reaching out of the mist near the base of the falls. And two hikers swore they heard someone calling their names from inside the forest."

Ridge frowned, leaning on the railing and scanning the area. "Have you noticed any physical changes? Water levels, unusual currents, anything like that?"

The emergency responder shook his head. "Nothing that would explain this. The falls look normal. The water quality checks out. But the reports keep coming in, and every single one of them has the same unsettling details."

Lynx peered over the railing, his sharp eyes narrowing as he studied the rushing water below. The sunlight reflected off the falls, creating a misty haze that clung to the surrounding rocks. "Have you looked behind the falls yet? Maybe there's something back there causing all this."

Seth nodded. "We sent a team to check the area earlier, but they didn't find anything unusual. Still, they said it didn't feel right—like they weren't alone."

The sheriff glanced at the brothers. "You three have any idea what this could be? We know your family's... resourceful when it comes to unusual situations."

Ridge exchanged a look with Lincoln and Lynx, a silent understanding passing between them. Lincoln turned back to the officials. "It's hard to say without getting a closer look, but it's clear something's out of the ordinary here."

Lynx tilted his head toward the mist, his tone thoughtful. "What if it's not just the water or the falls? What if it's something tied to the area itself—something we can't see unless we're looking for it?"

The park service official raised an eyebrow. "Are you suggesting this is... supernatural?"

Ridge straightened, his expression neutral but firm. "Let's just say we've dealt with strange things before. Whatever this is, it's affecting people in a very specific way, and that's not something we can ignore."

As they spoke, a faint whisper seemed to drift on the air, just audible above the roar of the falls. Everyone froze, the sound sending a collective chill through the group. It was indistinct, more like a murmur carried by the wind, but it left a lingering unease.

"Did you hear that?" Lynx asked, his voice low but sharp.

The emergency responder nodded, his face pale. "That's what people have been talking about. It's like... it's coming from everywhere and nowhere at the same time."

Lincoln glanced toward the trail leading up and around the falls, his instincts on high alert. "This isn't just a random occurrence. Whatever it is, it's deliberate."

Seth looked around nervously, his hand resting on the radio clipped to his belt. "So what do we do? Close off the area? It's already drawing too much attention."

Before anyone could answer, the whispering grew louder, mingling with the roar of the water. Shadows flickered at the edges of the mist, subtle but unmistakable. Ridge tightened his grip on the railing, his voice steady but urgent. "We need to get a better look. There's something back there, behind the falls."

Lincoln turned to him, his expression resolute. "If we don't, it's only going to get worse. We'll take a closer look—carefully. You all stay here."

Ridge nodded toward Lynx, who was already stepping back from the railing. Ridge leaned in and whispered, "Let's move. Callum and the others should be in position by now. If this thing's here, we're not going in blind."

As the trio prepared to descend the narrow path toward the base of the falls, the sheriff called after them. "Be careful. If this turns into something you can't handle, call for backup."

Lincoln glanced over his shoulder, a faint smile tugging at the corner of his mouth. "We'll be fine. Just make sure no one else comes down here until we're back."

The three of them disappeared down the trail, leaving the officials on the deck exchanging uneasy glances. The whispers faded once more, but the tension lingered, a heavy reminder that whatever was happening at Looking Glass Falls, it was far from over.

30

The roar of Looking Glass Falls grew louder as Ridge, Lincoln, and Lynx carefully navigated the final stretch of the slippery trail to the base of the falls. The air was damp and cold, the mist clinging to their faces and clothing as they approached the rushing water. The scene was mesmerizing—raw power cascading into a frothing pool—but the brothers weren't there to admire the view.

"Anything?" Ridge asked, raising his voice over the thunderous falls as he scanned the surrounding rocks.

"Not yet," Lynx replied, his eyes narrowing as he surveyed the area. He stepped cautiously onto a slick boulder, his boots finding uncertain purchase. "But there's something... off. I can feel it."

Lincoln nodded, his gaze fixed on the space behind the falling water. "That mist—it's thicker than it should be, almost like it's hiding something."

High above them, Callum and Varstyn remained concealed within the dense forest, their glowing forms barely visible in the shadows. Callum crouched low, his sharp eyes trained on the Beaumonts below. "They've found something," he murmured to Varstyn. "Stay ready. If anything emerges, we'll strike."

Varstyn nodded silently, his hand resting on the hilt of his blade as he kept watch.

Below, Lynx's attention was drawn to a faint, intermittent flash of green light emanating from behind the water. He tilted his head, his breath catching as the light flickered again, brighter this time.

"There!" Lynx pointed, his voice urgent. "Behind the falls. That green glow—it looks like portal energy."

Ridge squinted, following Lynx's gaze. "You sure? It could just be sunlight refracting off the water."

"It's not," Lynx said firmly, his tone leaving no room for doubt. "I know portal energy when I see it. We need to check it out."

The trio moved closer, their boots slipping on the wet rocks as they carefully approached the falls. The sound was deafening now, the sheer force of the water creating a curtain of mist that obscured their vision.

Lynx reached the edge first, the green light pulsing brighter as he peered into the narrow space behind the falls. "There's a gap back here," he called over his shoulder. "It's small, but I think I can squeeze through."

Ridge frowned, his protective instincts kicking in. "Be careful. If it's a portal, there's no telling what's on the other side."

Lynx shot him a grin, the tension in the moment failing to dampen his usual bravado. "You sound like Dad. Relax, I'll just take a quick look."

He braced himself against the slick rocks and slid into the narrow opening, the roar of the water muffling slightly as he entered. The space was cramped, the walls of the rocky passage pressing against his shoulders as he moved deeper. The green light grew brighter, illuminating the jagged walls with an otherworldly glow.

And then he saw it: a small, shimmering portal embedded in the rock, its edges flickering with unstable energy. Unlike the portals Lynx was familiar with, this one was smaller, almost like it had been hastily created or damaged. It pulsed faintly, the energy within swirling in chaotic patterns.

"It's definitely a portal," Lynx called out, his voice echoing faintly back through the opening. "But it's smaller than—"

Before he could finish, the portal flared to life, the green light intensifying as tendrils of dark energy erupted from its center. The tendrils moved with unnatural speed, snaking toward Lynx and wrapping around his legs.

"Lynx!" Ridge shouted, his heart lurching as he saw his nephew stumble, the tendrils pulling him closer to the portal.

Lynx grabbed at the rocky walls, trying to resist the pull. "It's the Umbralox!" he yelled. "Get me out of here!"

Ridge didn't hesitate. He lunged into the narrow gap, grabbing Lynx under his arms and pulling with all his strength. The tendrils tightened their grip, the energy crackling as it tried to drag Lynx back toward the portal.

"It's not letting go!" Lynx gritted through clenched teeth, his hands scrabbling for purchase on the slick rock.

Lincoln, realizing the severity of the situation, rushed to help. He reached into the gap, wrapping his arms around Lynx's torso. "Hold on! We've got you!"

The three Beaumonts became locked in a desperate tug-of-war, the tendrils pulling with an unnatural strength as Ridge and Lincoln strained to free Lynx. The portal's energy surged, the light flashing erratically as if feeding off the struggle.

"Don't let go!" Ridge growled, his muscles burning as he fought against the relentless pull.

Lynx gritted his teeth, the pain in his legs intensifying. "I'm not exactly enjoying this, you know!"

Lincoln shifted his grip, planting his feet firmly on the rocks. "One more pull. On three. One... two... three!"

With a final heave, Ridge and Lincoln wrenched Lynx free of the tendrils' grasp. The sudden release sent all three of them tumbling backward, their momentum carrying them out of the gap and into the freezing water at the base of the falls.

The shock of the icy water stole their breath, but they quickly scrambled to their feet, the adrenaline coursing through their veins dulling the cold. Ridge pulled Lynx upright, his hands gripping his nephew's shoulders. "You okay?"

Lynx nodded, coughing as he shook the water from his hair. "Yeah. Just remind me not to go exploring any more mysterious glowing lights."

Lincoln glanced back toward the falls, his eyes narrowing. The portal was still visible behind the cascading water, its energy dimming slightly but still active. "We need to figure out how to shut that thing down. If the Umbralox is using it to get through..."

Before he could finish, Callum and Varstyn emerged from the woods, their weapons drawn. Callum's sharp gaze immediately went to the Beaumonts, his expression grim. "What happened?"

"A portal," Ridge said, pointing toward the gap. "It's back there. Smaller than usual, but definitely active. It grabbed Lynx with some kind of tendrils."

Callum's jaw tightened. "The Umbralox is using the portal as a foothold. If we leave it open, it will continue to grow stronger."

Lincoln nodded. "We need a plan. Fast."

As they regrouped on the slick rocks, the sound of the falls roared around them, a constant reminder of the danger lurking just beyond the water. The portal pulsed faintly in the shadows, its sinister energy a silent threat that refused to be ignored.

Lynx, who had been keeping an eye on the viewing deck above, suddenly stiffened. His voice was tight with urgency as he called out, "Dad, we got a problem. The sheriff is getting ready to shoot our friends."

Lincoln and Ridge snapped their heads up toward the deck, their hearts racing. Three figures stood above them—Sheriff Bowen, Ranger Dixon, and the park official they had spoken to earlier. Each of them had their guns drawn and aimed directly at Callum and Varstyn, who had emerged from the woods to regroup with the brothers.

"What the hell?" Ridge muttered, his voice low but furious.

Without hesitation, all three Beaumonts moved as one, rushing to place themselves between the warriors and the potential threat. "Don't shoot!" Lincoln yelled, his voice booming over the roar of the falls as he threw up his hands in a gesture of peace.

Callum and Varstyn, realizing the danger, immediately dropped to the ground, their movements precise and calculated. They flattened themselves against the rocks, their glowing forms dimming slightly as if to make themselves less conspicuous. The warriors' training was evident, but the situation remained precarious.

"Stand down!" Ridge shouted, his tone sharp as he waved his arms to get the attention of the sheriff and his companions. "They're with us! They're not a threat!"

Sheriff Bowen hesitated, his gun still trained on the figures below. "What the hell are they, then?" he demanded, his voice carrying over the distance. "You didn't say anything about aliens being in our woods!"

"They're not aliens," Lynx interjected, his voice steady but loud enough to be heard. "They're our friends, and they're here to help. Put the guns down!"

For a tense moment, no one moved. The air was thick with unease, the roar of the falls only amplifying the weight of the standoff. Lincoln's heart pounded as he watched the sheriff's finger hover near the trigger.

"They're lying on the ground," Lincoln added, his voice firm but calm. "They're not even moving. Does that look like a threat to you?"

Finally, after what felt like an eternity, Sheriff Bowen lowered his weapon slightly. The others followed suit, though their movements were hesitant. "Alright," Bowen said, his tone still wary. "But you'd better have a damn good explanation for this."

"We do," Ridge assured him, his voice tight with controlled frustration. "But now's not the time. Let's talk down here, away from the edge. Just... holster your weapons first."

Bowen exchanged a glance with the others, then nodded. The three of them secured their guns and began descending the trail, their footsteps echoing against the rocks.

As they approached the halfway point, Lincoln turned to Callum and Varstyn, his voice low but urgent. "Now's your chance. Get out of here."

Callum hesitated, his glowing eyes meeting Lincoln's. "We don't run."

"You're not running," Lincoln replied firmly. "You're regrouping. Stick close to the road and head back toward the manor. We'll pick you up on the way. Look for the signal."

Varstyn glanced at Callum, who gave a reluctant nod. "Fine. But don't take too long."

With that, the two warriors moved swiftly and silently, disappearing into the woods as if they had never been there. Their glowing forms faded into the shadows, leaving the Beaumonts alone to face the approaching officials.

By the time Bowen, Dixon, and the park official reached the bottom, Lincoln, Ridge, and Lynx were standing casually near the rocks, doing their best to appear calm.

"What's going on here?" Bowen demanded, his eyes scanning the area as if expecting the warriors to reappear. "You're hiding something."

Lincoln stepped forward, his tone measured. "We're not hiding anything. Those two are part of a team we're working with to figure out what's happening here. They're... specialists."

"Specialists?" Dixon repeated, crossing his arms. "They looked more like something out of a sci-fi movie. What kind of specialists glow like that?"

"They're from out of town," Ridge said quickly, shooting his brother a warning glance. "Way out of town. But they've dealt with situations like this before, and we thought their expertise might help."

Bowen didn't look convinced. "You brought in people we've never heard of, people who don't even look human, to deal with a problem in our jurisdiction?"

Lynx stepped in, his tone more assertive. "Look, we get it. This is all really weird. But right now, the falls are acting up, people are getting spooked, and we're all trying to figure out what's going on. Let's focus on that instead of pointing fingers."

Dixon narrowed his eyes but said nothing, while the park official shifted uncomfortably. Bowen finally exhaled, his shoulders relaxing slightly. "Fine. But I want answers. And if I see those... 'specialists' again, they'd better not give me a reason to draw my weapon."

"They won't," Lincoln promised. "But we need to work together if we're going to solve this."

Satisfied for the moment, Bowen gestured toward the falls. "Let's take a closer look. Show us what you've found."

The brothers exchanged a glance, their unease lingering but their resolve firm. They led the way toward the narrow opening behind the falls, careful to keep their movements measured. Ridge kept an eye on the trail, ensuring no one noticed Callum and Varstyn slipping away.

As the group reached the edge of the water, Lynx pointed toward the faint green glow still emanating from the hidden portal. "There. That's what we're dealing with."

The officials stared, their expressions shifting from skepticism to unease. "What the hell is that?" Dixon muttered, his hand instinctively reaching for his holstered weapon.

"It's the source of the disturbances," Lincoln said carefully, stepping between the officials and the glowing light. "It's not natural, and it's what's causing all the weird things people have been experiencing. We're working on figuring out how to shut it down."

Bowen narrowed his eyes. "And you think those... 'specialists' can help?"

"They've dealt with similar situations before," Ridge replied. "Trust us, you want them on your side."

For a moment, it seemed like Bowen might argue, but he finally nodded. "Fine. But this stays between us. The last thing we need is a panic."

Lincoln nodded in agreement. "We're on the same page."

The group lingered for a moment longer, the sound of the falls filling the silence. Finally, Bowen turned back toward the trail. "Let's get out of here. This place is giving me the creeps."

As the officials began their ascent back up the trail, Lincoln let out a breath he hadn't realized he was holding. He glanced at Ridge and Lynx, who both looked equally relieved.

"Let's hope Callum and Varstyn made it out," Lynx said quietly.

"They're fine," Ridge said confidently. "Now let's get moving before anyone else decides to start asking questions."

The trio turned toward the woods, their focus shifting to the next step in their plan. The portal wasn't going to shut itself down, and the clock was ticking.

31

The drive back to Sage Manor was tense, the atmosphere in Ridge's Jeep heavy with the weight of what had just transpired at Looking Glass Falls. Callum sat quietly in the back, his glowing eyes focused on the road ahead, while Varstyn kept watch out the window, his hand resting near the hilt of his blade.

Lynx leaned forward in his seat, his elbows braced on his knees, while Lincoln and Ridge exchanged occasional glances, both of them silently processing the events.

As they pulled into the long driveway, the sun was starting to set and the soft glow of the manor's lights came into view. Ridge parked near the front steps, the engine rumbling to a stop as everyone exited the vehicle.

Callum immediately turned to Varstyn. "Go back to the perimeter," he instructed, his voice steady. "We'll need full coverage tonight. Thank you for your service at the falls."

Varstyn inclined his head, his glowing eyes flickering with understanding. "Of course." He moved swiftly, disappearing into the shadows as he made his way back to the other warriors stationed around the property.

Callum turned to Ridge, Lincoln and Lynx. "Let's go inside. Drexel will want to know we've returned, and the rest of your family needs to hear what happened."

The group moved toward the front door, their footsteps muffled on the gravel. Callum opened the door and stepped inside, his glowing form momentarily lighting up the darkening hallway. The familiar warmth of the manor was a stark contrast to the cold tension of the falls, but the unease lingered.

Callum ascended the stairs with the Beaumonts following close behind. As they reached the playroom, they could hear faint laughter and the sound of blocks being stacked. The children, oblivious to the dangers outside, were still engrossed in their games.

Drexel stood near the doorway, his tall frame alert but relaxed. He nodded as Callum approached. "Everything secure?"

Callum nodded. "Yes. Thank you for holding things down here while I was away. You can resume perimeter duty with the others. The family is safe, but we'll need to maintain vigilance."

Drexel gave a brief bow. "Understood." He turned and headed down the stairs, his movements silent and purposeful.

Once Drexel was gone, Lincoln glanced at Callum. "Come inside. We all need to talk about what happened at the falls."

Callum nodded and followed them into the playroom. Gran Celia, Francis, Bethany, Waverly and Lorinda looked up as they entered, their expressions a mix of curiosity and concern. Maya and Maddox briefly paused their play before returning to their blocks, their youthful innocence shielding them from the gravity of the situation.

Gran Celia stood, her hands clasped in front of her. "What happened out there?"

Lincoln exhaled, running a hand through his hair. "It's bad, mom. There's a portal behind the falls—active and unstable. Lynx nearly got pulled in by the Umbralox."

Bethany's hand flew to her mouth, her eyes wide. "What?" She immediately rushed to give Lynx a hug asking him if he was hurting anywhere.

"I'm fine, mom," he shrugged her off.

Callum stepped forward, his presence commanding attention. "It's smaller than the ones we've encountered before, but it's active. The tendrils of the Umbralox are using it as a foothold. If it's not closed soon, its influence will grow."

Francis frowned, her sharp mind already racing ahead. "What do we need to shut it down?"

Ridge leaned against the wall, arms crossed. "That's the thing—we don't know yet. The portal is different from what we've seen here and on Tanzlora or Arcmyrin. It's weaker, but it feels... fragmented. Like it's not fully formed."

Gran Celia's brow furrowed. "Could it be that the Umbralox is testing the waters? Establishing a presence here before launching a full attack?"

Callum nodded. "That's my fear. The portal's instability suggests it's a temporary construct, but even temporary access is dangerous. The whispers, the shadows—they're all part of its strategy to manipulate and destabilize."

The room was quiet for a moment, the weight of the situation pressing heavily on everyone. Ridge broke the silence, his brow furrowed in thought. "Do you think the defeat of the Umbralox on Tanzlora weakened them enough to make this just... a last-ditch effort? Like a final gasp before they're completely eradicated?"

Lincoln rubbed his chin thoughtfully. "It's possible. The Umbralox drew a lot of its power from Tanzlora's core. Cutting it off from that energy source would have crippled its ability to manifest fully. What we're seeing here on Earth might just be the remnants trying to hold on."

Waverly, who had been sitting quietly, nodded slowly. "That makes sense. The shadows here feel different—less substantial. When we faced the Umbralox on Tanzlora, it was this overwhelming force, like it was feeding off the planet itself. Here, it feels... fragmented. Weaker."

Gran Celia tapped her fingers lightly against the arm of her chair, her expression contemplative. "It could be that the Umbralox is grasping at whatever it can. Without Tanzlora's core energy, it may be unable to sustain itself fully. What we're seeing now might be its attempt to create chaos before fading completely."

Francis raised an eyebrow. "A cornered predator is often the most dangerous. Even if it's weakened, we can't underestimate what it might do out of desperation."

Lorinda, chimed in hesitantly. "But if it's true that the Umbralox is weaker now, then maybe that's something we can use to our advantage. If this is all it has left, maybe we can destroy it for good."

Lynx crossed his arms, his tone thoughtful. "If that's the case, we need to act fast. The longer it lingers, the more damage it can do. Even if it's not at full strength, it's already causing fear and confusion. That's exactly what it feeds on."

Ridge nodded. "So, we close the portal, eliminate its foothold here, and finish what we started on Tanzlora. If this is its last gasp, then we need to make sure it's its *final* one."

Gran Celia's eyes softened as she looked at her family. "You've already done so much. Tanzlora owes you their survival, and now Earth may need you to save it as well. But this time, you're not facing the full might of the Umbralox. It's diminished, and you have the strength—and the elemental spirits—to see this through."

Lincoln took a deep breath, his voice steady. "Then that's exactly what we'll do. This ends here and now. No more shadows, no more whispers. We're going to finish this—for Earth, for Tanzlora, and for the future of the Triad."

Ridge spoke up, his voice tight with frustration. "Did we mention that the sheriff and the rangers almost shot Callum and Varstyn? They saw them and freaked out. We barely managed to de-escalate the situation."

Both Waverly and Bethany gasped. Lorinda and Francis both said, "What?" in unison.

Gran Celia's expression darkened. "The sheriff? Shooting at allies? That's reckless, even for someone unfamiliar with the situation."

"They don't understand," Lincoln said, his tone even. "To them, this is all just... alien. They're scared, and scared people make rash decisions.

We managed to calm them down, but it's clear they don't trust what they don't know."

Callum's glowing eyes swept over the room, his expression thoughtful. "That makes our mission even more critical. If the portal isn't closed, the Umbralox's influence will only grow, and fear will spread. The people here will turn on one another before they even understand what's happening."

Gran Celia nodded, her voice resolute. "Then we definitely need a plan. Callum, what do you suggest?"

Callum straightened, his presence radiating calm authority. "First, we need to monitor the portal and ensure it doesn't expand. The warriors will maintain a close watch on the property and the surrounding area. Second, we must determine the best way to neutralize the portal. The daggers you brought back from Tanzlora may be the key."

Lincoln exchanged a glance with Ridge and Lynx. "The daggers are powerful, but we've never used them for something like this. If they're going to work, we'll need the elemental spirits' guidance."

Francis tilted her head thoughtfully. "The spirits are bound to the Triad. Would they even be able to intervene on Earth?"

Callum's expression softened slightly. "The spirits' connection is strongest to Tanzlora, but they are tied to you, the Beaumonts. If anyone can call upon their power here, it's you."

The room fell into a heavy silence again. Lincoln finally broke it, his voice steady. "We'll figure it out. We always do. For now, let's focus on keeping everyone safe and getting the information we need."

Callum stood near the playroom doorway, his glowing eyes fixed on Lincoln and Ridge. "Information," he said firmly. "That is what we need. Perhaps we should contact the elders on both Tanzlora and Arcmyrin to alert them to what is happening. They both need to be aware."

Lincoln nodded, "Agreed. We'll go to the chamber under the gazebo to contact Keelee and Elara. They'll want to know about the portal and the Umbralox's influence here."

Ridge joined him, grabbing his jacket from the back of a chair. "Let's go. Callum, you coming?"

Callum inclined his head. "Yes. I need to coordinate with the warriors on how to safely guard the manor and send two on a covert mission to monitor the portal at the falls. If the Umbralox is using it as an entry point, we need eyes on it at all times."

Gran Celia stood, smoothing her skirt as she addressed the group. "While you're doing that, we'll start settling in for the night. With more people in the manor, we'll need to sort out sleeping arrangements. Not everyone can fit into my suite."

Francis raised an eyebrow, her tone light despite the tension. "You mean you're finally kicking us out of your grand bedroom, Celia? I was getting used to that chaise lounge."

Gran Celia smiled faintly. "As much as I enjoy your company, Francis, I think we can all agree it's better to spread out for comfortable sleep while remaining safe. We'll still double and triple up to make it work."

Lorinda glanced at Monica, who was sitting quietly with Maya and Maddox. "Monica and I can take the room we've been using since we got here. It's small, but it's cozy."

"That's a start," Gran Celia replied. "Let's figure out the rest after we get the children ready for bed."

Lincoln turned to Callum as they stepped into the hallway. "We'll meet you back here after you've spoken with the warriors. Let's get moving."

As the three descended the stairs and made their way towards the chamber under the gazebo, Callum's mind was already at work. "The portal at the falls is a clear risk," he said as they walked. "I'll send two warriors to observe it from a distance. They'll stay hidden and report any activity. The rest will rotate shifts around the manor."

Ridge nodded. "Good. The last thing we need is those shadows finding another way to slip past us."

When they reached the chamber, Callum stopped near the entrance. "I'll join you after I've spoken to my warriors. We need a coordinated strategy for the night."

Lincoln clapped him on the shoulder. "Do what you need to do. We'll handle the communications with Keelee and Elara."

Inside the chamber, Lincoln and Ridge approached the central console, the glowing orb in the middle of the room pulsating faintly. Ridge placed his hand over the orb, causing it to brighten up and start emitting a soft hum.

"Keelee first?" Ridge asked.

Lincoln nodded. "He needs to hear about this portal. Then we'll loop in Elara."

Within moments, Keelee's holographic image appeared, his form flickering slightly before stabilizing. His expression was calm but expectant. "Lincoln, Ridge. What news do you bring?"

Lincoln wasted no time. "There's a portal behind the Looking Glass Falls here in the Pisgah National Forest. These falls are located close to Sage Manor. The portal is smaller than what we've seen here and on Tanzlora or Arcmyrin, but it's active and unstable. The Umbralox's influence is seeping through."

Keelee's expression darkened. "An enemy portal on Earth? This is troubling indeed. Its instability suggests desperation—but desperation can still be dangerous."

"That's exactly what Francis said," Ridge reminded Lincoln, "are we sure she isn't part Tanzloran? She sure can decipher all those ancient texts quickly."

Lincoln shot a glaring look at Ridge. "Focus, Ridge." Looking back at Keelee, he said "It's the desperation part that we're worried about too. We need to shut the portal down, but we're not sure how yet. Would the elders have any advice?"

"I will bring this to the council immediately," Keelee said. "In the meantime, monitor the portal closely. Do not engage until we have more information."

Lincoln nodded. "We'll stay on it. We also plan to contact Elara. The elders of Arcmyrin need to be aware of this too."

Keelee's image flickered as he inclined his head. "A wise decision. The Umbralox's reach must not be underestimated. I will update you as soon as I have more details from the council."

As Keelee's image disappeared, Ridge asked Lincoln, "Why didn't you tell Keelee that Callum has two of the Tanzloran warriors on a covert mission to monitor that portal right now?"

"Because I have a feeling that Callum would be in huge trouble for leaving the grounds of the manor especially if they knew that other humans besides us have seen the warriors. Not to mention that we almost got them shot."

"Is your 'feeling' based on something you know for sure or does it have anything to do with that last communication between myself and Lumorith right before we left Tanzlora?"

"Probably a little of both but we need to discuss this later, now is not the time."

32

Ridge activated the communicator orb again, this time linking to
Arcmyrin. Moments later, a tall, elegant holographic figure materialized—Elara, the liaison between the Arcmyrin elders and the Beaumonts.

"Elara," Ridge greeted. "We've got a situation on Earth."

Elara's luminous eyes focused intently on them. "Explain."

Lincoln detailed the events at Looking Glass Falls, from the discov-
ery of the portal to the shadows and tendrils that had nearly pulled Lynx
inside. "We think it's a remnant of the Umbralox, weakened after what
happened on Tanzlora but still trying to cause damage."

Elara's expression grew grim. "If the portal remains active, it could
serve as a foothold for more sinister forces. I will inform the elders of
Arcmyrin. They will likely have insight into dealing with a fragmented
portal."

"Thanks," Ridge said. "We'll need all the help we can get."

As the communication ended, Lincoln turned to Ridge, his expression thoughtful. "We're not alone in this, at least. That's something."

Ridge nodded. "Yeah, but it's still on us to handle things here. Let's
get back and see how Callum's coordinating the warriors."

Lincoln and Ridge watched as the chamber dimmed into its natural state of cool, reflective silence once Elara signed off communications. He ran a hand through his hair, his expression thoughtful. "We've got allies in Keelee and Elara, but we're the boots on the ground here. It's up to us to contain this portal and figure out how to shut it down before things get worse."

Ridge picked up his jacket from the floor and slung it over his shoulder. "Agreed. And let's not forget Callum and his warriors. If anyone can help us keep this under control, it's them."

The two brothers exited the chamber and crossed the lawn toward the house. The manor loomed ahead, its windows glowing warmly against the cool night air. The hum of quiet conversation inside was occasionally punctuated by the faint laughter of the children in the playroom. Despite the calm within, both men felt the weight of what lay ahead.

Inside the manor, they found Callum in the foyer, his tall frame illuminated by the soft glow of the chandelier. He was speaking quietly with Varstyn and Drexel, who had just returned from their rounds.

"Good timing," Callum said as Lincoln and Ridge approached. "We've made some adjustments to the perimeter. Two warriors will remain stationed at the front and back entrances of the manor, while Varstyn and Drexel will rotate between patrolling the grounds and observing the portal at the falls."

"Are they equipped for a long stakeout?" Ridge asked.

Callum nodded. "They've taken supplies and cloaking gear. They'll stay hidden and report back if anything unusual happens. The goal is observation only—we don't want to provoke whatever is using the portal until we're certain of the best way to shut it down."

Lincoln crossed his arms, his expression thoughtful. "Good. The last thing we need is to escalate things before we're ready. What about the warriors here at the manor?"

Callum gestured toward Drexel. "He'll take the lead on internal security tonight, ensuring the family is safe while the rest of us focus on the portal. We've increased the patrol frequency to every fifteen minutes."

Ridge exchanged a glance with Lincoln. "Sounds solid. What's the plan if the shadows make another move?"

"They won't get close," Callum said firmly. "But if they do, we'll be ready."

Satisfied with the plan, Lincoln nodded. "Thanks, Callum. We'll keep everyone inside for now and make sure no one strays near the edges of the property."

Callum inclined his head. "A wise precaution. I'll coordinate with the warriors to ensure the manor remains secure."

The brothers watched as Callum and Drexel moved toward the front door, their steps purposeful. Ridge turned to Lincoln, his expression serious. "They've got the perimeter locked down. Now we just need to make sure the family's prepared for whatever comes next."

"Agreed," Lincoln said. "Let's check on everyone upstairs."

They climbed the grand staircase, their boots barely making a sound on the polished wood. As they approached the playroom, the muffled laughter of the children became clearer. Maya and Maddox were sitting on the floor, still constructing elaborate block towers, while Monica watched from a nearby chair. Lorinda sat next to her, occasionally offering suggestions for the towers' designs.

Gran Celia and Francis were seated near the window, their conversation low but animated. The sight was a stark reminder of the normalcy they were fighting to protect.

Gran Celia looked up as the brothers entered. "How did it go? Did you get through to Keelee and Elara?"

Lincoln nodded. "We did. They're both aware of the situation. Keelee is alerting the Tanzloran elders, and Elara is informing the Arcmyrin council. They'll get back to us with any advice."

Francis leaned back in her chair, her arms crossed. "And what about the portal? Any progress on figuring out how to shut it down?"

"Not yet," Ridge admitted. "But Callum's got warriors watching it. If anything changes, we'll know."

Gran Celia sighed, her hands folded in her lap. "At least we have allies. That's more than most would have in a situation like this."

Lincoln glanced toward the children, who were blissfully unaware of the tension in the room. "How are they holding up?"

Lorinda smiled faintly. "Better than us, I think. They're completely absorbed in their game."

As the conversation shifted, Gran Celia rose to her feet. "We were just discussing sleeping arrangements for tonight. With all the family back under one roof, we'll need to make sure everyone has a place to rest."

Lincoln nodded. "Good idea. Ridge and I can help figure it out."

Gran Celia smiled warmly. "Thank you. Let's start by making sure the children are settled. Everything else can wait."

The family began organizing the sleeping arrangements, their efforts a small act of normalcy in the face of the chaos surrounding them. Despite the tension, there was a sense of unity—a reminder that no matter what came next, they would face it together.

Ridge stood near the window in Lorinda and Monica's room, his sharp eyes scanning the perimeter outside. The curtains hung heavy and still, but he gave them a quick tug to ensure they were drawn tightly. Satisfied, he stepped back and leaned against the wall, crossing his arms as he surveyed the cozy space. The soft hum of the shower running in the adjoining bathroom was the only sound in the otherwise quiet room.

Lorinda sat on the edge of the bed, watching Ridge with an expression caught somewhere between curiosity and gratitude. She could see the tension in his shoulders, the way his gaze lingered just a moment too long on the window and door. It was obvious he was carrying the weight of everything that had happened—both on Earth and Tanzlora.

"You don't have to keep checking," Lorinda said gently, breaking the silence. "We're safe here. I trust you."

Ridge gave her a small, sheepish smile, running a hand through his hair. "Force of habit, I guess. After everything we've been through, I just want to make sure."

Lorinda tilted her head, studying him for a moment. "You mean after everything you've been through. You and your family."

Ridge shifted, his arms dropping to his sides. "Yeah, about that..." He sighed, his expression softening. "I'm sorry, Lorinda. You came to us for help, for safety, and now you're stuck in the middle of all this chaos. The shadows, the portal, the warriors... it's a lot. And you shouldn't have to deal with it."

She shook her head, her voice firm. "Ridge, don't apologize. I came to Sage Manor because I felt like I had nowhere else to go, and I trusted you—your family—to understand. And you did. You've kept us safe when no one else could have. I'm not scared here. Not at Sage Manor. Especially not now that you're back."

Her words seemed to catch him off guard, his gaze locking onto hers. For a moment, his usual confidence faltered, replaced by something deeper, more vulnerable. "You're not scared?" he asked quietly.

Lorinda smiled, a faint blush creeping up her cheeks. "No. Not here. Not with you."

Ridge swallowed hard, his heart beating just a little faster. "That means a lot. And I promise, we'll figure this out. We beat the Umbralox on Tanzlora, and we'll do it again here. I won't let anything happen to you or Monica."

"I know," she replied softly. "And I believe in you—your whole family. What you've done, what you're capable of... it's incredible."

The room grew still, the air between them charged with unspoken tension. Ridge took a small step closer, his eyes searching hers as if trying to find the right words. Lorinda's breath caught as she felt the intensity of his gaze, her heartbeat quickening. For a fleeting moment, she was certain he was going to kiss her.

But just as the moment reached its peak, the bathroom door swung open with a loud creak, and Monica bounded into the room, her hair damp and her pajamas slightly askew. "All done, Mom!" she announced brightly, oblivious to the atmosphere she'd interrupted.

Ridge immediately stepped back, clearing his throat as he glanced toward the door. "Good timing, Monica. The room's all secure. You two should be good for the night."

Lorinda blinked, the spell of the moment broken. "Thank you, Ridge," she said, her voice a touch unsteady.

Ridge nodded, his usual composure slipping back into place. "If you need anything, I'm in the room right next door. Just holler my name."

He moved toward the door, pausing briefly to glance back at Lorinda. Their eyes met for a brief second, a silent understanding passing between them, before he stepped out into the hallway, closing the door softly behind him.

Lorinda exhaled slowly, her hand drifting to her chest as she tried to calm her racing heart. Monica climbed onto the bed, chattering about her shower, blissfully unaware of the moment she had interrupted.

Lorinda smiled faintly, pulling her daughter close and resolving to focus on the here and now—at least for the night.

Ridge stopped in the hallway outside his room, his hand hovering over the doorknob when he noticed Lynx standing there, arms crossed and an unreadable expression on his face. Ridge raised an eyebrow. "Can I help you?"

Lynx sighed dramatically, ticking off points on his fingers as he spoke. "Not my idea. Mom doesn't want me sleeping alone tonight. And since I'm not sharing a room with kids, my sister, my grandma, or Francis..." He paused, raising his final finger for emphasis. "You're the best choice."

Ridge stared at him for a moment, his lips twitching as he tried not to laugh. "Well, I feel honored," he replied, his voice dripping with sarcasm. He turned the doorknob and opened the door, motioning for Lynx to enter. "Come on, your highness. Let's get this over with."

Lynx strolled into the room, flopping onto the bed with an exaggerated sigh of resignation. Ridge shook his head, muttering under his breath as he closed the door. "Out of all the places I thought this night would take me, bunking with you was not one of them."

Meanwhile, across the hall, Lincoln and Bethany were tucking Maya and Maddox into the large bed in their room. The twins were already half-asleep, their small hands clutching their favorite stuffed animals as they snuggled under the covers. Bethany sat on the edge of the bed, brushing Maddox's hair gently back from his face.

"Do you think the shadows will come here?" Maya asked sleepily, her wide eyes looking up at Lincoln.

Lincoln crouched beside the bed, his tone reassuring. "No, sweetheart. Callum and the warriors are watching over us, and we're all together. Nothing's going to get past us."

Maya nodded, her eyelids drooping as she turned her face into the pillow. Bethany kissed both children on the forehead before pulling the blanket up to their chins. "Goodnight, my loves," she whispered.

In another part of the manor, Gran Celia emerged from her bathroom, her robe tied snugly around her waist. She stopped short when she saw both Francis and Waverly in her sitting room, their expressions sheepish.

Celia raised an eyebrow. "Can I help you ladies?"

Francis stood, smoothing her skirt. "We thought we'd stay with you tonight. Safety in numbers and all that."

Waverly grinned, though there was a hint of unease in her eyes. "Besides, you've got the best setup in the house. The rest of us are doubling or quadrupling up."

Celia crossed her arms, pretending to be stern. "And you think I'll just let you invade my sanctuary?"

Waverly shrugged. "I was going to let Francis take the bed with you since you've both already braved the chaise lounges. I'll sleep on one of the lounges this time."

Francis nodded. "Fair's fair. And it's better than trying to squeeze into another overcrowded room."

Celia shook her head, her lips twitching with amusement. "Fine. You win. But don't blame me if I snore."

Waverly laughed. "Deal."

As they settled into the room, the comfort of being together eased some of the tension that had lingered throughout the day. Celia climbed into bed, feeling grateful for her family and their resilience. She peeked her head out of her bedroom door, catching sight of Drexel standing watch in the hallway.

"It's Drexel, right?" she asked softly, her voice filled with warmth.

He turned, his glowing eyes meeting hers. "Yes."

"I just wanted to say thank you. For everything you and the other warriors are doing. I know danger still lurks, but I feel safer knowing you're here."

Drexel inclined his head respectfully, his expression calm but resolute. "It's an honor to protect your family. We will remain vigilant."

Celia nodded, her heart full as she retreated back into her room. She lay down, pulling the covers up as Francis and Waverly settled in. Despite the uncertainty ahead, she allowed herself a moment of peace, knowing that they were all together—and safe.

33

The sun rose slowly over Sage Manor, casting its warm light through the windows and filling the home with a quiet sense of calm after the previous day's chaos. The Beaumont family gathered in the large dining room, the smell of fresh coffee, sizzling bacon, and pancakes wafting through the air. Maya and Maddox sat at the head of the table, giggling as they competed to see who could stack the tallest tower of pancakes on their plates. This seemed to be a normal breakfast ritual for them and Monica watched it with a smile, clearly enjoying the energy of her newfound friends.

Gran Celia presided over the table, her presence grounding as always, while Francis poured orange juice for everyone. Bethany and Waverly moved efficiently between the kitchen and dining room, bringing out plates of fruit, eggs, and toast, while Ridge and Lincoln took seats near the middle of the table, discussing the day ahead. Lynx sat at the other end, half-awake but drawn by the promise of food.

Callum entered the room with Drexel and Varstyn close behind, their towering figures an unusual but welcome sight at the family breakfast. "You didn't have to prepare all this," Callum said as he took a seat. "The warriors and I can manage with rations."

Gran Celia waved a hand dismissively. "Nonsense. You're guests in this house, and we take care of our guests."

Maddox grinned up at Callum, holding out a plate of bacon. "Here, try this! It's the best."

Callum accepted the offering with a rare smile, his expression softening as he joined in the meal. The warriors, initially hesitant, soon relaxed in the warmth of the family atmosphere. Laughter and conversation filled the room, the bonds between everyone growing stronger with each shared bite.

After breakfast, Bethany and Waverly unveiled the surprise they had been preparing. "Sanodia sent something through the portal with us for the warriors," Bethany said, holding up a basket covered with a colorful cloth. "We thought they might appreciate a taste of home."

Callum's brows rose in surprise as Waverly lifted the cloth to reveal neatly packed containers of Tanzloran food—vibrant fruits, roasted root vegetables, and bread made from the grains of their homeland. "Sanodia sent this?" he asked, his voice tinged with both awe and gratitude.

Bethany nodded. "She wanted to make sure you were taken care of. She said the energy here is different, and you need nourishment that resonates with Tanzloran frequencies."

Callum stared at the food for a moment, his expression uncharacteristically soft. "That's... thoughtful. Very thoughtful. My sister always finds a way to surprise me." A hint of pride flickered in his glowing eyes. "Thank you for bringing this to us."

As the family prepared to deliver the food to the warriors stationed around the property, Bethany lingered beside Callum, a wistful smile on her face. "Your mother, Marellis, was the same way," she said quietly.

"She always thought of others, always made sure everyone was cared for. Even when she was dealing with so much herself."

Callum's gaze softened further, a rare vulnerability crossing his features. "She taught us well. Everything I do, I do to honor her."

Bethany placed a hand on his arm. "She'd be proud of you, Callum. Of all of you."

The family dispersed to deliver the food, each pair taking a section of the property to meet with the warriors. The sight of the vibrant Tanzloran food brought smiles and murmurs of appreciation from the warriors, who were touched by the gesture. It was a moment of connection, a reminder of the unity that bound them together, even across worlds.

Later that morning, Ridge and Lincoln gathered Waverly and Lynx at the gazebo, leading them down into the chamber beneath. The room with its sleek consoles and glowing screens was a familiar hub for their interstellar communications. Ridge activated the orb in the center of the chamber, the soft hum of its energy filling the space as the screens flickered to life.

Lincoln leaned forward, his elbows resting on the table. "Let's check in with Keelee and Elara. We need to know what the councils are advising about the portal."

Waverly nodded, her fingers brushing against the edge of the table. "I hope they've made progress. We need a clear plan."

As Ridge initiated the commnications, the screens flickered once more—but instead of Keelee or Elara appearing, swirling light filled the displays. The energy in the room shifted, and a faint breeze seemed to stir the air. The Beaumonts exchanged wary glances as the light coalesced into familiar forms.

The elemental spirits appeared on the screens, their glowing, ethereal shapes radiating a sense of power and wisdom. Mistara, the spirit of water, shimmered like sunlight on a lake. Terraveta, the spirit of earth, stood solid and grounding. Ambreela, the spirit of air, moved gracefully, her form light and fluid. Ignissa, the spirit of fire, burned brightly, her presence commanding.

Mistara was the first to speak, her voice calm and steady. "Beaumonts, Earth hangs in the balance. The portal at the falls is a remnant of the Umbralox's power, a foothold it seeks to strengthen. You must act swiftly to destroy it."

Ridge leaned forward, his brow furrowed. "We've been trying to figure out how. The portal is unstable, and we're not sure what will shut it down."

Ignissa's fiery form flickered as she spoke. "The daggers you carry are the key. They are attuned to the energy of the Triad and can sever the connection between the portal and the shadows that created it."

Ambreela's voice was soft but firm. "But you must act with precision. The portal's energy is fragile; too much force could cause it to collapse violently, spreading its influence instead of containing it."

Lincoln nodded, absorbing their words. "So, we use the daggers to close it. But how do we know the right time to act? The shadows are still using it."

Terraveta's voice was deep and grounding. "The shadows are weak without their source. Watch for the moment when their energy is stretched thin, when their influence falters. That is when you strike."

Waverly tilted her head, her gaze thoughtful. "And what happens after? Once the portal is closed, will the shadows still be a threat?"

Mistara's shimmering form seemed to ripple. "The shadows will scatter, their hold on Earth diminished. But vigilance will be needed. The echoes of the Umbralox's influence may linger, seeking new ways to take root."

The spirits began to fade, their light dimming as their parting words echoed through the chamber. "The strength of the Triad flows through you. Trust in your connection, and you will succeed."

As the screens returned to normal, the Beaumonts sat in silence for a moment, the weight of the task ahead settling over them. Ridge broke the quiet, his voice steady. "We've got what we need. Now we just have to make it happen."

The hum of the chamber's energy continued to fill the air as Ridge reset the console, initiating another connection. Within moments, two holographic figures shimmered into view—Keelee, standing tall with his glowing presence exuding calm authority, and Elara, her elegant form radiating a serene luminescence. Both envoys immediately focused on the Beaumonts gathered around the table, their expressions serious.

"Keelee, Elara," Lincoln greeted, leaning forward. "We've just spoken with the elemental spirits. They gave us guidance on closing the portal, but we need to know what your councils recommend."

Keelee nodded, his voice steady. "First, tell us what the spirits advised."

Lincoln recounted the conversation with the spirits, detailing their warning about the portal's fragility and the importance of timing. He explained the spirits' belief that the daggers were the key to severing the portal's connection to the shadows and how acting at the precise moment of weakness was critical.

When he finished, Keelee exchanged a glance with Elara, who stepped forward first to speak.

"The Arcmyrin Council is deeply concerned about the portal's instability," Elara said, her voice melodic but firm. "They agree that the daggers, as artifacts of the Triad, are the only tools capable of closing the portal without catastrophic consequences. However, they caution that using the daggers improperly could amplify the portal's energy instead of severing it. Timing will be everything."

Keelee inclined his head in agreement. "The Tanzloran elders share the same concern. The portal is a dangerous fragment of the Umbralox's power. While it no longer has the core energy of Tanzlora to draw from, it is feeding on Earth's environment. That makes it more unpredictable."

Ridge frowned, his arms crossed. "So, we can't just stab it and hope for the best."

"No," Keelee said gravely. "The elders recommend careful observation of the portal's behavior. It will weaken as its energy stretches thin, especially when its tendrils fail to connect to anything substantial. That is the moment to strike."

Elara nodded. "Additionally, the Arcmyrin Council believes that combining the power of all four daggers simultaneously will be necessary. Each dagger represents an elemental force, and their combined energy is what will sever the portal's connection completely."

Waverly's brow furrowed. "But what if the portal collapses violently before we're ready? The spirits warned us about that."

Keelee's gaze softened. "The collapse is a risk, but it can be mitigated. The elders suggest using the daggers to contain the portal's energy as it weakens. The containment will prevent a destructive outburst."

Elara added, "And that will also ensure the shadows' influence is truly eradicated from the area. If the portal is simply closed without severing the tendrils' connection, the shadows may linger, seeking a new foothold."

Lynx leaned forward, his expression intense. "So it's not just about timing; it's about precision. We need to be in sync, all four of us, with the daggers."

Keelee nodded. "Exactly. You will need focus, cooperation, and clarity of intent. The elemental spirits will guide you, but the execution is up to you."

Lincoln exhaled, his gaze steady as he looked between Keelee and Elara. "What about the portal itself? Once it's closed, will that be the end of it, or could it reopen?"

Elara's expression grew somber. "That depends on how it is closed. If the connection is severed completely, the portal will be rendered inert. But if any trace of the shadow's influence remains, it could reawaken under the right conditions."

"That's why the daggers are critical," Keelee added. "They are attuned to the elemental spirits and the Triad's energy. If wielded correctly, they will ensure the portal is sealed permanently."

Ridge glanced at the others, his jaw tight. "Then we don't have room for mistakes."

"No, you don't," Keelee said bluntly. "But you also have the strength and knowledge to succeed. The spirits have chosen you for this task for a reason."

Elara's tone softened. "And you have allies. Arcmyrin and Tanzlora stand with you, even from afar. We will continue to provide counsel and resources as needed."

The holographic figures began to flicker, signaling the end of the transmission. Keelee's final words carried a note of firm encouragement. "Trust in the spirits, trust in each other, and trust in the daggers. You are the Beaumonts—your legacy has prepared you for this."

Elara added, "The Triad depends on you, but you are not alone. Remember that."

As the holograms faded, the room fell into a heavy silence. The Beaumonts exchanged determined glances, the weight of their task clearer than ever.

Ridge finally broke the silence, his voice steady. "We've got everything we need. Now let's make it count."

The silence following Ridge's declaration lingered for a moment longer before Lynx broke it, his tone hesitant but thoughtful. "There's one problem we haven't addressed," he said, glancing at everyone around the table and then at the fading holograms of Keelee and Elara. "The area around the portal—it's tiny. Barely big enough for me to squeeze into when I checked it out."

Lincoln frowned, leaning back in his chair. "You're saying there's no room for all four of us to stand in there with the daggers?"

Lynx nodded. "Exactly. It's cramped. Even if we're as synchronized as possible, there's no way all four of us can fit behind the falls to activate the daggers at the same time. Unless we shrink, or..." He trailed off, his expression darkening. "...we blow the area open with dynamite."

34

The room grew quiet again as the gravity of his words set in. Keelee's holographic form flickered back into clarity, his brows furrowed in concern. "Blowing open the area with dynamite is not an ideal solution. The portal's instability could react violently to such a disruption. The entire area might collapse."

Elara reappeared alongside Keelee, her expression equally grim. "Lynx raises a valid point, though. The daggers must be used simultaneously, but the confined space creates a logistical challenge. We need another solution."

Waverly leaned forward, her tone curious but measured. "Is there any way to extend the daggers' reach? Could their energy be channeled into the portal without all four of us physically being right there?"

Elara tilted her head, considering. "The daggers are designed to work in unison. They draw energy from the elemental spirits and the wielder's intent. Distance complicates that connection, but it might not make it impossible."

Keelee's expression shifted slightly, as if struck by an idea. "There may be a way to channel the daggers' power from a slight distance, but it would require precision and a strong connection with the spirits. If one or more of you were positioned just outside the portal's immediate vicinity—perhaps just beyond the narrow opening—you could focus your energy through the dagger into the portal."

Ridge raised an eyebrow. "So, basically, we'd have to line up and shoot dagger energy into the portal like it's some kind of magical relay?"

Keelee's lips quirked in a faint smile. "In essence, yes. The daggers would act as conduits. It would require immense focus and trust, but it could work."

Lynx frowned, still skeptical. "What if we mess it up? If we're not perfectly in sync, wouldn't that risk destabilizing the portal even more?"

Elara's tone was calm but firm. "That's why your connection to the elemental spirits is vital. They will guide you, ensuring the energy aligns correctly. But you must remain focused and committed to the task. Doubt or hesitation could disrupt the flow."

Lincoln rubbed his temples, the weight of the situation pressing harder with every word. "And if the relay fails?"

Keelee's hologram flickered briefly as he replied. "If the relay fails, the portal may become further destabilized, but it would not immediately collapse. The spirits will act as a buffer to minimize risk—but you must succeed."

Waverly exhaled, her tone thoughtful. "So, we split the team. Two of us inside the portal chamber, two just outside. We align our focus, channel the energy, and hope it's enough to shut the thing down."

Keelee nodded. "Precisely. It is a risk, but it is also your best option."

Ridge crossed his arms, his jaw tight. "Great. A risky plan in a cramped space with unstable energy. What could go wrong?"

Lynx shot him a wry look. "Plenty. But at least we've got a plan now. Better than blowing things up and hoping for the best."

Elara's holographic form softened slightly as she addressed the group. "You have the strength and knowledge to overcome this challenge. Trust in the spirits, and in each other. The Triad stands with you."

Keelee inclined his head, his tone steady. "Prepare yourselves. The portal will not wait for hesitation."

As the holograms faded once more, the Beaumonts exchanged determined glances. The path ahead was fraught with danger.

Ridge leaned back in his chair, tapping a finger on the table as he looked at Lynx. "Do you think you and Waverly could squeeze into that portal space together? Enough room to maneuver your daggers?"

Lynx raised an eyebrow, his expression skeptical. "Maybe if we don't eat for a whole week. And even then, I'm not sure about this whole relay proposal. If Waverly and I are crammed in there, wouldn't we be in the way of the energy flowing from your dagger and Lincoln's?"

Waverly nodded in agreement. "He's got a point. It's not just about squeezing in there—it's about the alignment. The energy needs to flow freely, and if we're too close, we could disrupt it."

The group fell into silence, the weight of the problem settling over them. The flickering screens in the chamber offered no further guidance, and the air was thick with frustration and uncertainty.

Ridge broke the silence with a sigh, his tone laced with sarcasm. "Great. So, our best plan involves impossible spatial logistics and questionable physics. Anyone else want to throw in an equally insane idea?"

Before anyone could respond, a voice cut through the tension. "You've got a bigger problem to deal with right now."

They all turned to see Gran Celia standing in the doorway, her expression a mix of concern and exasperation. "There's a situation in the parlor, and it goes by the name of General Adamson."

Waverly groaned audibly, rolling her eyes. "Oh, good grief. What is he doing here?"

Lincoln didn't even try to mask his frustration, running a hand down his face. "The last thing we need right now is the U.S. military poking their noses into this."

Ridge frowned, looking between them. "Who's General Adamson?"

Waverly shot him a tired look. "He's one of those 'I'm in charge of everything' types. If he's here, it means the government is sniffing around, and they're not going to back off easily."

Lincoln stood, his chair scraping against the floor as he pushed it back. "Come on, little brother. Let's go meet the General. You wanted to know why Lumorith says the Triadorne is unsafe on Earth? This is your chance to see it up close and personal."

Ridge stood reluctantly, glancing at Lynx and Waverly. "Guess this is the part where I learn about the joys of keeping family secrets."

Lynx smirked, grabbing his jacket. "Welcome to the club."

The group followed Gran Celia out of the chamber and back up to the house. As they approached the parlor, the low hum of conversation became audible. The General's authoritative tone was unmistakable, carrying an edge that set everyone else on edge.

Gran Celia paused at the parlor doorway, turning to the family. "Remember, stay calm. Let me take the lead if he starts asking questions we don't want to answer."

Lincoln nodded. "Understood. Let's see what he wants."

The family stepped into the parlor to find General Adamson standing near the fireplace, his posture rigid and commanding. He turned as they entered, his sharp eyes narrowing slightly as he took in the group.

"Ah, Mr. Beaumont," the General said, his tone clipped. "And the whole family, it seems. How convenient."

Lincoln crossed his arms, his expression neutral. "General Adamson. What brings you to our home unannounced?"

The General's lips pressed into a thin line. "We've received reports of unusual activity in this area—disturbances, unexplained phenomena. I thought it prudent to pay a visit and see for myself."

Waverly scoffed under her breath, but Gran Celia shot her a warning glance. Stepping forward, Celia's tone was polite but firm. "General, this is private property. If you have questions, I suggest you state them clearly."

Adamson didn't miss a beat. "I've been briefed on your family's... unique situation. Let's not waste time pretending I don't know that something very unusual is going on here."

Ridge tensed, his hands clenching into fists at his sides. Lincoln placed a calming hand on his shoulder, his voice steady. "We're aware of the disturbances, General. We're handling it."

"And what exactly does 'handling it' mean?" Adamson's gaze was piercing, his tone leaving no room for evasion.

Gran Celia stepped in, her voice calm and disarming. "It means exactly what it sounds like. This is a family matter, and we're more than capable of resolving it without outside interference."

The General's eyes narrowed, clearly unsatisfied with her answer. "This isn't just a family matter anymore. Whatever's happening here is affecting the surrounding area. That makes it my jurisdiction."

Lincoln stepped forward, his tone firm but measured. "With all due respect, General, you're not equipped to deal with what's happening here. Interfering will only make things worse."

Adamson opened his mouth to respond, but Ridge cut in, his voice sharp. "Look, General, we get it. You're worried. But barging in here and throwing your weight around isn't going to solve anything."

The General's gaze shifted to Ridge, a flicker of curiosity crossing his face. "And you are?"

Ridge met his gaze evenly. "Someone who's not going to stand here and let you make things worse."

The tension in the room was palpable, but before the situation could escalate further, Gran Celia raised a hand. "Enough. General, you've said your piece. Now, unless you have actionable intelligence to share, I suggest you let us do what we need to do."

Adamson hesitated for a moment before giving a curt nod. "Fine. But I'll be keeping a close eye on this situation. If things escalate, I'll be back—and next time, I won't come alone."

As the General left, the family exchanged wary glances. Lincoln exhaled slowly, turning to Ridge. "Now you understand why we don't advertise who we are or what we do."

Ridge nodded, his expression grim. "Yeah. I get it now. Loud and clear."

Ridge wandered aimlessly near the gardens, his footsteps crunching softly against the gravel paths. The confrontation with General Adamson still played in his mind, the man's piercing gaze and veiled threats fueling Ridge's frustration. The cool mountain air should have been calming, but his shoulders remained tense, his hands shoved deep into his pockets as he tried to rein in his simmering anger.

He didn't notice Lorinda until her voice cut through the quiet. "Are you okay?"

Ridge turned to see her standing a few feet away, concern etched on her face. He hesitated for a moment before letting out a deep sigh, the weight of the evening visibly softening his stance. "I've been better."

Lorinda approached cautiously, her gaze steady. "I overheard what happened with the General. Francis and I couldn't help it—it's not exactly a quiet house." She smiled gently, her tone light. "I saw you come out here and figured you might need someone to talk to."

Ridge gestured toward a nearby bench beneath an arch of ivy. "Might as well sit down. It's better than pacing around and scaring the rabbits."

They sat in silence for a moment, the faint rustle of leaves and chirping of crickets filling the air. Ridge stared at the ground, his elbows on his knees, before finally breaking the silence. "It's just... exasperating," he said, his voice low but intense. "Earth's leaders—they're either so afraid of what they don't understand or so greedy for power that they won't even consider the possibility of something greater. Something that could help everyone."

Lorinda tilted her head, listening intently. "You're talking about what Lumorith said—about how Earth's leadership isn't ready for communication with benevolent entities?"

Ridge nodded, his jaw tightening. "Exactly. Tanzlora and Arcmyrin—they've advanced because they work with the elemental spirits, with each other. They embrace progress and connection. But here? It's like we're stuck in a cycle of fear and control. Every time someone like Adamson shows up, I'm reminded of how far we still have to go."

Lorinda was quiet for a moment, then placed a hand on his arm, her touch grounding. "I understand. More than you might think."

Ridge raised an eyebrow, his skepticism apparent. "Do you?"

She laughed softly. "I do. Maybe not entirely, but Celia and Francis have helped me see things from a completely different perspective. Before I came here, I was just... existing. Working, raising Monica, going through the motions. I didn't think about what could be out there or what it meant to really be part of something bigger."

He tilted his head, intrigued. "What changed?"

"Everything," Lorinda said simply. "Meeting your family, learning about Tanzlora, seeing what's possible when people—or planets—work together. It's been overwhelming, sure, but it's also been... good. A good change."

Ridge let her words sink in, the tension in his shoulders easing slightly. "You know," he said after a moment, "it's nice to hear that. Sometimes it feels like we're fighting an uphill battle, like the world's too set in its ways to change."

Lorinda smiled, her eyes warm. "Change takes time, Ridge. But you and your family are making a difference—here, on Tanzlora, across the Triad. That matters."

He glanced at her, his lips curving into a faint smile. "You're surprisingly good at this whole pep talk thing."

She shrugged playfully. "I've had good teachers."

The two of them sat there a while longer, the garden's serene atmosphere helping to soothe their frayed nerves. For the first time that day, Ridge felt a glimmer of hope that maybe, just maybe, things could change for the better.

35

Ridge and Lorinda walked back toward the parlor, their conversation fading into comfortable silence. The house was quieter now, the tension from earlier still lingering but softened by the calming atmosphere of the manor. As they approached the parlor doorway, Ridge froze mid-step, his eyes narrowing slightly.

Sheriff Bowen sat in one of the large armchairs, his hat resting on his knee. His expression was serious but not hostile, his sharp eyes flicking toward them as they entered.

"Well," Ridge muttered under his breath to Lorinda, "this just keeps getting better."

The sheriff stood as they entered, his large frame imposing but his demeanor calm. "Ridge. Miss Lorinda." He tipped his head in greeting, then glanced at the door behind them. "Your family around? I came to talk to all of you."

Gran Celia entered from the hallway, her expression neutral but welcoming. "Sheriff Bowen, good evening. We weren't expecting you." She gestured toward another chair. "Please, sit."

Bowen gave her a curt nod, settling back into his seat as Ridge and Lorinda took spots on the sofa nearby. "I came to warn you about the General's visit," the sheriff began, his voice low and steady. "But clearly, I was too late."

Ridge crossed his arms, his jaw tightening. "You could say that. He left a hell of an impression."

Bowen exhaled sharply, his frustration evident. "I don't want him or the military interfering in this investigation any more than you do. Neither does Ranger Dixon."

Gran Celia tilted her head, studying him. "Do you have any idea how he found out about what's happening?"

Bowen nodded grimly. "We've got a strong suspicion. Dixon and I believe it was one of the park rangers—Janet Holt. She's new, ambitious, and not exactly subtle about her aspirations. We think she flagged the incident at the falls to someone higher up, and it snowballed from there."

Waverly and Lincoln entered the parlor, having overheard the conversation from the hallway. Lincoln leaned against the doorway, his expression stern. "So this Holt just decided to report something she didn't understand to the military?"

"Looks that way," Bowen confirmed. "And now we've got General Adamson sniffing around, which is the last thing we need. I don't want him setting up operations here, causing panic, and stirring up trouble. This is my county, and I won't have it turned into a circus."

Waverly frowned. "Sheriff, why are you telling us this? Not that we don't appreciate the heads-up."

Bowen's gaze sharpened. "Because I need you to shoot straight with me. I've always suspected your family was... different. You've kept to yourselves, you don't cause trouble, but you've also helped this community more than anyone else I know. I want to help you, but I can't do that if I'm blind to what's really going on."

Ridge leaned forward, his tone skeptical. "What exactly are you asking, Sheriff? Because this isn't something you're going to find in a police handbook."

Bowen met Ridge's gaze evenly. "I'm not asking for a full history lesson. I don't need to know every detail. But I need to know enough to keep Adamson off your backs and protect this town. I may not understand all this... spiritual and supernatural stuff you're dealing with, and frankly, I'm not sure I believe in it. But I know government overreach when I see it, and I won't let the military trample over my county."

Gran Celia exchanged a glance with Lincoln, who nodded subtly. She turned back to Bowen, her voice calm but firm. "Sheriff, you've always been a fair and reasonable man. I believe you when you say you want to help. What we're dealing with is... complicated. It's not just about this county, or even this state. It's bigger than that."

Bowen's jaw tightened, but he didn't interrupt. Celia continued. "What happened at the falls is connected to something ancient and dangerous, something we're working to contain. If Adamson and his people get involved, they'll only make things worse."

Bowen leaned back in his chair, his brow furrowed. "How much worse are we talking?"

Lincoln stepped forward, his tone measured. "Let's just say the fallout could go far beyond Looking Glass Falls. This is delicate, Sheriff. If we don't handle it right, we're looking at a lot more than panic in your county."

Bowen nodded slowly, absorbing their words. "All right. I'll do what I can to keep Adamson and his people at bay. But you have to promise me one thing."

"What's that?" Ridge asked warily.

"Whatever you're doing to fix this," Bowen said, his gaze steady, "make sure it works. Because if it doesn't, there won't be much I can do to help."

Gran Celia nodded solemnly. "We understand. And thank you, Sheriff. Your trust means a great deal to us."

Bowen stood, placing his hat back on his head. "I'll keep you updated on what I hear about Adamson. Just... be careful, all of you."

As the sheriff left, the family exchanged heavy glances, the weight of his words settling over them. Ridge sighed, running a hand through his hair. "No pressure or anything."

Lincoln clapped him on the shoulder, his expression grim but resolute. "We've handled worse. Let's make sure this doesn't become another thing to add to that list."

As the door closed behind Sheriff Bowen, silence filled the parlor. The weight of his words lingered, settling heavily over the family. Gran Celia, standing by the fireplace, turned to face the group. Her calm yet resolute demeanor was a steadying force.

"Well," she said, smoothing her skirt. "It seems the stakes just got higher. We've dealt with the likes of General Adamson before, but with the portal and the shadows, this is a different kind of challenge."

Lincoln nodded, his jaw tight. "We need to act fast. If Adamson gets any more involved, it could complicate everything we're trying to do. The portal is the priority, but we can't let the military set up shop here. That kind of chaos will attract attention we don't need."

Waverly crossed her arms, leaning against the armrest of a chair. "Sheriff Bowen is on our side, which helps. But his hands are tied to an extent. We need to make sure we're ready for whatever happens next."

Ridge, who had been pacing near the window, stopped and turned to face them. "Ready how? The portal is unstable, the daggers might not fit in the space we have, and we're juggling shadows, government interference, and whatever other curveballs the Umbralox throws our way."

Lynx smirked faintly from his spot on the sofa. "Don't forget the whispering shadows. They add a nice creepy touch."

Ridge shot him a look. "Helpful, Lynx."

Gran Celia raised a hand, silencing the brewing tension. "We can't solve everything at once, but we can prepare. Let's focus on what we can control right now. Lincoln, Ridge, and Lynx, you've already made headway at the falls. That's where we need to start."

Lincoln nodded, his brow furrowed. "We need to go back, but this time with a plan. The spirits said timing is critical. We'll need to watch the portal carefully, wait for the right moment, and act decisively."

Gran Celia's gaze sharpened. "And what about the shadows? They're bound to interfere. You'll need to be ready for them, too."

"We'll use the daggers," Waverly said firmly. "The spirits already told us they're our best defense. If we can keep the shadows at bay long enough to close the portal, that should weaken their hold here."

Francis, who had been sitting quietly by the bookshelf, spoke up. "And what if it doesn't? What if closing the portal only pushes them further into the shadows, waiting for another opportunity?"

The room fell silent at her words. It was a sobering thought, one they all knew was possible. Lincoln broke the silence, his voice steady. "Then we'll deal with that when it comes. One step at a time. Right now, the portal is the biggest threat. If we can shut it down, we'll cut off their access point."

Gran Celia nodded. "Agreed. But we'll need to move carefully. The military is watching, and so are the shadows. We can't afford any mistakes."

Lynx leaned back, his arms crossed. "And how do we deal with the General if he decides to stick his nose in again? We can't exactly keep this under wraps if he starts snooping around the falls."

Gran Celia's lips tightened. "Leave Adamson to me. I have a few old friends in high places who might be able to remind him that this isn't his jurisdiction."

Waverly raised an eyebrow. "You're not going to call in favors with the President, are you?"

Gran Celia smiled faintly. "Let's just say I have connections. Trust me, I'll handle it."

The room fell into a tense silence again, each family member lost in their thoughts. Finally, Lincoln stood and clapped his hands together, breaking the quiet. "All right. Let's gear up. We're going to need everything we've got for this."

Over the next several hours, the family worked together to prepare for the surveillance at Looking Glass Falls. The Tanzloran warriors coordinated with Callum, who divided them into teams—one group to continue guarding the manor and another to take up vigil at the falls. Varstyn and Drexel volunteered to lead the team, their fierce loyalty to Callum evident in their determination.

Bethany and Gran Celia worked on preparing additional herbal mixtures to boost the warrior's energy and endurance. Sanodia had sent a fresh batch of Tanzloran herbs through the portal earlier that morning, and Bethany carefully blended them into restorative infusions.

"Make sure every warrior drinks this before they leave for the falls," Bethany instructed, handing a vial to each family member. "It won't last long, but it'll give them a boost when they need it most."

Waverly checked and double-checked the daggers, ensuring they were secured in their sheaths but easily accessible. She glanced at Lynx, who was leaning against the counter, twirling his own dagger absently. "You ready for this?" she asked.

He gave her a crooked grin. "I was born ready. You?"

She smirked. "Always."

Ridge, meanwhile, was outside with Callum, discussing potential strategies for dealing with the shadows. "If the shadows show up in force, we'll need to divide their attention," Callum said. "You focus on the portal; we'll handle the rest."

Ridge nodded, his jaw set. "We'll do our part. Just make sure your warriors stay safe. We can't afford to lose anyone."

As night fell, the family gathered in the manor's dining room for a quick meal. The tension was palpable, but the shared meal offered a moment of solace amidst the chaos. Maya and Maddox chattered excitedly about the warriors' glowing weapons, oblivious to the weight of the mission ahead.

After dinner, the family retreated to their respective rooms, each of them preparing in their own way. Ridge sat on the edge of his bed, staring at the dagger in his hands. Its glowing green gemstone seemed to pulse in rhythm with his heartbeat, a constant reminder of the responsibility he carried.

Lincoln checked in with each family member, offering quiet words of encouragement. When he reached Ridge's room, he paused in the doorway. "You good?" he asked.

Ridge looked up, his expression resolute. "I will be."

Lincoln nodded. "Get some rest. Tomorrow's going to be a long day."

At dawn, the family gathered in the foyer, their gear packed and their expressions grim but determined. Callum and his warriors waited outside, their glowing forms a stark contrast to the dim morning light.

Gran Celia stood at the door, her hands clasped in front of her. "Be careful," she said, her voice steady but laced with worry. "And remember—you're not just fighting for Earth. You're fighting for the Triad."

Lincoln stepped forward and embraced her. "We'll come back," he promised. "All of us."

As the family and warriors loaded into the vehicles and drove toward Looking Glass Falls, a sense of resolve filled the air. The shadows might be lurking, the portal might be unstable, and the General might still pose a threat—but the Beaumonts were ready to face it all.

Together.

SECRETS OF SAGE MANOR

BOOK 3

BATTLE FOR PISGAH

AVAILABLE NOW AT WWW.AUTHORLGRICE.COM

Thank you to all the readers who have journeyed with the Beaumont family - your presence made this story come alive.

I'm so excited to share their story with you.

I appreciate you for taking the time to read it.

Sincerely,

LG Rice

Visit my website: www.authorlgrice.com
Contact me at hello@authorlgrice.com

www.ingramcontent.com/pod-product-compliance
Lightning Source LLC
Chambersburg PA
CBHW071918130726
47909CB00014B/2068